DEAD LINE

DEAD LINE

A Sage Adair Historical Mystery
of the Pacific Northwest

9/22/15

Susan L. Stoner

S. L. Stoner

Yamhill Press
P.O. Box 42348
Portland, OR   97242
www.yamhillpress.net

Dead Line
A Sage Adair Historical Mystery of the Pacific Northwest

Dead Line is a work of fiction. Names, characters, places and incidents are the products of the author's imagination or are used fictitiously. Any resemblance to actual events, locales, or person, living or dead, is entirely coincidental unless specifically noted otherwise.

A Yamhill Press Book

Copyright © 2015 by S. L. Stoner

Cover Design by Alec Icky Dunn/Blackoutprint.com
Interior Design by Josh MacPhee/AntumbraDesign.org

Printed in the United States. This book may not be reproduced in whole or in part, by any means, without permission. For information contact Yamhill Press at www.yamhillpress.net.

Edition ISBNs
Softcover ISBN 978-0-9907509-0-1
Ebook ISBN 978-0-9823184-3-0

Publisher's Cataloging-in-Publication

Dead Line / S.L. Stoner

pages cm. -- (A Sage Adair historical mystery of the Pacific Northwest)
1. Northwest, Pacific--History--20th century--Fiction. 2. Sheep ranching--Fiction. 3. Land fraud--Fiction. 4. Detective and mystery stories. 5. Martial arts fiction. 6. Historical fiction. 7. Adventure stories. I. Title. II. Series: Stoner, S. L. Sage Adair historical mystery.

PS3619.T6857D43 2015   813'.6   QBI15-600021

This Story is Dedicated to
Denise L. Collins, A Beautiful Soul
Who Keeps Her Moral Compass Well-Polished
and in Fine Working Order
and to
Labor Union Attorneys Everywhere,
Especially Those Who Practice in the Pacific Northwest.
It Has Been An Honor to Know You

"Only perform those acts which your soul approves."
—Buddha

ONE

Sage grabbed at the Seat rail when a hoof slipped and the horse's rear end dipped. A raspy guffaw rang out, riding breath laced with stale booze.

"Least you're of a mind to get flattened like a Johnny Cake, you'd do a mite better leaping off 'n the top instead of holding on for dear life. If this rig decides to turn bottom up, you don't want to ride her over," the stagecoach driver advised. He guffawed again before spitting a brown arc of tobacco juice over the side where it disappeared in the dust churned up by the wheels.

Bone dry, barren land as far as Sage could see. Something out there would, no doubt, welcome the moisture in that vile stuff. Not for the first time, he studied the parched landscape with distaste. He was a mountain man at heart. Give him trees and ferns and even dripping rain. This bleak rolling plain threatened death by thirst, snakebite or boredom.

"Besides, it won't do us any good you grabbing hold of that rail if things turn a mite tricky," continued the driver. His name was Dexter Higgenbottom. He'd been, he'd said, "whelped in the Ozark Mountains of the fine State of Missouri."

Sage pulled out a kerchief and raised his hat to wipe the sweat off his forehead. That blasted sun made him feel like he was being skewered to the seat. "Tricky?" he repeated, turning to look at the man. And, what did Dexter mean, "do us any good?"

Keen blue eyes, nesting deep in sun-burnt wrinkles, studied him. If the furrow between the man's brows was any indication, 'ole Dexter was having some doubts. Like maybe he'd invited the wrong man to ride atop his stagecoach.

Dexter answered the unspoken question as if Sage had asked it aloud. "I figured, from the look of you, that maybe there was a bit more weathering under your hat brim than the others. Them other passengers ain't suitable. The fellow's a citified sales drummer. That mother gal is coming back from nursing relatives in Portland. She'd likely do but she's tuckered out from taking care of sick folks. I wouldn't mind sharing my seat with that back-east school marm. She's a looker but she's got no experience. Says she's planning on teaching and homesteading so she'll be learning prairie ways. But right now, she's greener than a spring tomader. You know how to shoot that rifle you got shoved down in your pack?"

Puzzled, Sage glanced around the countryside and saw only rock-strewn prairie, tufts of sparse grass and gray clumps of sagebrush. Unless they came upon a stone outcrop close to the road, there was little chance of any holdup men. The more likely calamity was snapping an axle in one of the deep ruts they bounced into and out of with some regularity. Though mystified he answered, "Yup, learned how to use it in the Yukon. Up there, plenty of critters think a fellow's just grub on two legs," Sage said before clamping his lips shut. No sense in saying anything more until he got a notion of where Dexter was headed.

"Hoped that was the case. You take a look-see at my shotgun down there." He tipped his head in the direction of a scabbard tied between his right foot and Sage's left foot so that the gun stock was ready to hand.

"She's loaded with double-ought buckshot. Won't be too long before we head down into Cow Canyon. That's a darn rough road, narrow and steep as all get out. More than one team," he nodded toward the horses, "has run off the edge." Dexter sent another brown squirt over the side, giving Sage time to set the image in his mind.

"Fact is, friend of mine by the name of Hector Stubbs, was driving his coach down the canyon a few days ago. Something scared the horses. He tried getting them under control. Instead, the coach hit a rock and he got his self tossed off." Dexter fell silent.

Sage cleared his throat. "Did Mister Stubbs make it?"

"Nope. Wheels rolled right over him. Squashed his skull flat. Right there in the middle of the canyon."

Sage glanced at the driver's face. It was all hard lines and pale eyes staring westward toward the distant Cascade range.

"Sorry to hear that," was all Sage could think to say. He looked down at the twin triggers of the double-barreled shotgun, still wondering why he might need to pull them.

Dexter glanced at Sage. "Heck was a damn fine man with the reins. He was my counter driver. I'd be heading south same time he'd be heading north and vice-versa. We liked to meet up at the Willowdale station. Have a smoke, nip a bit from the flask and do a spot of jawing. I figure something made his horses bolt. Something about halfway down the canyon bottom."

"You thinking it was a rattler?" If so, Sage thought, we are definitely in trouble. Shooting a coiled snake from up here atop this bouncing seat would be a challenge. Way harder than dropping a charging moose in his tracks.

"Nah, snakes ain't the problem. Sure, there's plenty of rattlers in this country but the horses are used to them. Besides, this rig makes so much noise I think every snake within a mile hears us a'comin and skedaddles. Nah," he said again, "I'm thinking coyote."

"Coyote?" Sage repeated, skepticism in his voice. That rangy critter was famous for being man-shy. They disappeared whenever they sensed humans. Working in the woods, he'd heard them howling most every night but never saw them except at a distance.

Again, Dexter interpreted Sage's reaction exactly. "Yup, normally, coyotes ain't no danger. They'll bring down a rancher's sheep or calves but they stay away from humans. But lately, rabies has gotten into the animals hereabouts. And, a rabid coyote turns mighty different. They'll charge anything and everything that's a'moving. Best rule of thumb out here on the prairie is 'if a coyote heads your way, shoot 'em dead. If you can't do that, you better get your feet a-flying in the opposite direction'."

Dexter switched the reins to his left hand so he could reach inside his capacious vest and extract a metal flask. In a practiced, one-handed move, he unscrewed the top and tilted his head back. Sage watched the man's Adam's apple bob between his grizzled chin and the red kerchief around his neck. Dexter's eyes never left the road during this maneuver.

"Want a swallow?" he asked, holding the flask out to Sage. "Don't mind if I do," Sage responded. Why not? He asked himself. It's not like I have anything to do other than keep my seat and shoot a rabid coyote or two. The whiskey burned its way down his throat and into his belly. He grimaced. The stuff was no kin to the smooth heat of Kentucky bourbon.

"I don't go with that fancy stuff," Dexter declared. "Rot gut whiskey has carried me over many a rough road. It's cheap. Everybody sells it. And, the best thing is, it don't never spoil you for nothing worse, 'cause there ain't no such thing," Dexter finished, before taking one final gulp and tucking the flask away.

Once the flask w a s secure a n d another hunk o f tobacco chaw settled in his cheek, Dexter rein-snapped the horses into a slightly faster pace. He continued his explanation. "Reason I'm thinking it was a rabid coyote is that I seen signs of one in the canyon. A rabid coyote will go after wood if he can't find nothing warm-blooded to bite. My last run, I seen that some critter had gnawed on the wood post holding up the toll station sign. Those gnaw marks was down low on the post. That's what made me think 'coyote'.

"Which means, once we're down in that canyon, you'll need to keep a sharp eye out. If I was by my own self, I'd lay that shotgun across my lap and pray like hell I could hold the horses and hit the coyote at the same time. You sitting up here makes everybody safer. Once we reach the bottom of the canyon, you pull that ole shotgun out and keep it ready. You see a coyote heading our direction, just shoot him dead. Don't be wondering about whether he's sick or not. 'Cause, I got to tell you, them horses get a good look at him, it'll be hard to hold 'em. That gol' durn trail's steep, narrow and rocky—they take it in their heads to bolt, we could lose our seats. More'n one runaway team's smashed its wagon to bits."

Sage shifted on his seat, eyeing the gun butt. At least, the shotgun's scatter pattern didn't require a sharpshooter's aim.

"You know much about teamstering?" Dexter asked Sage some minutes later.

"Can't say that I do," Sage answered honestly. "Course I've ridden on stagecoaches and wagons but never driven more than a single horse buggy. I'm more used to riding the rails, sledding, canoeing—though mostly I've traveled by shanks' mare," he said, thinking of the hundreds of miles he'd trudged through the Yukon's stunted forests.

"Them rails is exactly what's killing my profession," Dexter said glumly. "Once they laid track to Shaniko, in 1900, the stage route from The Dalles went dead. Next line we lose will be this here piece, between Shaniko and Prineville. They're even talking about laying the rails from the Columbia River clear south to Farewell Bend."

Dexter sighed and squinted at the distant mountains as if contemplating his doomed profession. Then he straightened, glanced at Sage and said, "Well, if you don't mind, I'll just give you the teamster basics. Just in case."

Sage nodded his assent. Dexter had done a fine job of making the descent down Cow Canyon sound as perilous as a spring thaw run down the Yukon River.

Gesturing at the horses, Dexter said, "First you need to know the horses' jobs. The two up front are the leads, these two back here, are called wheelers. That's on account of them being closest to the coach wheels. The front ones are the smartest. These wheelers are the strongest. Them bells on the leads are not for show. With these narrow roads we need to warn folks that we're a'coming. 'Specially since we travel a mite faster than the freighters. Up to seven miles an hour on the flat stretches." That last sentence held pride.

Sage studied the muscled haunches of the four horses. Their shiny manes stirred in the breeze of their movement. They looked well-cared for, unlike the coach they pulled. That contraption rocked, squeaked and groaned at every bump. It was a miserable, road-worn affair. Grimy twine tied up stained canvas window shades. The narrow bench seats sported a few worn velvet buttons anchored to thin cushions. The canvas pad Sage sat upon was twice as thick.

Dexter's voice broke into his thoughts. "Now each horse has a rein. But, if you can only keep hold of two, you want them to be the lead reins. That's 'cause these wheeler horses are attached to each other and to the lead horses. That keeps them in place. Whatever them lead animals take it into their heads to do, the wheelers will more'n likely follow right along.

"If you look down beside the box there, you'll see a long handle. There's one on each side. Them's brake levers. If I holler 'brake' I expect you to grab that lever on your side and pull back with every bit of strength you got. It likely won't stop the coach or a bolting team, but it might slow us down a bit until I can get things under control."

Sage mulled over the instructions. Grab and pull if Dexter yelled "brake" and dive for the lead reins if, God forbid, Dexter dropped them.

They jostled along, with only the coach's rattles and distant bird calls breaking the silence. Sage glumly surveyed the landscape as sweat streamed down his back and sides. The crystalline air and cloudless sky offered no protection from the sun's heat. Only the breeze stirred by their passing, dried his sweaty brow whenever he lifted his hat for relief. Even without the discomforting heat, the dry prairie desolation would have lowered his spirits. Given a choice, he wouldn't be here.

Dexter interrupted Sage's dark musings by clearing his throat to ask, "So, Mr. Miner, what's brought you into this country?" For the first time, Sage wished he'd picked a different alias. Feeling a little silly at the coincidence of his false name and his pretend occupation he said, "Thought I'd try a little panning up on Scissors Creek, outside Prineville. I heard tell color's been found there. And, I figured I might like the ponderosa pine and empty spaces thereabouts."

Dexter nodded. "Yup, some years' back folks found a few nuggets up that way all right. 'Course Ashwood's the place where most folks prospect these days."

Sage had heard of the big mining operations outside Ashwood. But, Ashwood wouldn't do. It was too distant from the place and people he needed to investigate. Unable to share that reason with Dexter, he said, "Naw, too many people up around Ashwood. I'm used to panning in the back of beyond. I don't like bumping into another man every few feet."

Dexter laughed. "That for sure is Ashwood. I drove stage into there for awhile. These days, it's got more bustle than Prineville. Gold, silver, copper and now they're saying, mercury. They've been finding all of it. Hard to believe there's treasure in those hills. 'Course thinking there's ways to get rich quick, brings out some pretty bad fellows. Hope you know how to handle yerself?"

Sage gave the stagecoach driver a mirthless smile. The other man's gaze sharpened. "Why, I 'spect you do, Mr. Miner," he said, answering his own self as he nodded. "I rightly 'spect you do," he repeated under his breath.

Ahead, the road seemed to disappear into the sky. Dexter pulled back on the reins, bringing the stage to a gentle stop. In the sudden quiet, a breeze jostled dry roadside grasses and the horses blew and snorted, their hooves softly thudding in the dust. The coach rocked and creaked as the three passengers clambered out, exclaiming as they moved cramped muscles. No doubt they were glad to walk out the nausea and aches caused by the coach's pitching from side to side.

Sage climbed down off his perch, as did Dexter who said, "I'm going to check the harnesses and straps. Make sure everything is right 'n tight," He turned away and began tugging the nearest harness buckles.

Sage wandered ahead of the coach. He'd be more a hindrance than a help where the horses were concerned. He'd met few horses he liked. Most tried to throw or knock him off. Thirty paces farther on and the Cow Canyon abyss lay at his feet. Far below a dry streambed twisted through a narrow ravine. Ahead, tumbled rock cluttered the high ground between two parallel ruts that plunged downward toward a sharp, hairpin turn. Now he saw the reason for the coach's tall wheels. They were needed to clear the road's high center and its scattering of stray rocks.

Brush and grass dotted the ravine. How did they find sufficient moisture to survive on a hillside of rock scree and parched gravel? He listened and heard only the muted voices of the passengers and the faint buzz of insects. Mostly, the silence felt like a physical weight pressing against his ears. A shadow raced across the road at his feet. He looked up. Two huge birds wheeled soundlessly overhead. Turkey vultures, those harbingers of death. Despite the heat, he shuddered. Runaway horses, coiled rattlers, rabid coyotes. Who knows what other dangers lay ahead? Maybe those circling birds would get lucky.

"There she is, Cow Canyon, worst dang stretch on the whole route." Sage jumped at the sound of Dexter's voice. The driver didn't seem to notice. "She drops 1,400 hundred feet in less than five miles," he continued. "Every single foot of it bone-jarring rock. Few places, the rocks are so bad that if you hit 'em wrong, our whole kit-and-caboodle will tump over and roll downhill like an empty milk can."

"I sure hope we don't meet any wagons coming the other way," Sage commented.

"Ain't much danger of that," Dexter assured him. "That down there is just too steep for the horses to pull uphill, even with a light load. Most every wagon heading north, including the other stage, takes the Antelope cutoff and comes at Shaniko the long way."

With that, Dexter headed back toward the coach saying, "No need to hurry. Folks need some time to visit the necessary." He gestured toward a large boulder that stood a few paces back from the road. Sure enough, the older woman was making her way behind it, gripping a stout stick like she knew what she was doing. A rattler strike while doing the necessary would be a very bad thing.

Sage returned to staring down into the desolate canyon. Why the hell was he here in this god forsaken place anyway? The answer rode on the sage tangy breeze that had suddenly sprung up, "'Cause I got no choice. No choice a'tall," he said aloud, mimicking Dexter's Missourian accent and turn of phrase.

TWO

Portland, Oregon, three days earlier.

IT BEGAN AN HOUR AFTER the noontime dinner ended. The dining room was empty at Mozart's Table. Shortly, the city's wealthiest women would arrive to engage in their daily ritual of tea, cakes and gossip. It was a ritual Sage studiously encouraged by flattering them with heavy doses of charm. Usually he enjoyed the game. It was a good opportunity to obtain useful tidbits of information concerning their husbands' business activities. Though, on rare occasions, he'd also felt ashamed of his deception.

Boredom weighed heavily as Sage totaled up the restaurant's midday receipts. It had been three weeks since President Roosevelt's train pulled out of Union Station heading north. Roosevelt's fourteen-thousand-mile train trek had been an unqualified success. The president returned to Washington astride a tidal wave of popular support. People liked his trust-busting, square-deal speeches. They were grateful he thought them important enough to warrant whistle-stops in their small western towns and cities.

Few knew how close Roosevelt had come to being assassinated in Portland. Sage doubted the President himself knew the whole story. Certainly no newspaper printed the tale of how a ragtag group of hobos, Chinese tong members and labor union activists had thwarted the attempt. Instead, the press simply parroted the official downplayed version of a lone crazy. No one wanted Portland to have Buffalo, New York's reputation as the scene of a sitting president's assassination.

Sage stood, stretched and refilled his coffee cup from the carafe sitting on the nearby sideboard. God, he missed action. It wasn't always like this. Working as an operative for labor union leader, Vincent St. Alban, could be downright exciting. There were times when he did more than play the wealthy restaurant proprietor gleaning helpful information from society matrons. Sometimes he was scared. Sometimes he got hurt. But still, he also felt most alive when in the midst of a dangerous mission.

Sighing, he sat again just as the front door opened, letting in the rattle and creak of the freight wagons that endlessly rolled down the street's wood block pavers.

At first glance, the man seemed a typical, prosperous customer. His gabardine suit and the gold watch chain draping across an embroidered silk vest looked expensive. Yet, those were cowboy boots. Polished, yes. But nevertheless, pointy-toed, high-heeled, cowboy boots. Sage's gaze sharpened. This was neither a salesman nor a businessman. That hawkish face wore the bronze weathering of an outdoors man. Narrowed eyes coolly took Sage's measure and catapulted Sage from idle boredom into sharp unease.

Sage rose, wearing his genial host smile. "The cook's taking a break but I can get you some coffee and pie," he offered, though sure the man wasn't there to eat or drink.

The stranger nodded pleasantly but said nothing. Instead, he grabbed the chair across from Sage, slid it back and sat. His quick smile failed to soften the pale blue eyes. "You're a hard man to corral, Mr. Adair. It's taken a few days to catch you alone." The words were spoken in an unmistakable Texas Panhandle twang. Sage knew it well. Briefly, he'd slowly passed through that part of Texas, vowing never to travel such barren land again unless aboard a train or some other fast moving conveyance.

Sage tensed but resumed his seat, keeping his legs un-
crossed and both feet planted firmly on the floor. Fong always
said, "Keep two feet on ground when danger threatens." Sage
usually followed Fong's advice. The Chinese man was amazingly
skilled in an oriental fighting art he called the 'snake and crane'.

He studied the man across from him who looked nearly
fifty, eighteen or so years older than Sage. The expensive suit
didn't conceal the wide shoulders and strong wrists that told of
intense physicality. And, the controlled ease of the man's movements signaled an ability to move fast.

This assessment occurred in the few seconds between the
end of the man's statement and Sage's adoption of a quizzical expression as he said, "Don't know why you didn't just come in and
introduce yourself. This isn't a private club." He reached across
the table, "Name's John Adair. I own this restaurant." The other
man's shake was firm, his palm slightly rough. No doubt about
it. This stranger knew hard labor.

"Yup, I know who you are. But I figure it's best if other folks
don't see us together. City this big, there's a lot of folks about and
no guarantee they won't turn up somewhere else and remember
who they saw. And, human critters sure do like to jabber."

Although instinct told him it'd be futile, Sage tried denial,
saying, "Well, sir, I don't believe you've informed me of your
name but I am sure you have me confused with someone else. I
cannot imagine why you would need a secret meeting with me.
As you can see," here he waved an airy hand at the empty room,
"I merely operate this eating establishment. No need to act all
'cloak and dagger' I am sure."

The other man studied him, then grinned. "Pretty good
show," he said before leaning forward, "Now, Mr. Adair, you best
stop with the silly palaver. We both know that rings true as a
church bell without its clapper."

That pithy observation stopped Sage. What did this stranger
know about him? Had he seen him in his undercover labor operative persona, John Miner? Only to later recognize him in his
role as John Adair, proprietor of Portland's fanciest restaurant?

No. Because the stranger's next words were, "I had me a long chin wag with Otis Welker. Just before he got himself killed down there in 'Frisco. So, I know you are a hell of a lot more than some soft-shoed restaurant owner. You work for the unions. You've got a Chinese sidekick who can take down ten men twice his size. And maybe your ma works alongside you as well. Welker wasn't too sure about that last but he suspected. Said the two of you have the same eyes. I haven't studied her up close so I don't have an opinion. Truth be told, I don't rightly care."

The air around Sage thickened the instant the stranger spoke the name "Otis Welker." Memory hit him like a bucket of cold water so that every word the stranger spoke after that seemed to enter Sage's ears muted, as if from a far distance. Once again, Sage was back a year ago, when Welker's icy eyes had stared into his—right after he'd arranged for Sage's murder.

But Sage hadn't been thrown from the train bridge in the middle of the Willamette River. Fong rescued him in the nick of time. Instead, it was Welker who'd died just days later. Newspaper reports said someone deliberately shoved the timber company agent beneath a San Francisco carriage.

Sage dropped all pretense and openly studied the man sitting across from him. It was then that the man's easy grin finally reached his eyes. "Nope, it wasn't me that shoved Welker. I didn't like him. I'll admit to that. Sometimes worked with him, at the Dickensen Agency, until he decided to hire out on his own to the timber companies. Never cottoned to his methods, before or after he left the agency. So don't be thinking I'm like him. I mean you no harm. I plan no trickery."

"You're a . . . ," Sage started to say but the other man interrupted.

"Yup, I'm still with the agency." He pulled a solid silver badge out of his vest pocket. Sage leaned forward to read "Dickensen Detective" engraved across the star. The man replaced the badge and continued talking, "Don't know how much longer I'll be working for them since I'm getting more than a little disgusted by their shenanigans. Name's Charles Lloyd Siringo, Mr. Adair. Friends call me 'Charlie.' And, I've got me a big problem. I'm thinking you're the only man who can help me find a way out of it."

"It'll be a damn cold day in hell before I help any Dickensen agent," Sage said, anger turning his face hot. The detective agency was responsible for the death of his grandfather, uncle and a whole slew of other Appalachian coal miners. Good men murdered because they tried to ease their families' poverty.

"Yup, I figured being a union man, you'd consider the Dickensen agency your worst enemy. Can't blame you for that. But, I ain't asking for the agency. In fact, the last thing I want is for them to know we're even talking. That's why it's taken me so gol' darn long to meet up with you."

Sage searched the man's face, trying to grasp what Siringo meant and intended. Siringo's return gaze remained steady in his calm face. There was no liar's sideways glance.

Oh well, Sage thought, it was pointless to pretend any longer. He was now well and truly curious. He raised a cautionary finger, saying, "I warn you, I can't imagine agreeing to help a Dickensen man under any circumstance. That said, go ahead. Tell me your story." Sage sat back and crossed his arms. He'd listen but he had no intention of being roped in by this cowboy.

Siringo scooted his chair closer, confident now that he knew Sage would listen. "Dickensen's sent me here to assist Governor Chamberlain. There's a deadly situation brewing east of the Cascade range."

Sage shook his head. He wanted nothing to do with events in eastern Oregon.

This time it was Siringo who raised a warning finger. "Please, Adair, hear me out. The cattlemen don't have enough grazing land. They've started blaming the sheep ranchers."

Siringo sighed, removed his derby and dropped it on the table. "Silly, useless citified thing don't deserve to be called a 'hat.' Keeps neither sun nor rain off a man's face," he grumbled before continuing, "The reason they're short grazing land is far more complicated than sheep. But, they see the grass disappearing and their cattle dying in fields stripped by the woolies. So, they've started killing sheep and they're talking about killing sheepherders as well. One old shepherd, a fellow who worked for the Kepler brothers, has gone missing. I'm surmising he's been murdered. And, someone's burned the Kepler's barn and feed out in the Ochocos.

"Now the cattlemen have started blazing dead lines all over. They say they'll shoot any sheep or shepherd that crosses the line. I hear the sheepmen, both shepherds and ranchers, are thinking to retaliate. My job is to identify who's stirring folks up on both sides, find the missing shepherd and report to the Governor so he can deal with the situation. That might sound simple but it's not."

Sage remained silent. This was interesting but why the hell did Siringo think Sage would help? He let his skepticism suffuse his face as he waited for Siringo to come to the point.

The Dickensen agent seemed not to notice Sage's expression, because he continued his tale. "I've been out there, horse trading, all around Prineville. That's Central Oregon's biggest town. Horse trading's my cover because I've been a cowboy and know horses better than most. Once they saw I could break a horse with the best of them, there's been no trouble getting accepted by the cattlemen. But that's just half the problem. Every day that passes, the situation is getting more dangerous for the shepherds and their animals.

"The governor swears he's doing everything possible to get Roosevelt and the Secretary of the Interior to intervene and straighten things out. He says the federal government made the darn mess, so they should fix it. As of yesterday, the governor still hadn't heard back from Washington D.C."

Siringo's forehead wrinkled in the effort to make Sage understand. "My problem, in the meantime, is that I sure can't straddle two horses going in different directions. If the cattlemen accept me, the sheepmen sure won't. Despite plenty of provoking, they've kept their anger reined in. One reason for that is the shepherds often work alone with only a herd dog for company. The only protection they pack is a varmint rifle. They can't move fast because all they have is a bulky camp wagon, a mule and a flock of slow moving sheep. So, there isn't much they can do when attacked by armed men on horseback. They sure can't outrun them. Still, the sheep ranchers' patience is wearing thin. From where they sit, Governor Chamberlain isn't doing anything and neither is the federal government."

Siringo tapped his fingernail against the edge of Sage's saucer—the sound musical in the silence. "It's mighty complicated, Adair. So many parts to it. The sheepmen also haven't retaliated because there's a division amongst them. Some are local fellows. They want to get along with their cattlemen neighbors. Other sheepmen are strangers just passing through, herding their sheep to and from the shearing sheds at Shaniko. Some of them come from as far east as Idaho and as far south as Klamath Falls. The men killing the sheep don't seem to be making any distinction between the two groups."

Sage nodded. He'd heard about immense flocks of sheep crossing Central Oregon. He could see why that might upset the cattlemen. Still, it was open range—federal land. "I understand. The newspapers report that a range war's starting up over there," he said.

The other man plucked a ready-made cigarette from a metal pocket tin. "Mind if I smoke?" he asked. Sage shook his head. Lifting his cup he pushed the saucer forward. "Go ahead. But you better get moving with your story. The teatime ladies will be arriving and once they do, I can't give you any more attention."

Cigarette lit, Siringo leaned forward and lowered his voice. "Last month, I was passing through town after giving my preliminary report to the Governor. My train east to Shaniko got delayed so I decided to drink a beer at Slap Jack's, down near the rail yard. I was sitting back in a corner when an hombre I know too darn well ambled in. Name of Pat Barry. He's an operative for Dickensen's but we aren't friends. Far from it. While back, I caught him beating an innocent man. He wanted the fellow to confess to a crime Barry himself had committed. I knew that cause I'd watched Barry do the crime. Anyway, I broke up the beating and reported Barry to the Dickensen superintendent. Not a gol' durn thing happened to Barry. I had to keep my hand on old Colts 45 the whole time I stayed in Denver 'cause Barry's sworn to get even." Siringo sat back, drew deeply on his cigarette, exhaled and watched the smoke drift upward before leaning forward again.

"Anyway, not wanting any trouble in Slap Jacks, I pulled my hat brim low and pushed my chair further back into the corner. Few minutes later, a skinny young fellow came in. He dressed like a cowpoke—boots, hat, shiny buckle and all. I had a vague recollection of his face but couldn't place him. Anyway, this cowboy straightaway sat down across from Barry. At the end of their jawing, I saw Barry shake the fellow's hand and give him some money. That was a sure sign they were up to no good. Barry only gives away other people's money.

"I studied the fellow's face so I'd remember it. Still, I figured Barry had something going here in the city with that young fellow. For certain it was something sneaky but I didn't think no more on it. I boarded the train and headed back to the Prineville area." Siringo pulled on his cigarette, letting the smoke slowly trickle out his nose.

"You saw Barry or the young fellow again, I expect," Sage said, trying to nudge the story along.

"Not Barry. The young fellow. Darned if he didn't ride the same train back to Central Oregon. So, I made his acquaintance. Turns out his name is Tom Meglit. Fact is, since then, I've been hearing too darn much about him. Not here but across the mountains in Prineville. That's where he's from and that's where he's stirring up sheepshooter trouble."

"Trouble? Sheepshooters?" Sage echoed, caught up in the story despite harboring a strong resistance against Siringo's purpose in telling it.

"'Sheepshooters' is how some of the cattlemen have named themselves. With Meglit hanging around the cowboys and cattle ranchers, I decided to learn a bit more about him. I figured, if he was up to something, maybe I could find out what."

"And did you?"

"That boy ain't any more than 21 years old. But I've got to tell you Mr. Adair, what people have to say about him scares the holy bejesus right out of me. I ain't proud of everything I've done in this life but I'm thinking there's something real bad about that kid. He rides a mean streak that runs a mile wide and a mile deep. Folks say he's right fond of words like 'dry gulch' and 'ambush.' Likes to brag, he does."

"Dry gulch?" Sage'd heard the term but wasn't sure what it meant except that its victims died.

Siringo's lips twisted. "It means tying a man up behind a horse and dragging him until he expires from being hauled across the rocks and bushes."

Imagining that painful death, Sage shuddered. "Well, I can see you got a problem with Meglit, the sheepshooters and the sheepmen but I don't see why I should get involved," he said. He began stacking his paperwork into a neat pile, readying to stand.

Siringo reached across the small table and grabbed Sage's forearm with just enough force to arrest its motion. "Look Mr. Adair, Dickensen has me acting the honest front man. I'm doing my best to stop trouble. Keep people safe. Meantime, Dickensen has Pat Barry and this young Tom Meglit, working behind the scenes. They're making sure it's all going to turn worse. I figure the Dickensen Agency is stirring up trouble just so they can keep collecting from the Governor. The situation is a cow they plan to keep milking. I've seen them do it before."

There was no mistaking the desperate plea in Siringo's face as he said, "I need someone I can trust out there in Central Oregon. Someone who can get next to the sheepmen. Otherwise, some decent folks will get themselves into a passel of trouble. And, I sure the heck can't ask Dickensen for help. Fact is, I suspect that if the agency figures out I've discovered their game, they'll give that Meglit kid a chance to practice his dry gulching on yours truly."

"Well, I'm sorry for the fix you're in but I don't see why I should get involved. I have this business to run. I don't know Central Oregon. I'm sure no cowboy. I don't even like horses. And, the only sheep with which I'm acquainted, arrive in lightly seasoned soup or coated with a pineapple glaze." He heard himself say the words, but to his own ears, they didn't sound all that convincing. A bad situation was indeed developing in Central Oregon, one that needed to be stopped.

Inwardly he chuckled at the realization he was feeling sorry for this Dickensen agent. Still, it had to be said. "I'm sorry, Mr. Siringo. I wish I could help but I'm needed here. I can't leave." This was the truth. Sage had to remain available in case St. Alban needed to send him on another mission. He couldn't go haring off to the Central Oregon prairie.

Siringo sat back, saying, "She kinda thought that might be your answer."

"She, who is she?" Sage asked, his throat tightening. Somehow, buried in the pit of his gut, he knew the answer even before Siringo opened his mouth to say the name.

The cowboy pulled a white envelope from an inside pocket and tossed it onto the table. "Lucinda Collins," he said, but his voice was gentle as if he knew the name would hurt.

Sage watched his own hand reach out and pick up the envelope. His fingers fumbled as they broke the seal and unfolded a single sheet of paper. He recognized the handwriting. And so he should. For a few months last year, she had sent him loving notes and other messages. Up until just days before she'd left town.

His mind's eye replayed that last scene again—crisp fall sunlight snagged by honey-colored hair. Her stepping into an expensive carriage—riding away beside another man. Later he'd learned she'd headed to Chicago, leaving her upscale bordello in the capable hands of a trusted employee. Leaving Sage behind.

He read the few words twice over, "Please come. We need your help. Otherwise, good people will get hurt. L."

Sage looked up into the face of the man across the table. "Is she all right?" he asked.

Siringo shook his head. "Nope, can't say that she is."

Sage rose from his chair, both hands flat on the table as he leaned toward Siringo. "What do you mean, man? Is Lucinda in trouble? Is she in some kind of danger?" he demanded.

Siringo's smile twisted as he said in his slow Texas drawl, "Wahl, now, I guess you'll need to cross the mountains to find that out, won't you Mr. Adair? And, I ain't going to tell you exactly where to find her until you turn up Prineville. I know that's harsh but I've got to have help."

THREE

So now here he was, staring into a desolate canyon, far from
Mozart's and all that was familiar. Sage took one last look down
the road before turning back and climbing onto the stagecoach.
The sales drummer also climbed back aboard and swung the
coach door shut. They were ready to go. Dexter grabbed his flask,
tipped it up, and then offered it to Sage who shook his head.
Years of such whiskey tippling probably allowed the slightly
drunk Dexter to respond well in emergencies. Sage could not say
the same about himself. Bad whiskey, merciless heat and glaring
light were already a mind-dulling mix—even before throwing in
a dose of fright.

Flask tucked away, Dexter yanked down his stained hat and
picked up the lines. Gently shaking the reins he called, "Heigh
now, let's git a goin' boys." With huffs and snorts the horses
stepped out, the leads soon cresting the canyon's edge.

As the coach tilted, Sage pushed stiff-legged against the kick
board. "What was the coach's weight?" he wondered. Besides five
people, it carried a pot-bellied stove atop a full rear boot, an iron
strongbox anchored beneath the driver's seat and suitcases and
parcels piled high on its roof. Tied atop that mound was an iron
plow. On a flat grade, the horses had strained to set it rolling.

He glanced over his shoulder. The roof top items looked
secure. But, had the whole load just slid forward? If a rope broke,

that pile would surely sweep them both off the seat. "Breathe" he told himself. Dexter would have made sure those ropes were tight. Best to ignore the looming mound. So, he looked ahead but was not reassured. The horses' haunches were already bunching in an effort to restrain the weight. How long could the animals prevent the whole kit and caboodle from breaking loose?

Beside him, Dexter straightened and locked his own boots against the kick board. He shot Sage a crazy-eyed, clenched-toothed grin as he leant backward to keep a steady tug on the reins. He gave no sign that he'd noticed Sage's nervous survey of the coach's rooftop.

"It's hard on the horses to go downhill before a heavy load. The trick here," he said, "is to keep them moving slow. Pretty soon we'll reach the first hairpin turn. There are seven, sharpish switchbacks 'afore we reach the creek bed. Each one of them's a grizzly bear. We'll be needing your hand on the brake fairly soon," he added.

Sage glanced to his right. A steep hillside fell away from the track. The front wheel on his side of the coach mounted a rock and then slammed down making the coach cant sharply first to one side and then the other. Cries sounded from inside the coach. He wasn't the only one eyeing the precipice at his elbow.

He studied the wooden brake handle, all smooth and shiny from use. He hadn't noticed that earlier. By the time they reached the first switchback, they'd gained speed. Sage "hopped to" when instructed, yanking the lever back to jam the rubber-covered brake block against the rear wheel on his side.

Dexter pulled hard on the reins while muttering some incoherent invocation. At the sloped corner, their high perch tilted sharply. Sage worked the brake lever and felt his toes trying to grip the footboard through his boots. Only empty space showed between the pricked ears of the lead horses. Once the corner was rounded and the stagecoach was again plunging down a straightaway, Dexter ordered him to ease off the brake. He cautioned Sage to remain ready to grab and "pull for all his worth."

Sage relaxed somewhat once they'd made the turn. Now, the upward slope was on his side. "At least," he reassured himself, "if I have to jump off, it won't be over the edge." Then he felt ashamed. The passengers wouldn't have that option if the coach broke loose. He took a deep breath, relaxed his legs and studied the canyon. Not much to see. Just rock, dirt, stunted juniper, scrub bush and tufted bunch grass. A shadow passed over the road ahead. The same two turkey vultures wheeled in tight circles directly above, their wing spans huge against the solid blue sky.

Dexter seemed to sense his nervousness because he chuckled and said, "You did real good, Mr. Miner. Just six more of those turns to go." Suddenly Dexter started frantically pulling on the reins. Before Sage realized the reason for Dexter's action, a huge boulder tumbled down the steep slope. Hitting hard and fast, it bounded out of sight over the edge nearly hitting the lead horses, causing them to snort and jerk their heads.

"Whoo-wee, that was a mite close," was the driver's only comment. His hand twitched toward the flask but he apparently thought better of it and tightened his two-handed grip on the reins instead.

They made it around the remaining switchbacks with only a few more heart-lurching moments and no more bounding boulders. That didn't mean their trials were over. Ahead, the road was little more than a winding path through the dry streambed. The task of keeping it open had to be endless. Whatever water traveled the course would shift the rocks.

Around a bend, Sage saw that a rock outcrop made for a passage too narrow for the stagecoach to pass through. Dexter turned the horses to one side, starting them up a rocky path. This time the horses strained to pull the load, breaths gusting from their heaving chests. After reaching the outcrop's top, the stagecoach plunged down the other side. Once again, Sage levered the brake block tight against the wheel while Dexter did the same on the other side.

Finally, they returned to the relative safety of the streambed. It still sloped sharply downward but at least there were no drop offs on either side. Sage rubbed the shaking muscles of his arm and relaxed.

His relief was short lived. "You'd best cradle that there shotgun," Dexter said, nodding toward the weapon still in its scabbard. "Hereabouts is where we can expect to see that rabid coyote. The toll station is just a half mile ahead. Keep a sharp lookout."

Sage did as told. He grabbed the gun and began scanning their surroundings. He wondered whether sand-colored coyote fur would stand out against the drab brown of rock and dirt. As if to make his job harder, the uneven ground beneath their wheels set the coach slewing side to side. Sage clutched the shotgun with one hand and the iron side rail with the other.

The horses saw the coyote first. Or, maybe, they smelled it. The head of the lead horse on Sage's side snapped up and sideways. Its ears pricked forward. Sage saw the huge brown eye widen until white showed and the horse snorted loudly. He'd seen those signs before. Usually just before the horse he was riding bolted.

Sage released his grip on the side rail, braced his feet against the kick board and, with a single smooth move, raised the gun aiming it at the spot where the horse stared. Sure enough, a rough-coated coyote staggered out from behind a boulder, white froth dribbling from its muzzle. Sage felt the stagecoach slowing as Dexter started hauling back on the reins.

Sighting on the coyote, Sage's arms held steady. He made himself wait. The damn coyote was still too far away but it was coming on, crazed determination driving it forward, its fangs glistening. Sage sucked in air and then slowly released it. Fong's voice sounded in his head for the first time that day. "Relax, Sage. Be one with weapon." Sage relaxed as much as he could. The seat bucked beneath him as the horses reared and plunged and Dexter's curses blued the air. Inside, the frightened passengers squealed with alarm.

The commotion seemed muted, distant and out of focus. For him, there was only the coyote advancing toward the end of the gun barrel. It was twenty yards away and closing fast. Fifteen yards. Any closer and a shotgun pellet might hit the horse. Sage snugged the gun butt tightly against his shoulder and fired. The kick slammed him backward, but his training with Fong let him move and turn with the force. Still, it hurt.

At first, the animal kept coming. Then it dropped in mid-stride as if hitting an invisible wall. Once down, it didn't move.

The danger was over but the horses didn't know it. If anything, the loud boom of the shotgun spurred them into greater hysteria. Apparently the lead horses became of one mind for suddenly their hooves slammed down onto the rocky bed, their hind legs dug in and they shot forward. With a jerk, the stagecoach catapulted after them. It careened past the coyote's carcass, plunging down the streambed so fast that it felt like the whole contraption was flying apart.

Dropping the shotgun into the scabbard, Sage reached to help Dexter haul back on the reins. Just as he did so, the plow strapped atop the suitcases snapped free. It slid forward to slam into the back of Dexter's head and sent his hat flying off into the dust. The plow followed.

Dexter's body slumped and his nerveless fingers released the reins. Sage threw himself across the driver, stopping him from following the hat and plow. At the same time, he grabbed for the reins. Too late. They slithered over the kick board's edge and out of his reach to land atop the left wheel horse, having somehow caught on a harness buckle. Keeping his body across Dexter, Sage clutched the kick board and stretched as far forward as he could. Not far enough. The reins lay a foot beyond his finger tips.

Meanwhile the team was picking up speed. The coach wheels seemed to be jumping from rock to rock. Tilting first to one side and then the other, each tilt becoming more extreme. They had to be just seconds away from tipping over. At the speed they were traveling, everyone on the coach could die.

In that moment, Sage remembered Dexter's instructions to jump before that happened. Yah, right, he thought ruefully. The unconscious man slid forward, his dead weight pushing against Sage's back. Shoving the driver onto the floor, Sage prayed Dexter was wedged in tight enough to stay.

Turning toward the horses, Sage saw that the reins were still there, still snagged and still just out of reach. All four of them.

"Never have liked horses all that much," he muttered through gritted teeth just before he jumped, flying out over the wheel horse's back, arms and legs spread.

Landing with an "oopmh," his hands grabbed for the harness strap around the creature's midsection. The horse shied at the sudden weight, sending Sage in a backward slide until his legs dangled off its rear end. Using the harness straps, he inched forward again, finally latching onto the heavier strap around the horse's chest. The critter's mane slapped his face but he barely noticed. He was too busy scrabbling for the reins. At last he had them in his clutch. Slowly, he pulled himself upright until he sat astride the horse's back, gripping its heaving body with his knees. Beneath him, the animal settled into a steady run as if somewhat calmed by the familiar sensation of having a man on its back. Sage hauled on the reins, hoping that his offside position wouldn't cause the lead horses to stumble. All around him the sound of crashing hooves and rattling coach filled the air. The passengers' cries had stilled.

He looked forward, thinking for the first time that maybe he could slow the coach before it rolled over or got smashed to smithereens. That hope was replaced by horror. Ahead, a huge boulder sat squarely in the middle of the road.

FOUR

Sage frantically hauled on the reins, until his arms and shoulders burned and his body arched backward over the horse. The team finally began slowing but too little and way too late. At this speed, if the lead horses split and tried to thunder past on either side of that boulder, the coach bottom wouldn't clear it. They'd overturn for sure. The only hope was for the lead horses to pass by one side or the other. Figuring out which reins would pull the horses to the right, he hauled on those even harder. It seemed to make no difference.

Suddenly, two men on horseback came galloping around the bend on the far side of the boulder. They swept past the boulder only to halt and turn their horses sideways, creating a solid barrier of man and horseflesh.

Maybe it was seeing others of their own kind or, maybe Sage's hauling on the reins had finally penetrated their terror, because the team immediately slowed to a sedate trot. When they passed around the obstruction, the coach barely tilted.

Sage glanced back. Dexter's body still lay behind the kick board. The jostling hadn't bounced him off. With no way to climb back onto the driver's seat, Sage remained astride the wheel horse, his body as sweaty as that of the lathered animal beneath him. He reached forward to scratch between its ears, "Good job, Mister Horse," he said.

The two cowboys rode up on either side to provide an escort. One was a young fellow, his hands browned by the sun. His weathered, wide-brimmed hat shaded laughing blue eyes and grin of white teeth. "Well, now. That must have been one thrilling ride," he said. Sage could only nod.

Their entourage rounded the bend. There sat the toll station. Unpainted plank sides, a few windows and a bumpy shake roof said this was an outpost of necessity. Behind the small building, snug against the rock wall of the canyon, stood an equally rough building. Shelter for the station's livestock and feed. Farther away was a third structure, this one built partially of rock and open on one side. Large tongs hung on the back wall behind a blackened anvil. Yah, you'd need to do some blacksmith work in Cow Canyon alright, Sage thought.

Still, there was pride in the surroundings. A row of tall Lombardy poplars caught the breeze and shaded the station's south side. A flagstone path bordered by lumpy canyon rocks bisected a tidy dirt yard. The path ended at the steps of the building's wide-roofed veranda.

The horses halted of their own accord and lowered their heads. Their blowing and the murmuring of the three passengers were the only sounds. Coach rocking, doors flung open, the passengers scrambled out on either side. In an act of discourtesy, the sales drummer didn't hand the women down from the coach. Instead, he took off at an undignified run toward a distant privy.

A beige cloud of drifting dust overtook the two women who were straightening their skirts and adjusting their outerwear.

"Hee-hee," came a weak chuckle. Dexter was struggling upright. He raised a shaky finger, pointing at the privy just as its door banged shut. "They say a scared coyote will crap himself. Happens to men too, I seen it more than once. 'Specially on this here Cow Canyon run."

Once again atop his seat, Dexter took charge. "Toss up them reins and then we'll see about getting you safely off the back of that horse. They're still a might skittish."

Sage tossed him the reins. Dexter spoke soothingly to the animals while one of the cowboys held the horse's head.

Sage carefully slid off its back. When his boots hit the dirt, his knees sagged.

"Sorry I done slept through the most exciting part," Dexter said, taking Sage's elbow and steering him toward the station. "I did manage to see that you got that pesky coyote but I'm afraid I missed the rest. Lathered up as the team is, I suspect they still don't believe that critter is dead."

Sage cleared his throat. "It was the shotgun blast that really seemed to set 'em off. Can't say that I blame them. It boomed mighty loud off those canyon walls."

"I see you remembered what I told you about keeping a'hold of the lead reins," Dexter said, patting Sage's back. "Well, I think our little adventure calls for a whiskey or two," he added. Dexter grimaced, reached up and ran a hand across a nearly bald head. "I expect we'll tarry here a bit. Someone's got to go up canyon. We need that plow and my durn hat. And, the team needs some heavy watering and a bit of calming."

The station's interior was simple. Three small plank tables with ladder-backed chairs nearly filled the front room. A potbellied stove and a cookstove stood in opposite corners. A doorway in the rear wall led into what had to be the station master's private quarters. Another doorway, in the sidewall, opened into a lean-to add-on. Sage saw plank bunk beds inside, no doubt for travelers' use. The main room's sole light came from the veranda-shaded windows on either side of the door and a small one over the kitchen's enamel basin. Sage didn't mind the gloom. It was a relief to be away from the sun's glare. Besides, it was marginally cooler inside.

Dexter said something to the station master who hurried up with a full whiskey bottle and a tray of glasses. He set three glasses on a nearby table and poured a small amount in each glass.

The two women took seats together at that table. The older one spoke firmly to the younger in words that carried a slight German accent. "Now, grab hold of your nerves, young lady. Think of it as a great story. You rode in a runaway stagecoach and you're alive to tell about it. That's a 'hello' from this country you'll never forget. Years from now, you'll be telling your kids the story. Wipe away those tears, now. Swallow this whiskey."

The young woman snuffled, wiped her face but shook her head mutely. "I don't believe in spirits. My folks were against them," she mumbled.

The older woman was having none of it. "Oh! Such nonsense," she said. "You've had a shock and this will help. It's medicine, girl. Can't go missish in this land. It won't do. Homesteading, you'll see worse things. It's a tough land. No place for the chicken-hearted."

That argument seemed to work. The younger woman straightened, grabbed the glass and threw its contents back in one smooth move. She immediately began coughing and her eyes again watered.

The older one chuckled affectionately and said, "All right! I can see you've got some grit. You'll do," she said. The girl's response was a weak smile but she straightened in her chair.

The station master brought the rest of the glasses and the bottle to Sage's table just as the two cowboys clumped into the small building. Sage stood and offered his hand. "Here's the fellows who saved the day," he said to Dexter. "If they hadn't ridden up and turned the horses, we'd have hit a huge boulder square-on."

Sage gestured to the cowboys and said "Have a seat. We're all having a little whiskey to calm our nerves and I'd sure like to buy you both a shot or two."

The cowboys removed their hats and made slight bows toward the ladies, "Howdy Missus Fromm and Miss," said the older one. The younger one merely grinned, but his dancing blue eyes stayed on the young woman so long she blushed.

"Why, it's nice to see you fellows again. It's been awhile. I'm thinking it must have been at the jack rabbit shoot last summer," said Mrs. Fromm.

"Boy howdy," said the talking cowboy, "That was some fun. And so was the schoolhouse dance afterward."

That little exchange over, the two cowboys introduced themselves as Jim Brown and Randy Taylor. The older cowboy,

Brown, was the talker of the two. "We were riding in and fixing to dismount, when we heard all that racket coming down the canyon. When the wind is low, you can hear a pine cone drop around here. Not that there are any. Old Perry Cram, there, he come running out the station hollering 'runaway' and waving his hands in the air like a demented holy roller. So we just kicked our horses and headed up canyon."

"If you hadn't, we would have hit that boulder square on for sure," Sage said.

The station master, a short, anxious-seeming man, spoke for the first time. "That boulder rolled loose yesterday. I tried moving it myself this morning but it's too heavy. What in tarnation set the horses off?"

Here Dexter jumped in, "Rabid coyote. Same one that set Heck's team off, I'm betting. Don't worry, that varmint won't be charging anyone else. Mr. Miner here, nailed him with a single shot of double-ought. Suspect you can find his carcass. Just look for those circling vultures. Those dadgum birds knew something was going to happen 'cause they stayed above us all down the canyon."

Cram nodded. "I'll head up real soon and bury him deep. Cow Canyon doesn't need rabid critters running around. You boys and your horses be willing to help me by moving that boulder?" he asked Brown and Taylor.

The men exchanged looks and Brown said, "Sure, our boss ain't expecting us anytime real soon."

"What outfit are you fellas with?" asked Dexter. For the first time, Sage detected a hint of reservation in the older cowboy's answer. "Hay Creek," he said. "The boss runs a small cattle herd, just to keep his hand in," he added.

Sage looked toward Dexter, one eyebrow raised. Dexter obliged by explaining, "Hay Creek's a sheep ranch in the area. It raises the biggest breed. 'Rambouillet' is what they call the critters," he said the name with a French-sounding flourish. "Not everybody hereabouts likes the sheep business," he added.

Ah hah, Sage thought to himself. My first opportunity to hear firsthand about the cattle and sheep problem. "Why, what's wrong with sheep, besides their smell?"

The two cowboys seemed to relax. After a small sip of his whiskey, the older man answered. "Well, you sure ain't from Central Oregon," he began, his tone still friendly. "These days, some of the cattlemen hereabouts hate sheep ranchers, even ones as rich and settled as John Edwards, our boss." This confirmed what Siringo had told him. Sage kept his face interested and ignorant.

The cowboy began to drawl a further explanation. "Hay Creek's been running sheep since the 1870's. It's a damn big spread, over 50,000 acres right in the midst of government range. Plenty big enough to keep the flock moving so's not to over-graze the land." The cowboy sighed and took another sip. The women had fallen silent.

"Recent years, though, lots of folks have jumped into the wool business," the cowboy continued, "And that's sent heaps more sheep trailing up to the shearing sheds at Shaniko. Now that Shaniko's a railhead, there's a straight shot to river shipping at The Dalles. Fact is, they say that The Dalles is the third biggest wool port in the country."

Sage leaned forward to add more whiskey to the man's glass. The cowboy nodded his thanks. "Problem is, not all the wool is raised local. Instead, the sheep flocks are coming from as far south as Klamath Falls and as far east as Boise. Every spring, they herd those sheep to Shaniko. Along the way, they graze the open range down to dirt," he said.

The cowboy tilted his glass up and drained it. Without saying a word, Sage grabbed the bottle and refilled the glass. Brown continued his explanation. "Sheep ain't like cattle. Cattle spread out, chomp off the grass tops and move on. The grass grows back in two or three years.

"It's different with sheep. They herd tight together. For safety, I suspect. All that competition means they crop close to the ground. Sometimes they even yank the grass out by its roots. And not just grass. Every darn green thing they see.

After a thousand head of sheep move through, it takes too long for the grass to grow back. Sagebrush and weeds take hold instead. Once that happens, the grass is gone forever."

The cowboy shook his head. "Folks think those huge herds of woolies ruin the range for cattle. As a cow man, I can't disagree. Local sheepmen, like our boss, understand the problem. Outsiders, though, don't plan on staying and don't care what happens, long as they can get their flocks to and from Shaniko."

Taylor, the younger cowboy piped up, his voice higher than Sage expected, "Our boss says it's the traveling sheep that's the problem. And, once the traveling sheep get sheared at Shaniko, they turn around and head back to their summer pastures, eating everything they missed when they was a'comin."

Silence fell on the group. Sage contemplated plains of sweet grass transformed into a wasteland of prickly clumps of inedible sage. "I guess I haven't seen much grass so far, come to think of it," he said.

The older cowboy nodded. "Yup, that'd be the sheep mostly. And, to be honest, the cattle ruin some of it too. Old timers say that, before us whites came, the bunch grass grew so thick and high that it snagged a man's stirrups. That's all gone now."

He sighed and returned to his explanation of more recent history, "Afore the Shaniko railhead, homesteaders and the Forest Reserve Act, things were kinda balanced between the local sheep and cattlemen," here he paused and addressed Mrs. Fromm, who'd shifted at his words as if to speak. "No offense to you, ma'am. Homesteaders like you are fine folk and we are glad to have you as neighbors. But, to prove up his claim, a homesteader has to plant crops and once he gets crops in the ground he has to fence them off to keep animals from eating or trampling them."

Turning his attention to the men at his table, he continued, "So, the homesteaders fence off the flat range land. At the same time, that damn Forest Reserve Act closed the slopes of the Cascade Mountains to grazing. Now, we hear they're planning to do the same in the Ochocos. With the Shaniko railroad drawing thousands of woolies in, there's way less grazing land for all the animals."

The younger cowboy spoke again, his voice subdued and less lively than his flashing smile had been. "The cattlemen had a real hard, double winter not so long ago. They lost most of their herds to hunger, thirst and cold. They've been working to build them back up. Losing government range land to the sheep and homesteaders makes it hard to keep the cattle fed and able to survive the winter."

Brown interrupted to agree, "Yup, just about the time the cattlemen started to recover from that winter, they started losing grazing land to the sheep. They're plenty mad. There's been a bunch of threats thrown around about driving out the local sheep ranchers if they let their sheep graze on government range. Every time you turn around another one of those dead lines is thrown up. It's got so bad that we need to carry weapons for more than shooting rattlers and four-legged varmints. Matter of fact, we're on our way to Shaniko. We have to escort our shepherds and the sheep back from the shearing sheds. Five years ago, we could have stayed home and let them wander home on their own."

"Are all the cattlemen making threats?" Sage asked, hoping for some names.

"Enough of them. And something worrisome has made it worse. An old shepherd and his dog disappeared awhile ago down south in the Ochoco Mountains," the cowboy said glumly.

Siringo had mentioned the Kepler brothers' missing shepherd. "What's a dead line?" Sage asked, remembering Siringo also mentioning something about the practice.

The young cowboy jumped in to offer the explanation. "It's a line they make across the open range. They nail little signs showing a skull and cross bones to trees. And sometimes they just carve a big X in the tree bark. It means if they find you or your sheep on the other side of that tree, they're going to shoot to kill."

Before any more was said, the sales drummer crossed the threshold. His first words, as he settled into a chair at the women's table, drove all thoughts of dead lines, sheep and cattle from Sage's mind.

"They still got that smallpox epidemic going on in Prineville?" the salesman asked, then continued, "Because I'm thinking I might just go up to Charlie Clarno's place instead. He's steam boating on the John Day River. There'll be a lot of travelers heading into and out of the prospecting area. There was a whole bunch of miners in The Dalles planning on heading over to the Sumpter gold fields, near Baker City. They'll travel on that steamboat too. Maybe, they'll purchase some of my notions and such."

The remainder of the man's comments passed into Sage's ears but sounded muffled, as if submerged in a bucket of water, while the words, "smallpox epidemic going on in Prineville," kept echoing sharp and clear.

Lucinda was in Prineville. That is what Siringo had said. For the first time, Sage understood why the Dickensen man wouldn't say Lucinda was alright. His hand suddenly ached. Looking down, Sage noticed his knuckles had gone bone-white from squeezing his glass. Slowly he eased his grip and glanced around. Apparently no one had noticed his reaction.

FIVE

"How come no one in Shaniko talked about there being smallpox in Prineville?" Sage asked Dexter once they were again underway. He couldn't recollect the group's discussion after the sales drummer shared his news. All he could think of was Lucinda. Did she carry the telltale pits of smallpox on her body? He couldn't remember. A sudden stab of fear hollowed his stomach.

"I figured you'd heard about it. Everybody hereabouts knows about the pox. It was in all the newspapers. Anyway, it's been a few months now. The scare has pretty much died down. Only Prineville still has a case or two. They got themselves a pest house going in the local bordello. Far's I know, no new cases have sprung up. A doctor came down from Portland and vaccinated lots of folks."

"Local bordello," Sage echoed, his fear increasing. Sure, Lucinda operated a high class, elegant bordello in Portland. But, if she was in a Prineville bordello, how the heck did that happen? His mind flailed to find an explanation. The last he'd known, she'd left for Chicago in the company of a wealthy man. Her leaving had been Sage's fault. He'd pushed her away.

Dexter talked on, oblivious to Sage's mental churnings. "Yup, the madam moved her ladies out and turned the whole place into a hospital while the town fathers ran back and forth like chickens running from the axe. She's got herself a couple of helpers. They been nursing the sick night and day."

After again hawking brown spittle into the road, Dexter said, "'Course, now that the danger's nearly over, the mayor and councilmen are throwing their shoulders out of joint patting themselves on the back. You watch. Once the smallpox is gone, everybody in town will lickety-split forget what Miz Xenobia Brown did for them. But, I tell you," here Dexter's weathered face turned fierce, "Me and some other fellows sure won't forget any time soon."

❀ ❀ ❀

The stagecoach rolled out of Cow Canyon and into a small valley where leafy trees bordered a meandering creek. The Willowdale Station sat at the creek's edge in the shade of tall oaks. Both women deboarded. Mrs. Fromm stepped into the arms of a weathered man who had two half-grown children standing by his side. He hugged her so hard she squealed like a little girl. The new school marm shyly stood to one side. Mrs. Fromm finally struggled loose, grabbed t h e young woman's hand and pulled her close.

"Good," Sage thought, "she won't be left on her own." But that was just a passing thought. Mostly he was impatient, eager to get going. Dexter must have felt the same because he didn't tarry. The coach rolled south as soon as the horses drank their fill. Sage kept his seat atop the stagecoach, although the compartment below was empty of all but the sales drummer. Dexter's friendly chatter failed to override worrisome thoughts. Where was Lucinda? Was she okay? Those two questions became a chant in his head. He tried to ignore the horrific image of her lively, bright face scarred and waxen.

Relief came when Fong's voice sounded in his head. "Worry with no chance to find solution, is like trying to catch handful of air. Walk on. Time will provide answer." So, Sage mentally "walked on" by thinking about his promise to Siringo. As the cowboy exited Mozart's, he'd echoed

Lucinda's written words:"There's mighty fine folks in Central Oregon who will suffer if the two of us don't put a stop to the shenanigans."

Now that Sage had a met a few of those good folks, he felt that familiar claw of obligation and loyalty grab hold. He liked the cowboys who'd saved them. Plain speaking, humble, the kind of no-frills hardworking people he himself came from. And, he'd admired Mrs. Fromm and her kindness to the teacher. And there was that young woman, determinately heading into a life as foreign to her as the moon's backside. His mother, Mae Clemens, would feel right at home with these tough-spirited folk. His mother. He wished she were here. Her pithy little sayings always bucked him up.

"What do you hear about placer gold on Scissors Creek?" he asked Dexter, hoping to distract himself. He might as well start practicing his role of would-be gold prospector. No way he could pretend to be a cowboy. He couldn't ride worth a darn. And, he knew nothing about sheep. Gold panning, however, was something he knew inside and out. After a year in the Klondike, sluicing in the chill waters of Rabbit Creek, he'd become both expert and rich.

"You'd do better heading east over to the Sumpter gold fields with that sales drummer," Dexter said. "Folks have found some color in the Scissors but it's so piddling small, it's hardly worth the bother."

Of course, Sage wouldn't pan long. He couldn't investigate a range war while standing in a remote creek. Tiny nuggets from his Klondike strike were stashed deep inside his pack. He planned to spend a few days up in the mountains, maybe get seen up there by someone and then hit his "strike." No one would think it odd to see a prospector, gold burning a hole in his pocket, hanging around town.

The stage stopped briefly at the prosperous Hay Creek Ranch with its gigantic barn. Barbed wire fences ran away across rolling hills. A burnt-orange ridge marked its northern boundary. The road they'd been traveling continued due east. It was the second route to Ashwood.

The sales drummer, deciding he wanted no part of smallpox-infested Prineville, left the stage at Hay Creek. He planned to travel east through Ashwood and then north to Clarno.

Puzzled by the fact Dexter hadn't even gotten down off the seat, Sage asked why they weren't stopping over, if for no other reason than to stretch their legs.

"Well, Perry Cram back in Cow Canyon told me that there'd been a case or two of smallpox here at Hay Creek. After a couple of stagecoach drivers caught it and died, I got myself vaccinated but since I don't know about you, I figured we best not linger," said Dexter as he clucked the horses into action.

Their road trailed south up a fairly steep grade and past a distant water tank before settling down into a level route carved from the side of a gently rolling hill. Sheep grazed high in a pasture on the right side. Two gray mule deer bounded away downhill on the left. Bird song filled the air, the calls and chirps louder than coach rattles and horse clops. They rumbled onward, the stagecoach's high wheels trapped in deep parallel ruts. In the wet or the winter, this would be a treacherous road. Sage said as much to Dexter.

"That's for sure," the driver agreed. "Many a time we've all had to give a shove. The mud grabs like wet cement. Turns this here stretch into a very long eight miles. It's a fine thing to round the corner and see Morrow's place. 'Course when its dry like this, a fellow could pretty near take a nap and let the wheels follow the ruts."

Reaching the Morrow's farmhouse, they dropped off mail and boxed goods before continuing south. A few miles farther and they were rolling into Grizzly, a few stores sitting at the base of a tree-dotted mountain Dexter called "Grizzly Butte." Its few buildings faced north toward rolling grasslands. Far in the distance stood the snow-capped Cascade Range, with Mt. Hood looming highest. Dexter unloaded the deadly plow at the small general store. "Can't say I am sorry to see that farm implement gone," he commented as he fingered the lump on the back of his head. "If that blade had hit my noggin instead of the handle, I might of lost what little I have left of my marbles."

No passengers boarded at Grizzly. "Folks are still steering clear of Prineville because of the pox. There's plenty sickness hereabouts as it is—diphtheria, typhoid, scarlet fever and the like. If that pox took hold, these folks would be in a heap of trouble," Dexter explained as the coach started rolling south, skirting Grizzly Butte.

❀ ❀ ❀

In deepening dusk, they rolled out of sweet-scented pine woods into an area of low hills and along a small bluff over-looking a large, flat valley. Scored rimrock, its vertical walls black against the darkening sky, bounded the valley's northern and western edges. At the base of the rimrocks, sage covered slopes dropped to the valley floor. Green clad hills rose in the distant east. Dexter told him those were the Ochoco Mountains. To the southeast, a hill and a golden plateau formed an opening for a river to flow northward in a twisting silver ribbon. By now, the late-June snow melt would be winding down and with it, the river's water level. The deep green grass on either side meant the river had overflowed its banks earlier in the year.

Below, the town stood on the valley's western edge. It was the first real town they'd seen since Shaniko. On its west side, the town was reachable only by a wooden bridge across the river. From there it spread east into the valley with plenty of flat land for expansion. The streets were laid out in a grid pattern with structures on every block. The road crossing the bridge inter-sected a commercial main street lined by two-story wood-frame and brick buildings. He could see cross-topped power poles. Someone must have hauled an electric generator down Cow Canyon. He shook his head at the thought.

"There they be, Prineville and the Crooked River," Dexter said, letting the reins go slack so he could fish for the flask he'd left untouched since the canyon. He offered Sage the first swig and Sage took it, hoping the fiery liquid would calm his nerves.

Dexter took his gulp, sighed with satisfaction and stowed the flask. "Fine little town," he told Sage. "There's timber in the

Ochoco's. Grass and water for the livestock. It's the busiest little town in Central Oregon. Cowpokes ride in from as far away as the French Glen ranch, just to wet their whistles, pick up ranch supplies and enjoy a bit of civilization. Don't know what'll happen if Sam Hill builds his railroad to Farewell Bend instead. But, I expect the Prineville folks will think of something."

"What's the best place to stay in Prineville?" Sage asked.

"Well, the two fanciest hotels are the Poindexter and the Prineville. That last's where they say the pox got started. A Pennsylvania timber cruiser carried it in. Like I said, they haven't had a new case now for a couple of weeks. All the hotels have been disinfected top to bottom. I've hauled enough of sulfur powder in the last month to dust the whole town twice over."

Dexter glanced sideways at Sage, "You ever been in a town that's got smallpox or been vaccinated for it?" he asked.

Sage shook his head. "Nope, that is one experience I've managed to miss," he said.

"Hmm, you certain sure you want to go into town? I could find you somewheres out here to stay and tomorrow you could catch me running back up to Shaniko. Wouldn't even charge you none," Dexter offered.

Sage wondered at the man's hesitation. Surely the town had taken measures and it seemed that those efforts had been successful if the problem was dying down. "Naw, I want to see Prineville, collect a mule and supplies. I've come too far to turn back now," Sage said.

In the silence that followed, Sage asked, "Where's that quarantine house? On the outskirts of town?" The first thing he intended to do was to figure out if Lucinda was in that whorehouse-turned-hospital.

"Naw, Miz Brown's 'boarding house' as she calls it, sits smack in the middle of town. She's always been a kind woman. Treats her girls right and proper. Even gives them a trousseau and a party when they decide to leave the sporting life for a cowboy or a homesteader. I'm hoping that once the plague passes, folks will treat her better. But, you know how they are, specially the women folk. They tend to forget they pull their drawers on, one leg at a time, just like the rest of us," he said. Twitching the reins, he clucked at the tired horses. They stepped forward smartly, eager for a well-earned rest.

Sage knew exactly what Dexter was talking about. Strolling with Lucinda, he couldn't miss the glares Portland's high society matrons had sent in her direction. She'd never commented but the tightening of her fingers on his forearm meant she'd noticed. As the prosperous, bachelor owner of an exclusive restaurant, Sage was excused for such social transgressions. Lucinda, however, remained a social "untouchable." Ironically, the women doing the shunning were the real beneficiaries of prostitution. Their husbands owned the very buildings in which Portland's five hundred brothels thrived. Noses in the air, they paraded around town wearing gowns bought by prostitution's profits.

The horses' manes fluttered in the breeze as they trotted eagerly toward the livery stable. Sage studied the town as the same questions cycled through his head. "Why was Lucinda out here in the middle of Central Oregon? What is she doing here? Would he find her? Did she have smallpox? Was she still alive?"

Though his eyes stared down at the town, the image in his mind was of Lucinda's laughing face the last time they'd been together. She'd been wearing the latest fashions, each hair strand in place. Still that wasn't his most treasured mental image. Instead, it was the day he'd come upon her as she scrubbed a cookstove top. She'd been wearing faded gingham, a smudge of coal black on her cheek, wisps of hair, loosened by her vigorous scrubbing, framing a gentle, private smile.

SIX

THE STAGECOACH RATTLED OVER THE planks spanning a wide creek Dexter called the "Ochoco." The town's electric power plant sat on the far side. Cords of bark-covered slab wood filled the plant's yard on all sides. Black wires webbed the air between the building's rooftop and street poles.

Dexter noted Sage's interest in the electrical plant. "'Ole Steve Yancy hauled in Mr. Gates' two generators and a steam boiler. Brung it down in bits and pieces. Made seven hair-raising round trips from the railhead through Cow Canyon. Folks hereabouts are mighty proud because Prineville's the first Central Oregon town to have electricity. Got it back in May of 1900. 'Course the power only runs from dusk to dawn. But, still, folks figure it's a start."

They turned onto Main Street, rolling to a stop at the Hamilton Stables on the corner of Fourth. Sage dismounted, his body stiff. Dexter also clambered down after snatching a canvas mailbag from beneath the seat. He tossed it over to a postal clerk waiting on the boardwalk. The clerk strode away up the street.

A well-dressed, smiling man approached Sage and said, "Howdy Mister, you plan on staying long?"

The man's smile reached his eyes and Sage answered easily, "Why, I figures to stay for a few days. I have to collect a few things for a trip into the gold country over east, near Scissors Creek."

This wasn't the exact truth. He hoped to stay in town much longer once he invented an excuse to do so.

"Well, I suppose you know that we've had a little problem with the smallpox here in Prineville, of late," the stranger commented.

Sage glanced at Dexter, catching an expression of shame, flitting across the stagecoach driver's face. "Yes, I only learned of it on the trip down here from Shaniko," Sage answered truthfully.

"And yet, you chose to come anyway," the smiling stranger said. "Tell me, have they vaccinated you for smallpox in the past?"

That question gave Sage what his mother called the "crawlies." For the first time he wondered if this little Prineville trip was more complicated than he'd been led to believe. "Why, no, they sure haven't," he answered truthfully.

The other man stuck out his hand, "Well, sir. Let me introduce myself. My name's Dr. Rosenberg and my job is to vaccinate and fumigate your person."

Sage took an involuntary step backward. "Wait a minute, I'm not sure . . ."

The doctor shook his head, "I'm afraid you have no choice. Since you are now in an area of official pestilence quarantine, I am required to vaccinate and fumigate your person. Don't worry. It won't take long and then you'll be free to go wet your whistle at the saloon.

The doctor gently took hold of Sage's elbow and began guiding him away, saying. "You come with me alongside the stable here. We've got the fumigating station all set up and I can vaccinate you at the same time."

Dazed by the sudden turn of events, Sage allowed the doctor to lead him around the edge of the building. There stood a large wooden shipping crate stamped "Piano" in big black letters. The doctor whipped off his suit coat and quickly donned a white one. "Got to look official," he said grinning, as he gestured for Sage to enter the crate. Once Sage was inside, the doctor followed, flipping a blanket down over the entrance. The doctor picked up a vacuum can and told Sage to cover his eyes. Once Sage obeyed, Rosenberg pumped dusty clouds that landed on Sage's face, hands and clothes. The dust stank and Sage held his breath, hoping the ordeal would end before he lost consciousness.

He felt a tug. "You can uncover your eyes and exit the crate," he heard the doctor say. Sure enough, Sage dropped his hands to find that the blanket had been flip ped back atop the crate. The doctor already stood outside gulping fresh air. Sage charged through the opening. As he inhaled, he felt a burning sensation in his nose and smelled a mix of vinegar and glue. The doctor was grinning at him. "I've learned the less time you have to think about it, the better it goes," he said, leading Sage to a nearby wooden bench. Sage sat. The doctor opened a metal box while saying cheerfully, "Now that you've had the formaldehyde dusting, we'll have the smallpox inoculation. Don't worry, it won't hurt a tough fellow like yourself."

The doctor's hand emerged holding a syringe. "You'll have to take off that coat and loosen your shirt," he said, pointing the sharp needle skyward.

Sage shrugged off his coat, unbuttoned his shirt and pulled it aside, exposing his bicep. The doctor swiftly stabbed him with the needle, depressed the plunger and removed it. It stung but not bad.

As Sage buttoned up his shirt, the doctor gave him the last bit of information. "Now, you are free to walk about town. Since we haven't had any new cases, we've stopped isolating newcomers. But, you also can't leave town until we know for sure that the vaccination took. That means you'll be staying around Prineville for more than a "couple" of days. Eight at least. More, if it doesn't take. Once it takes, you can come and go as you please. Sorry. I know you were hoping to leave sooner. But only those who've had the pox or been inoculated successfully are permitted to leave or enter our fair city."

Sage smiled. This was the first good news he'd heard since rolling into Prineville.

❀ ❀ ❀

Dexter Higgenbottom stood in the White & Combs' Saloon, anchoring one end of a long bar. The stage driver had no choice but to stand. There wasn't a stick of furniture in the whole place. Sage walked up beside him, signaled the bartender for a beer and asked, "What kind of watering hole is this? Where's the furniture?"

"Wahl . . . " Dexter's Missouri drawl was more pronounced and slurred. Evidently, he'd tucked away a few whiskey shots while Sage was getting fumigated and punctured. "'Cause of the pox, they didn't want folks congregating too long," he answered. "So they ordered all the saloons to remove their furniture. Don't worry, the bartender here told me they'll be bringing it back soon 'cause the pox outbreak is about over."

Sage swallowed his beer and nodded to the bartender. Pretty good beer. They'd passed a large building sporting a "Prineville Brewery" sign. Locally brewed beer tended to be better, he realized. Maybe because the brewer himself had to hear the complaints if it wasn't. He turned to Dexter, "So, Dexter, why didn't you warn me about the piano crate, the shot and having to stay around?"

Dexter's watery blue eyes stared into Sage's. "Wahl now Mr. Miner, I used to do that for passengers. Then they'd fret and stew the whole trip. Ask me question after question I couldn't answer. I didn't want to have to tell you to ride inside. I liked your company up there on the box."

Sage knew an honest answer when he heard it. He slapped Dexter on the back, signaled the bartender to refill the stagecoach driver's glass and said, "Yeah, you're probably right. I would have come anyway and you did save me hours of fretting."

A few drinks later, Dexter staggered off to bed. He said his return trip to Shaniko started "mighty early" the next morning. Before he left, he told Sage how to find the whorehouse turned hospital. "A fella can step off the Poindexter Hotel's back porch, right into the back yard of Miz Xenobia Brown's boarding house," he said. "But you can't go in, of course. Nobody but the doctor and them with pox can go in nowadays. There's a fellow name of Ed Harbin who carries messages to and from the house. He sits right outside, in front."

Dexter eyed Sage suspiciously for the first time. "You sure are awful interested in a place most folks won't even talk about," he said.

Sage shrugged. "I was talking to the doctor. Something he said made me think maybe someone I know is in that pesthouse, that's all," he lied.

"I surely hope not. I'd rather be chased down Cow Canyon by a pack of rabid coyotes than step into that house." For a minute, Dexter's rheumy eyes clouded. He drained his glass and set it down hard on the counter. "A partner of mine died from the smallpox. It's a god awful way to go. That pox-carrying easterner wrapped up in a blanket when he rode in the coach. My friend was the driver. That night, he rolled up in that blanket to sleep. He didn't know the back East fellow was sick."

Sage laid a hand on the driver's shoulder but said nothing. The man had lost two friends in short order. No words could close those wounds.

After a rueful smile, Dexter headed toward the door only to turn back. He put a strong hand on Sage's shoulder. "See here, Miner. I won't never forget that you saved my life. You ever need any help, any help at all, you know where to find me. I'm driving either to or from Shaniko every day except Sunday." With that, the driver staggered across the unfurnished floor and out onto the boardwalk.

He could tell The Poindexter Hotel was short on guests since most of the room keys were still in their slots. Mr. Poindexter repeatedly assured Sage that, without fail, the hotel was disinfected every single day from top to bottom. Sage hadn't asked and didn't care. Tired from the long trip, he just wanted to sleep. Still, he did want the answer to one question. "Who is this Ed Harbin fellow folks are talking about?" he asked.

"Oh my, oh my." The hotel keeper's round face glowed with pride. "Our Mr. Harbin is quite the hero in these parts," he said. "Why, he's built a little visitors' stand that sits in the street next over. Right smack dab in front of the pesthouse. You can't miss him. There's a white flag with a red cross hanging above a little crate. Folks want to get a message, food or any old thing to a pox victim, they just take it to Ed and off he goes. Delivers messages and medicine to the pesthouse but also bicycles things out to folks quarantined on farms and ranches. Harbin says he's already had the pox, so there's no worry he'll catch it again. The man's neglecting his shingle-making business something awful. He tells everybody that he's just doing his duty. The Poindexter, the Prineville and the town's other restaurants, we take our turns at keeping him fed."

When Sage asked for a room at the back of the hotel, Poindexter gave him the key to one on the second floor. I t w as typical—iron bedstead, tall wardrobe, porcelain wash bowl and cushioned chair. A narrow window overlooked the house behind the hotel. Sage pulled the chair next to the window. Moonlight glinted dimly on the house's tin roof. The yard was deep and narrow. He could see a covered porch, squat bush, leaf tree and privy outbuilding. He wished he could see through walls. He wished he could hear the voices that must be speaking inside the house.

Tomorrow, he would make the acquaintance of Prineville's newest hero. "Tomorrow," he promised himself, "Tomorrow, I'll know whether she's inside."

SEVEN

SAGE JERKED AWAKE. EVERY JOINT in his body protested as he struggled up from the chair. Peering at his pocket watch, he could just make out that it was four in the morning. Too early to go looking for Lucinda. He untied and removed his boots before staggering to the bed. Falling on it, he yanked the coverlet over his shoulders as his head hit the pillow.

The whap of a privy door shutting woke him the second time. Sunlight shone brightly through the window's rectangle. The room had grown too warm for the coverlet. He flung it aside. His watch showed close to eight o'clock. Stepping to the window he looked out just in time to see a woman's skirt swish out of sight beneath the back porch overhang. "Damn," he muttered.

Splashing water on his face, he decided not to shave, although his moustache drooped and whiskers darkened his chin. Not exactly how he'd like to look when Lucinda set eyes on him for the first time in almost a year. But John Miner, gold prospector, needed to look rough. Besides, it wouldn't be the first time she saw him that way. She knew of his double life. More than once, she'd helped him switch from John Adair, Mozart's proprietor, to John Miner, itinerant worker.

Less than an hour later, Sage exited the hotel to stand in the shade of its covered porch. They'd served a plentiful breakfast. No doubt hard-working cowboys expected a ranch-style breakfast whenever they came to town. A giggling gaggle of girls, dressed in ankle-high walking dresses, wheeled past on their safety bicycles. As one, their young appraising eyes turned toward Sage. Then, like a school of fish, their attention snapped forward as their bicycles formed two lines. They pedaled by on either side of a fire cistern's wooden cover that anchored a nearby intersection. A call drifted back to him, "Maisy Bell, I saw you a'look'n. Don't you be shopping. Billy won't like it!" More giggles trailed behind them as they rode up the street.

Sage stepped into the street, taking in the hodgepodge of false-front clapboards and new brick buildings. Definitely a bustling place. In the distance, a dramatic jut of yellow rimrock stood against a blue, cloudless sky. Sage slowly turned, surveying this spot people had picked to build a town. Plentiful water flowed in lazy loops across the fl at, gr assy va lley. Pine dark mountains rising in the east meant lumber and firewood were close to hand. A tree-dotted hill and a majestic plateau cupped the valley on the south. It seemed a sheltered place.

For the first time, he felt the beauty. A spare, merciless land, yes. Yet there was an awe-inspiring grandeur, too. It reminded him of those times he'd stood on a mountainside above the tree line, his eyes following the dramatic granite upthrusts that stretched away into the distance. The big sky and expansive landscape seemed to stretch a man's thoughts out, make them bigger.

"Well, Tourist," came a familiar drawl, "you stand there gawking too much longer and those sheep are going to plant you into the dirt with their pointy little feet."

Sage whirled. The lanky figure of Charlie Siringo leaned against a porch post. Behind Sage came a baaing and bleating that was growing louder. Sure enough, a flood of dingy white wool rounded the street corner, flowing toward him up the wide dirt street. Sage joined Siringo on the porch.

Bells tinkling on their leaders' collars, the noisy herd advanced in a rush, two dusty men keeping pace on either side. Black and white dogs raced along the edges, keeping the noisy critters tightly bunched and moving forward. The woolies' slanted eyes, in their black triangle faces, were fiercely intent.

People appeared on the boardwalks to watch. Some onlookers were merely interested. A greater number scowled. A few spat into the dusty street before returning inside, their backs stiff.

Sage looked toward Siringo. The cowboy's narrowed eyes were scanning the scene, his face expressionless. The man looked every inch a cowpoke just ridden off the range. His brown, wide-brimmed hat was sweat-stained. A dark blue kerchief set off the faded red of his long sleeved shirt. Well-worn denim trousers were tucked into scuffed, pointy-toed, boots. He looked like he'd been born to wear the outfit.

"More and more folks are taking exception to those animals trotting up Main Street," Siringo said out of the side of his mouth. More softly he said, "Since I saw you last, there's been some mighty big saloon talk." Siringo's mouth twisted in disgust, "And some fool folks are listening. Never ceases to amaze me just how many folks are right glad to turn their thinking over to somebody else. They're not much different from those sheep. Damn, glad you got here," he finished up.

"She's in the pesthouse, isn't she?" Sage asked. "Is she sick?" The Dickensen detective tore his eyes away from the street scene to study Sage, his gaze sharpening. "No. She's tired but she doesn't have the pox. When folks took sick, Xenobia cleared out her house and started nursing. Next day or so, Ms. Lucinda Collins arrived on the stagecoach. She went right to helping out. She didn't stop at the hotel or nothing. Went straight into the pesthouse and hasn't been out since."

Siringo looked away, "She tells me she had the pox as a kid, same as me. 'Course it hasn't been easy. Folks are mighty sick. Some have died. And, she can't leave since the house is quarantined. I guess you know why I didn't tell you."

"You thought I wouldn't come if I couldn't even talk to her," Sage answered dryly.

That comment brought a nod from Siringo. "I am doing all I can with the cattlemen but I got no one on the sheep side that I can trust. Since I saw you last, more sheep are dead. Worse, a young shepherd and his dog were murdered a few days ago. That's one barn, two flocks of sheep and one, maybe two shepherds and their dogs killed. I don't know how much longer the sheepmen will hold back."

The detective looked straight at Sage. "The violence is building. Those dead lines are going up all over. Hell, I've tacked up a few signs my own self just to prove I'm a true blue, sheep-hating cowboy. I'm still trying to figure out which group of cattlemen might be involved in the violence. I need someone to learn whether the sheepmen are planning to retaliate. I'd sure the heck be thinking about it if I wore their boots."

He paused to study the street. The sheep had disappeared around the far corner and most of the observers had turned back inside. Stepping closer he told Sage in a low voice, "There's a fellow that's part owner of the Rimrock Saloon. His name's Asa Rayburn. He used to work for Charles Bellingham, a sheep rancher up north. He doesn't strike me as an upright fellow but he knows all the sheepmen hereabouts—ranchers and shepherds. I'm thinking you might spend some time getting to know him. Maybe, through him, you can get in with the sheepmen."

Just then a group of men exited the hotel behind them. Siringo touched his hat brim, turned and clumped away down the boardwalk. Watching Siringo leave, Sage murmured to the man's back, "You were wrong, Siringo. I would have come anyway."

❀ ❀ ❀

The two-story clapboard house sat low, needing only a single step to reach its covered porch. There a man sat on a wooden chair. Only his bare shins and feet basked in the morning sun. He seemed to be dozing. Ten feet into the street stood a wooden freight box with a single pole nailed to one corner. The pole held aloft a limp flag, white with a single red cross. Willow baskets sat atop the crate. Two small kegs were on either side, evidently serving as stools for the stand's attendant and guest. No one was there.

Sage went to the stand. Inside one basket he saw folded notes addressed to various people. In another, a jagged rock held down sheets of blank paper. A nearby jar held a collection of hand-sharpened pencils. He gazed up and down the street. It was empty of life except for a sand-colored dog. It trotted onto a neighboring porch and lay down with a sigh, its pink tongue lolling in the heat. Sage sat on one of the empty wooden kegs.

"Ed took medicine out to the Carter place for Doc Belknap. After that, he's delivering a few groceries. He'll be back shortly," called a voice from the porch. The dozing man had woke and stood, his hand on the doorknob.

"Wait," Sage called as he jumped up. Maybe this man, who looked like some kind of accountant with his black arm braces and wire-rimmed glasses, could at least confirm that Lucinda was inside. But the man raised a hand, "I'm not supposed to be out here. Just had to get some fresh air. Rough night." He gave a tired wave before disappearing inside and closing the door softly.

"Oh, hell's bells," Sage said.

Ten minutes later a solitary, smallish fellow peddled up the street. Reaching the stand, the man hopped off his safety bicycle, leaned it against the box, dusted down his clothes and turned to Sage, saying cheerfully, "Howdy, stranger. Ed Harbin's my name. Can I help you?"

Sage reached out a hand, "John Miner's mine. I am sure hoping you can help me out. I've heard tell of your great doings during this epidemic."

As they shook, Sage studied the small man who was in his early fifties. He had a full head of scruffy hair dusting a smooth brow above straight eyebrows, wide-spaced eyes, snub nose and square jaw. The total package was a likeable face that would appear youthful no matter what his age.

"Yup, I suppose so," the man acknowledged without a trace of pride. "Already had smallpox myself so's I can't get it again. Folks need to communicate with those who've got the pox. Keep their spirits up and maybe mend fences that got broke down some time ago. And, the sick need medicine and food and some-times, may God protect, burying," Harbin's voice trailed off.

Sage let the man work through his memories and out the other side. And Harbin did sort it out because, after taking a deep breath, he continued, "So here I am, delivering messages, medicine and such. I suspect you're wanting a message carried?"

"Mr. Harbin, I really would like to get a message to someone I think is inside the pesthouse over there," Sage nodded toward the house. "Her name is Miss Lucinda Collins."

The man's eyes widened and brightened at the name. "Oh, she sure is there all right. A real vision," he said. "Not that I get to see her much. They're supposed to stay inside, you know. You a friend of hers?"

Sage had thought long and hard about how he was going to answer that particular question. If he claimed too close of an acquaintance, his activities might place her in grave danger. On the other hand, he had to have a good excuse for seeing her. "I'm a friend of her brother actually. Only met her once, briefly. But I told him I'd look in on her. Make sure she's all right," he told Harbin.

"Far's I know, she's doing fine, if a bit overworked. There's just the three of them in there taking care of folks—Miss Collins, Frank Hart and the house's mad . . . ah, proprietor, Miz Xenobia Brown." He looked at Sage speculatively before saying, "She arrived right after the quarantine started. Said she'd had smallpox and was an old friend to Miz Brown. She insisted on going inside and helping. Been there some weeks now."

"So, she's still healthy?"

"Was the last time I saw her, a few days ago. She's gone a bit pale and skinny but you'd expect that. You want me to take her a message?" Harbin asked as he gestured toward the blank paper in the wicker basket. "I'm the only one allowed on the porch, other than the doctor. Can't bring a message out though. People think smallpox can be carried on paper. That's why the postmaster in Silver Lake rejects all Prineville mail. It's causing all sorts of problems."

"A good idea, Mr. Harbin. I'll write a note," Sage said as he sat again on the nearest keg. Harbin stretched his arms over his head and then twisted his waist like a pugilist loosening up before a fight. Reaching for the paper and taking up a pencil, Sage asked. "You stay here all day?"

"Pretty much. I'd just started up a whipsaw mill when the epidemic struck. Figure, once it's over, I'll be back to feeding wood through the planer. I go home at dark, of course, but I'm right back here first light in the morning. Daytime, the hotels and restaurants take turns bringing me food. So, I pretty much stay put here at the box unless I'm gone on deliveries."

"How soon do you think it will be over?" Sage asked. He hated the idea of not being able to talk privately with her. She was so close after all these months when he'd wondered where and how she was. His fault of course. At least, that was the point his mother had made repeatedly.

Harbin raked stubby fingers through his thick hair. "Well, right at the start Dr. Hutchinson come in from Portland. He brought vaccine. Gave shots to over 2,000 people hereabouts. Dr. Rosenberg's kept up with it after that. The vaccinating and fumigating seems to have slowed the disease pretty good. We've only had one new outbreak in the last two weeks. Everyone else has either died or is on the mend. I've been delivering medicine out to the Carter place. Both of them are better. The fellow inside also seems to have made it through last night. He's the last one who took ill with it. I expect I'll be back at my mill soon." The man sighed, an expression of regret flitting across his face.

Prineville's shingle maker was going to miss his role of town hero. Sage understood. Having a higher purpose in one's life was more satisfying than the humdrum of merely making a living.

As Harbin talked, Sage wrote, "Dear Miss Collins. My name is John Miner. You may not remember me since we only made acquaintance one time. I am a friend of your brother, Philander. He asked me to stop in Prineville and ascertain that you are all right and have no unmet needs. I await those reassurances. Your servant, John Miner."

He handed the note to Harbin who promptly folded it without reading it and hopped down from his keg. "I'll run it over there right now," he called over his shoulder as he strode toward the pesthouse.

EIGHT

IT TOOK FOREVER FOR THE door to open and for her to step across the threshold onto the porch. Her eyes shone bright in the pallor of her face. Beneath a faded calico dress, her figure seemed slight, lacking its customary roundness. Her hair was a piled jumble atop her head. Their eyes met and locked. Sounds of robin warble and prairie twitter muted. Lucinda's eyes flicked to one side and he realized that Harbin was avidly observing this meeting between brother's friend and brother's sister.

Lucinda recovered first. "Mr. Miner, how nice to see you again." Her clear voice was warm, carrying just a hint of laughter.

He stepped toward her only to have Harbin hustle forward to block any further advance. "Here, now. The sheriff and Doctor Rosenberg issued very strict orders. There's to be no mingling between folks outside the house with those inside the house. I could already get in trouble with the Doc for letting Miss Lucinda come out onto the porch. Don't you move any closer, Mr. Miner."

The urge to smack the fellow upside the head was strong until Sage reminded himself that Harbin was Prineville's hero of the hour. It wouldn't do to get on the wrong side of him. So instead he said, "Oh, sorry Mr. Harbin. I forgot. Smallpox is something new for me."

"Precisely why it is all the more important that you be extra careful," said Harbin, a smile softening the bite of his words.

Over the man's shoulder he could see Lucinda grinning. When Harbin turned to look, though, her face had already composed itself into one of polite interest.

Harbin turned back, his broad forehead creased. The man was clearly receiving weak signals from his something's-not-exactly-right intuition. "If you'll promise me that you won't take another step closer, I'll let you two converse a few minutes more," was all he said.

Sage held up both hands in surrender. "Not one step closer, Mr. Harbin. I won't move one step closer," he promised, stifling his own grin.

Harbin nodded and then turned on his heel, strolling toward the end of the block.

"How are you doing, Lucinda?" was all Sage could think to say.

Her hands went to her hips and she said with some exasperation, "Well, really Sage. After over a month cleaning up messes and changing bed linen, I can't say I'm feeling my best!" The sternness vanished as she flashed him a smile, "And you, how are you? You don't exactly look like a cowpoke from around these here parts."

He laughed at her attempted cowgirl talk. "Well, that's because I am a gold panning fool, looking to make my fortune in the Ochocos over east of town, Ma'am," he added, with a shy duck of his head.

She stepped forward to the edge of the porch and for the first time the sun struck her full on, catching at the rich honey glints of her hair and the cornflower blue of her eyes. There was welcome in her face. She was happy to see him.

She chuckled. "Smart choice. You'd have a hard time pretending to be a cowboy since you're afraid of horses. And, how was your trip out?" she added primly.

"Well, I had a runaway stagecoach ride down Cow Canyon. That left me with a few bruises. And, despite two scrubbings,

I swear that fumigating powder is still on my hide. Other than that, I can't complain."

He saw her eyes shift to one side so he followed the direction of her gaze. True to his word, Ed Harbin had turned and was slowly ambling back in their direction.

"Listen," Sage said hurriedly. "We need to talk without our chaperone hanging on every word. "I'm in the Poindexter, right behind the house here. Any chance of meeting, after dark tonight, in your back yard?"

She nodded. "I'll head to the outhouse at ten-thirty. You know we can't stand close to each other, right?"

He nodded grimly. More than anything he just wanted to wrap his arms around her and hold her tight until they reached that place where things had been right between them.

She must have read his thoughts because her smile turned sweet and wistful even as she raised her voice to say loud enough for Harbin to hear, "I thank you for stopping by and bringing me word of Philander. Please let him know that, if there are no new smallpox cases in the next few days, we expect Dr. Rosenberg to lift the quarantine. Then I can travel on. I just couldn't leave my good friend Xenobia to fend for herself once she decided to turn her boarding house into a hospital."

"Is it just the two of you doing all the nursing then?" Sage asked.

"No, we also have a man helping us, Frank Hart. He's an accountant who was traveling through and he's also had smallpox. Between the three of us, we've nursed ten people back to health. Only one man died, early on."

Harbin reached them and stood nervously by Sage's side. Clearly he was afraid the doctor would catch them conversing. Their goodbye's said, Lucinda entered the house and softly closed the door.

Sage stood in the dirt street, staring at the door until Harbin cleared his throat to say, "Mighty fine looking woman there. She's done Prineville an awful good turn, especially seeing as how she doesn't know but one of us."

Slapping his hat back onto his head, Sage looked at Harbin. "Yes," was all he could think to say to both comments.

The restaurant attached to the Poindexter Hotel lobby was nearly full when Sage decided he'd seen all there was to see in Prineville and that it was time to stop the stomach growls. On his tour he'd passed a few window signs that declared, "We Promise to Have White Cooks Only." Sage puzzled over the sign until he remembered. Many restaurants in the West had Chinese cooks. Evidently the owners of the establishments displaying that proclamation thought that open prejudice would attract more customers. For Sage, that sign meant he'd take his business elsewhere.

His town tour hadn't taken long. Its few commercial streets mostly sported clapboard false fronts. But, here and there were newer, stone and brick buildings. Elsewhere, streets were lined by wood-framed houses. Plenty of buildings, commercial and residential, were under construction. That explained the brick works and the sawmill at the edge of town.

Prineville was a cow town. There were cowboy outfitters, harness makers and hitching rails for cow ponies outside most businesses. Still, few ponies were tied up and few people were walking or riding along the town's wide dirt streets. Undoubtedly the epidemic was keeping folks away. People living in the outlying areas were likely traveling to Farewell Bend, thirty-five miles south, when they wanted to frolic or make purchases. The epidemic had to be a hard hit to Prineville's commercial interests.

The Poindexter's food was decent, though not quite as good as Ida's. It seemed that only Ida knew how to butter fry potatoes so they weren't greasy. He had his fork to his lips when two men in suits appeared in the lobby archway. The head waiter bustled over to seat them, his manner declaring these were important guests, "Congressman Thomas and Dr. Van Ostrand, how are you gentlemen today?" he queried as he ushered them to a table at the room's center. His subsequent banter indicated the two were regular customers. Once the waiter departed, though, the men quickly sobered. They leaned across the table toward one another as if fearful of being overheard.

When the waiter came to refill his coffee cup, Sage asked, "Did I hear you say 'Congressman'?"

The energetic fellow puffed up a bit as he answered, "Why yes, that's our local Congressman, Newt Thomas—the fellow wearing the red bow tie. He lives here in Prineville when he's not back in Washington D.C. The other fellow with him is Dr. Van Ostrand. He's our local dentist."

"Looks like they are discussing important business." Sage said, hoping to trigger more revelations. It worked.

"Well, I guess that would be right. They're in the stock business together."

"Cattlemen?"

The waiter shook his head. "Nope, they're sheep ranchers. They have a big flock, out on the range east of town. They used to lease sections from the toll road company but this year, the road company pulled those leases."

"Here I was thinking Prineville was a cattle town," Sage said.

"Oh it sure enough is," the waiter assured him. "But, there's a passel of sheep hereabouts, some say up to a quarter million. Lots more than there are cattle."

"That's got to cause hard feelings, when the cows and the sheep try to eat the same grass. From what I saw on my trip down, there's not a lot to eat out there."

For the first time, the waiter's features seemed to close down and his brown eyes squinted as he looked at Sage "I am new in town" he said. "Still, I've seen some fights and heard some pretty rough words exchanged between the cowboys and the herders. Best thing to do mister, is keep your nose to yourself and not ask too many questions. Stick to your gold panning." With that, he walked away leaving Sage staring into a full coffee cup.

Forthright advice. He realized Prineville was not Portland. There'd be no cruising its saloons and shops asking questions unless he wanted to trigger speculation. He'd said nothing to anyone at the Poindexter about gold panning—yet the waiter was clearly informed about Sage's business. The best plan would be to keep his mouth shut and his ears wide open if he wanted to learn more about the budding range war.

Sage studied the two sheep ranchers. Their faces looked somber. No wonder. They'd lost their grazing land just when sheep shootings, barn burnings, shepherd killings and dead lines were on the rise. Definitely a rough time for sheepmen. Studying their tense faces out of the corner of his eye, Sage wondered whether those two were plotting the retaliation Siringo feared.

Groggy after an early afternoon nap in his hot hotel room, Sage ordered coffee from the saloon's morose barkeep. Despite the open door and windows, it was stifling inside the Rimrock Saloon. He stood at the bar, as did the few other subdued patrons. The saloon was strictly complying with the ban on tables and chairs.

His coffee cup empty, Sage waved off a refill. Instead he ordered a sarsparilla, its cool sweetness proof that the barkeep had managed to ice it down. A man stood a few feet further along the bar. He wore the low heeled boots and leather vest of a sheepherder. From the sag of his shoulders it was clear that troubling thoughts weighed heavy on him. Sage cleared his throat to get the man's attention. "Say, mister, it looks like you're having a hard day of it. Can I buy you a beer or a sarsparilla? Don't know about the beer but this soda's mighty cool on the throat."

The man lifted his head, his face uncomprehending. Then his thoughts seemed to travel back from a far distance and his gaze sharpened. "Why, I guess that would be all right," he told Sage in an accent straight from Ireland's green pastures. "I'm drinking birch beer since I don't care much for the rooty taste of the sarsparilla."

He moved closer and thrust out his hand. "My name's Twilleran Parnell McGinnis. 'Parnell' for that great Irish nationalist, too soon departed. Call me 'Twill' for short. Mayhaps

I will switch to straight beer. I plan to get blootered this day and night. In memory of a lost friend, don'cha know? So it's gratitude I have for your offer. Would you care to partake in the imbibing of sociable drinks?"

McGinnis was a tall man, standing maybe two inches above Sage's six feet. He was black-haired and blue-eyed like Sage. He had a s quare jaw, wide mouth, and smooth brow above sweeping dark eyebrows. Though he was broody about his dead friend, his face showed good humor and kindness.

Sage soon learned that Twill had indeed traveled to Oregon from County Cork in the old country. His story was simple. "There's a band of us who came to Oregon to herd sheep. John G. Doherty, has the big spread, up in Morrow County. He sent us a special invite to Oregon—paid our way. He knew us Irish boys are well and truly trained in the fine art of shepherding. He traveled his own self from the Emerald Isle. Only other men who know sheep as well, are the Basques. They're the small brown fellows from the Spanish mountains. But the Basques work further east, over toward Baker City and beyond. Of course, they walk through here when they deliver their sheep to Shaniko for shearing. Got to know a few."

Sage signaled for a beer, saying to Twill, "People's spirits here in the Rimrock seem a little low today. Is that because of your friend?" At Twill's nod, Sage said, "I've heard that you shepherds are a quiet bunch compared to cowpokes riding off the range. You're not planning on taking revenge are you?"

Twill looked at Sage, his face suddenly watchful. "Well, I can see from looking at you that you're no cowboy. What might you be doing in Prineville?" he asked, ignoring Sage's question.

Apparently, the Prineville gossip telegraph did not extend into the Rimrock. So, Sage told Twill about his intention to pan for gold in Scissors Creek.

Twill looked doubtful. "I've heard that trout's the only thing to be found in that creek. They might be having a bit of gold color on their scales but I'm thinking it's not the metal kind."

Sage laughed, "Yah, that's what I've been hearing. But I'm here now and my poke is getting low. I need to find something to do."

"Well, don't contemplate sheep herding," Twill said. "You're right about us feeling sorrow. Two days ago someone shot ewes and lambs over at Gray's Meadow. Shot them when they were penned up and couldn't get away. The bastard also killed the herding dog. And he murdered the herder, my friend. Twill raised his glass and shouted, "Here's to Timothy O'Dea, a grander son of Ireland was never before seen upon this godforsaken plain!" "Hear, hears" echoed and Twill raised his glass again, "And here's to his loyal dog, Felan. No herding dog was ever finer!" Another chorus of "hear, hear" rolled along the bar.

Twill wasn't done mourning his friend. He ordered a round for himself and Sage before saying, "The real heart ringer is that Tim was planning to give up herding. He and Felan were going to leave the flocks. Settle down and farm. Tim was excited about it. He'd managed to lay claim to some land up there in the Ochoco's and was going to start proving it up."

"I thought it cost money to file a claim."

The Irishman was nodding, "Tim didn't spend much money. He was such a fine fellow. Do anything for you. Liked to laugh, he did. But shy, you know? Especially with the ladies. Ah, What for? I ask you, what was it for? Timothy and Felan are gone, dead and gone. My glory is I had such friends." Twill didn't seem to notice the tears coursing down his cheeks, onto the bar and into his beer.

After a few moments of silence, Sage turned to the barkeep. "Say, I notice that sign on the wall says there's bunking space for rent upstairs. I'm staying at the Poindexter but that's more than I can afford. You got any space left?" After making the arrangements, he ordered another round. Might as well keep the Irishman company for a while longer. It was the least he could do.

❀ ❀ ❀

Miles from town, far out on the rolling vastness of dry prairie, Charlie Siringo carefully slid out of his saddle. He'd stripped off his spurs, knowing that he'd have to step stealthily once the man he trailed reached his destination. Putting a calming hand on the horse's velvet nose, he tied its reins to a scrub bush. To the south, straight ahead, the crown of a solitary juniper tree stood beneath moonlight dulled by a thin cloud layer. The yellow flicker at the tree's base meant this was the meeting place.

He dropped into a crouch, freezing as the sound of a horse blowing nearby broke the quiet. Another horse and rider were approaching from the west. The dull moonlight meant the meeting tree was easy to spot, but it also meant any hombre trying to sneak closer could also be seen—especially by those traveling in from the dark. He'd have to wait until they'd all arrived. Wait until their attention was focused on each other, the fire blinding their night vision. Only then could he creep close enough to hear what they were planning. Siringo carefully pulled a tobacco pouch from his pocket before lowering himself down. He stretched out on his belly, his narrow hips squeezed between two rocks. He breathed in the tang of sage and sun dried bunch grass, tucked a wad of chew into his cheek and watched the distant fire flicker as he waited for the Crook County sheepshooters' meeting to begin.

NINE

SHORTLY AFTER TEN O'CLOCK, SAGE wandered out the Poindexter's front door. He left behind a snoozing desk clerk and the quiet snores of a cowboy who hadn't made it past the lobby. Country folk were early risers. He moved north, along the front of the hotel, until he reached a break in the storefronts. After looking carefully around, he slipped into the gap. Stepping over rusted tin cans and garbage that had found a final resting place, he reached the back of the buildings. Once there, he moved cautiously until he was between the pesthouse privy and the hotel's rear porch. He hoped that someone in the rooms above wasn't gazing out his window.

He didn't have long to wait. Loose glass in the pesthouse's back door rattled as it was softy opened and shut. Ears straining, he could hear the scuff of shoes and squeak of the privy door. As if he would have waited in there!

Her voice softly called, "Sage?"

"Here, behind the privy," he whispered loudly. Then she was there, her face a pale oval in the cloudy moonlight. He wished the clouds would drift away so that he could see better. He squinted and slowly her features resolved. She looked tired, thin, lovely. He took a deep breath and let it out. At last they could talk. It had been a long time. He was so full of unspoken words that all he could manage was "Hi. Nice night."

Her response was to squint her eyes, her brow creasing, before she stepped closer. "Good heavens," she whispered. "What happened to you?"

Involuntarily, he reached up to gently finger his mouth. Siringo had planted him a good one. "I'll tell you in a minute," Sage said. "First, I want to make sure we can meet this same time and place every night. Then I want hear what you have to say about what's been going on around here."

She nodded and said, "All right. We can meet here every night you are in town. If you have to leave, tie a rag on that bush." She pointed to the stubby shrub. "Thank you for coming, Sage," she said without a smile.

"Did you think there was any chance I wouldn't?"

This time her smile seemed wistful. Maybe it was the lack of light? He stepped forward, trying to see better.

She didn't seem to notice. "I really didn't know. I hoped you'd come, if for nothing more than for old time's sake," was all she said as she also stepped forward—stopping close enough that he could smell her perfume but still far enough away that he could not touch her. He moved forward. She jumped back and held up a hand. "No Sage, you're too close. This meeting is dangerous enough. You don't want to catch smallpox. I would never forgive myself. And neither would your mother," she added.

He smiled and stepped back. "She misses you. She'd blame me, not you. Besides, I am sure you would nurse me back to health in no time," he said.

This time she shook her head slowly. "I wish that were true but people have died in this epidemic. One of them in this very house. We did everything we could and nothing we did saved him. He was young, healthy and dead within a few days." For a moment she stood silent. In that pause a faint breeze flowed through, rustling the leaves of the back yard's lone tree.

She seemed to tuck away the sadness because her face transformed from pensive to alert. "He's the reason I thought Charlie needed your help," she said.

"Charlie? You mean Siringo?" How had the Dickensen man gained her confidence so quickly? When had they even had a chance to talk?

This time, her lips twisted sideways in that rueful quirk of hers. "Charlie's a longtime friend of Xenobia's. He always visits her whenever he's in Oregon. I had already planned to see her on my way back to Portland. When the epidemic broke out, she had him hustle up to The Dalles to meet my train from Chicago. She didn't want me exposed to smallpox. She already had the hospital up and running."

"And so, of course, you immediately insisted on traveling back to Prineville with Siringo to help your friend in her hospital," Sage finished for her.

Her face tightened but all she said was, "Well, of course. Charlie said it was a big outbreak and Xenobia had no one helping her. Frank came along to help after I did. 'Anyways,' as your mother would say, I'd had smallpox as a child so it made sense. Later, during an outbreak in Spokane, I learned how to nurse people with the pox. And," she added, "I was in no hurry to reach Portland."

That last statement hit like a blow. So, Lucinda had not been planning a grand reunion with him. Sage swallowed his hurt and asked, "So tell me about the fellow who died."

"He was a young man up from Missouri in the last year or so. He worked as a ranch hand for a while but then tried to find work here in town. That's when he came down with the pox. We took him in, but at the last he became delirious. Most of what he said made no sense at all. He keep asking me for forgiveness. He thought I was a nun or something because he kept calling me 'sister.'" She paused and turned her face up to the clouds, the glitter of unshed tears in her eyes.

When she looked at him again, she said, "It sounded like he'd had a hand in some really bad business and was carrying a lot of guilt about it. He talked about dying sheep. And, he mumbled something about an old guy. Whenever he talked about him, he'd start crying. He never said directly, but I think someone must have died."

"Siringo told me there's been sheepshootings and an old shepherd is missing," Sage said slowly, as he tried to work out the timing.

"Yes, I thought of that old shepherd too. But, that's the thing. That's why Charlie needs your help. The young man, his name was Harry Perkins, also kept saying that it wasn't over. He begged me to stop it but he never said what 'it' was. And over and over, he said he should have made up his own mind, not followed. He kept saying he'd broke the moral compass his mama gave him. Sometimes he swore that he'd just given his compass 'away'." Her voice had thickened with unshed tears, making it difficult for her to speak. She drew in a shaky breath. "He was so ravaged by guilt, Sage. I think that's why he died. He just couldn't bear to live with whatever it was that he had done."

Sage wondered whether the dead man had been a sheep-shooter. Next he caught himself wishing Lucinda wouldn't call Siringo "Charlie" with such easy familiarity. He quickly shut down that last thought. Now was not the time to add jealousy to the already complex state of affairs.

Lucinda sighed. "That's about all I know. Now suppose you tell me how Mr. Fong's number one student managed to get that fat lip?"

A squirt of malicious anticipation made Sage smile. "'Charlie' did it," he said.

That day's late afternoon had been sweltering. Sage had sat on the hotel's veranda, hoping for a breeze. His head felt mud-dled by the heat and by the beer he'd drunk in Twill's company. Woozily he perused the columns of the *Crook County Journal*. His eyelids drooped. Just as he decided that a nap might be the best way to beat the heat, a commotion broke out about a block away. A group of men, their boots and dress declaring them to be members of the cowboy tribe, encircled another man. Their drunken shouts and laughter sounded threatening. Sage rose and began ambling in their direction. As he did so, he chastised himself for getting involved in something that would surely be gossiped about. He also reminded himself not to use any of Fong's fighting techniques. People didn't need to know that the would-be prospector, John Miner, was trained in an exotic fighting art. That'd really get their tongues wagging.

The cowboys were shoving someone from one side of the group to the other. For a brief second, Sage saw that they were picking on a tall, black-haired man. He quickened his pace. When he was within twenty feet, he heard the familiar Irish lilt. "I'm seeing that you Missouri boyo's are cowards. Can't take on a wee Irishman unless there's a crowd of you!"

No doubt about it. Twill McGinnis was taunting the cowboys. Sage increased his pace only to nearly miss a step when he recognized Charlie Siringo standing on the far side of the cowboy circle.

"Which one of you cowardly cowpokes killed my friend, Timothy O'Dea? You think you want a fight, then? I'm ready to knock your pans in! I haven't had me the pleasure of busting craniums in a while." Twill was in full-throated Irish rage. Doubtless he'd continued his wake for his dead friend and was far from his clear-headed best.

Sage had no choice. Besides, a calculating voice inside his head also murmured, "And this might be just the way to earn a place among the sheepmen."

Reaching the circle, Sage raised his voice. "Well, now, is this the way to cool off on a hot summer day, my friends?" As one, the cowboys turned to look at him and even Twill ceased his taunting. Then, realizing help had arrived, Twill sprang into action. He took a swing at a cowboy who promptly returned the favor. Sage hadn't done any bare-knuckle fighting since meeting Fong, so his first swing was somewhat clumsy. Then he got into the rhythm and landed quite a few punches. Fong's endless lessons in how to sense an attack and stand firmly rooted paid off. Soon he and Twill were back-to-back and holding their own. That all changed when Charlie Siringo stepped forward and unexpectedly slammed a fist into Sage's mouth. Sage hit the street's hard-packed dirt, his lips forming a questioning "what?" Before he could regain his feet and go after Siringo to return the favor, the fight was over.

"Break it up, I said! Or you'll all end up spending the night in the calaboose! It's too damn hot for this nonsense," shouted a man looming over Sage. Sunlight glinted on a silver star pinned to the man's lapel. Prineville's sheriff had arrived. Slowly rising to his feet, Sage turned to help Twill up as well. The cowboys were already slinking off, heading toward the nearby White and Combs Saloon.

It was only then that Sage noticed that the sheriff was holding a pistol by the barrel. Once the sheriff holstered his gun, he said, "You two get off Main Street, now. If, you need to wet your whistles after this dust up, head over to the Rimrock. I don't want to see either of you in the White's."

"But, those cowboys . . ."

The sheriff didn't let Sage finish. "Those cowboys . . . ." he interrupted, "just rode 180 dusty miles up from the FrenchGlenn Ranch. They got in this morning and have been drinking ever since. You stay out of their way until they've got the trail out of their system. They don't like sheepmen and they're spoiling for a fight." With that, he turned his back and walked away.

Twill stuck out a hand. "I am more than grateful for your assistance, Mister John Miner," he said. "I was putting up a brave front but preparing for the worst. You helped even things up a bit. I do believe we held our own and then some."

Sage laughed, only to feel the smarting of a torn lip.

"Let's go over to the Rimrock, like the sheriff suggested," said Twill, as he slapped his dusty hat against his leg.

"Tell you what," Sage replied, "I'll just go get some ice from the hotel and maybe put on a clean shirt and meet you over there."

When Sage reached his room, he noticed the door slightly ajar. Cautiously, he pushed it open. Charles Siringo sat in the chair, staring out the window. He showed no surprise at seeing Sage. Instead he said, "Sorry about the punch. Looks like it will hurt for a bit."

Sage pressed an ice-filled cloth against his lip. "Yes, remind me to thank you for that," he said. "Maybe I can return the favor sometime."

Siringo held up a hand. "Now, don't be getting mad. It was either my fist on your mouth or the sheriff's gun butt on the back of your skull. I didn't have time to ask you which you'd prefer."

"He was going to brain me? Why would he do that?" Sage asked.

"Darn tootin' he was going to brain you. For two reasons. First, he's a cattleman, through and through. And second, he wanted to stop the fight. It was either take on you and the Irishman or all them cowboys. The sheriff knows how to add and subtract. Two's a much smaller number. Besides," he added with a slow smile, "I've now become somewhat of a hero with my new friends since I'm the only one who was able to knock you on your butt."

Lucinda's spurt of laughter sounded louder than it should have. Even as he shushed her, his spirits rose. He could still make her laugh. He'd missed laughing with her and so much more. He reached out.

Maybe it was his reaching hand or maybe she sensed his thoughts because she sadly shook her head and then she was gone. He was again alone behind the privy. He stared up into a mess of clouds backlit by the moon. "Yah Ma, I know. That's what I get for being an idjit," he admitted.

TEN

FRYING BACON WOKE HIS STOMACH and set it to growling. Sage lay atop a thin pad of blankets. Overhead, the arches of exposed rafters ran the loft's length. Unglazed window openings at each gable end offered the only outlet for the rising heat. He was sweating. Definitely not the Poindexter Hotel, he told himself. He sat up, groaning as frozen joints shifted. It had been an uncomfortable night with the wooden floorboards growing harder each passing hour. Looking around he saw that the loft was empty. Everyone else was already gone.

The Rimrock Saloon's sleeping accommodations were Spartan. Twenty-five cents bought the right to spread your own bedding on the floor. For the wealthier customers, seven-foot high partitions with blankets over the partition openings, created two rooms on one side. These cost seventy-five cents a night, which bought you one-half of a double bed to share with a stranger. He should have spent the seventy-five cents, but, he'd wanted to appear poor as the shepherds he hoped to befriend—someone "short on cash and long on making do" as his mother would say.

His nose led him down the outside stairs and back into the Rimrock Saloon. Tables and chairs now crowded the floor. In the kitchen corner, a Chinese cook bustled, his movements quick and sure. Sage's loft mates were shoveling in fried potatoes, eggs, bacon and slightly burnt toast.

At a nearby table, Twill was leaning back in his chair, hands folded across his stomach, an empty plate before him. Seeing Sage, he grinned, shouting, "Hey now, John, I'm thinking that your belly is ready to converse with the best the Rimrock has to offer! Have a seat and I'll keep you company. Praise be the saints, they've lifted the ban on tables and chairs."

The Irishman's exuberance was less than pleasurable. Sage's head throbbed above his eyebrows. Too many beers last night. The frustration he felt after his brief meeting with Lucinda had made him drink too much. Sage carefully slid onto a chair.

Twill was nothing if not insightful. "Ah ha! I can see I best be quieting my cheerful patter this morning, boyo. You aren't looking so good. No wonder, I'm thinking. You were full drunk and blootered when you stumbled off to bed."

The Chinese cook reached Sage's side. "You like bacon, eggs, toast?" he asked, with that familiar accent so welcome to Sage's ears. Damn, he sure missed Fong. How about that? In his mind, he saw his best friend smile at the thought.

"Yes, please," Sage said, as Twill rose and walked over to the bar to speak to the bartender. He returned with a mug of coffee. "Drink this up, it's got a wee hair of the dog that bit you," he instructed.

The coffee contained more "dog" than "wee hair." After choking a bit, Sage said, "Thanks, this might actually help."

Twill nodded sagely, quoting, "It seems that you have 'very poor and unhappy brains for drinking' and should seek 'some other custom of entertainment'."

Sage groaned. At evening's end, they'd taken to testing each other on old Willie Shakespeare's words upon discovering they shared a liking for the English bard's various works. This was despite Twill's increasingly adamant opinion that Shakespeare was only second best, "No one can beat our own William Yeats when it comes to words that sing," said Twill, repeatedly.

Now Twill laughed, chiding, "Ah! So, your inability to joust over the great Bard's words this morn is but an admission that, you did, indeed, 'out sport discretion last night.'"

Those were fighting words. Sage had his Princeton training to defend. He straightened, took a huge swallow of the enriched coffee and said confidently, "The play is *Othello* for both quotes. Cassio is the speaker both times. He's explaining his hangover."

Twill roared delightedly and slapped Sage's shoulder, nearly knocking him from the chair. Sage winced and raised both hands. "Alright. Stop. I give up. Enough of Shakespeare. I admit it. I need peace and quiet or my head's going to split like a dropped watermelon," he was saying as his plate arrived. It looked unappetizing and though his stomach shrunk with revulsion, he forced himself to eat.

Looking up from his plate, he saw Twill eyeing two men just entering the saloon. He looked alert and expectant. It was the two men Sage'd seen dining at the Poindexter, that dentist Van Ostrand and the congressman, Newt Thomas.

For a minute he was puzzled, and then he remembered and straightened. They were sheep ranchers. The bartender hurried over to serve them. Important sheep ranchers, if the bartender's hustle meant anything, Sage concluded.

"Hey, Twill, how come there's so many shepherds hanging about town?"

"Shearing work up to the Shaniko sheds is mostly done," Twill answered absently. "Some of them are shearing hands, passing through on their way back home. They got trapped by the quarantine and are waiting to see if their vaccination has took. Besides, nobody is hurrying to get out into the back of beyond. There's plans a'brewing." The chair scraped as the Irishman rose to his feet. "Excuse me a moment, boyo. I need to talk to my bosses."

Twill ambled across the room and pulled out a chair to sit at the sheep ranchers' table. As Sage ate, he eyed the three of them, but looked away when he saw Twill gesturing in his direction. Sage was evidently the topic of conversation. While he ate, Sage strained to hear what they were saying. No luck. They kept their voices too low. He wondered if their discussion had anything to do with the "plans." Maybe Siringo was wrong. Maybe O'Dea's death had snapped the sheepmens' restraint and they were going to retaliate. How could he find out? More important, what could he do to stop them?

Across the room, Twill stood up and headed back toward Sage. "Say, boyo, my bosses might be interested in hiring you for a bit o'work," Twill told him.

"But the doctor says I can't leave town. I'm willing to learn sheep herding but I'm thinking there aren't many sheep grazing Prineville's streets."

Twill chuckled. "True be, though a few backyard sheep have been known to go for a wander, same with the milk cows." Then he got back to business. "It's not herding they're wanting. They need someone who's smart enough to do a bit of book work and letter writing."

"But, Twill, that's surely a job you can do," Sage said. Why didn't the shepherd jump at the opportunity to stay in town and make money, he wondered.

Twill sighed and sat down. "That's just it, boyo. I can't do the job because I never learned my letters. When it comes to reading and writing, my head is thick as a fieldstone wall. Every time I try, the words look like squiggling black worms and my head aches worse than the morning after a night of bad whiskey."

Astounded, all Sage could think to say was, "But you quote William Shakespeare verbatim. Better and more accurately than any Shakespearean scholar."

That observation made Twill shrug. "Well it's a blessing and curse that every darn thing I hear gets 'screwed to my memory'," he said. At Sage's arched eyebrow, Twill added, "Cymbeline, that evil Jachimo. Not surprising you wouldn't remember it. Not one of our bard's best plays."

Twill leaned closer, ready to confide. "Truth be, when I worked in Morrow County, I tended the woolies with an Englishman whose only book was Shakespeare's Collected Works. Fancied himself a theater player, he did. Always read aloud. I must have heard every play at least three times."

"Now, that could be a kind of torture."

The Irishman shook his head. "Ah, nay. He was pretty good at reading. Dramatic, don't you know? Lots of different voices. Besides, the best thing about shepherding is that there is always call to wander off to check on the flock. That time with Jack was the best herding job I ever worked. Made me think on things I'd never considered before."

Congressman Thomas's jovial call from across the room interrupted their conversation. "Mr. McGinnis, are you making any progress there?"

Twill looked at Sage and asked, "Will ye be talking to them?"

The two sheep ranchers were all smiles and handshakes when Twill and Sage joined them. "Mr. McGinnis tells us that you are a man of many talents, maybe just the fellow we need to help us out," said the congressman with a warm, ready smile.

"I am certainly willing to try. What is it you need?" asked Sage, scooting closer and thinking this might be a way right into the middle of the sheepmen.

"We run a sheep ranch as well as our other businesses," said the dentist without warmth or smile. Impatience laced his words and gestures. "Our bookkeeper took his family to Portland for a visit. While he was absent, this damnable smallpox outbreak happened. Now he refuses to return until they lift the quarantine. Meanwhile, we've business to conduct and neither one of us has the time to straighten out the finances and get us back on track. Do you know anything about keeping books?"

The question wasn't unusual. The West was full of men possessing various skills and levels of education, hunting adventure, wealth or escape from a sticky situation back East.

Truthfulness gave Sage's voice confidence. "Matter of fact, I have extensive experience in the art of keeping books. Can't say that I like the work, but I can do it fairly well."

"Twill told us how you stepped in and saved him from those cowboys," said the congressman. "A man with your skills and courage is the kind of man we need in

Prineville and in Central Oregon. You thinking of settling down here?"

That question brought a rueful smile to Sage's lips but before he could find an appropriate answer, Dr. Van Ostrand interrupted, "Yea gods, Newt. Stop trying to butter his bacon. The man's quarantined here in Prineville. He was staying at the Poindexter. Now he's sleeping on the floor upstairs—his funds are obviously low." Van Ostrand waved a dismissive hand at the interior of the Rimrock and said, "Why on earth would he turn down temporary work that pays well?"

Because he didn't like his new boss, was Sage's silent response.

The dentist turned to Sage, bluntly saying, "Miner, if you're interested, we'll pay you ten dollars for a five-day week and buy you a decent suit of clothes. We can't have you looking disreputable if you're handling our finances. We're in a pickle because Oliver's been gone over two months. And, we also have research that needs to be done at the country courthouse—something that you can probably do. You want the job?"

"Well, I can't promise you that I'll stay for longer than it takes Dr. Rosenberg to release me from the quarantine," Sage answered. "He said it'd be about eight days. After that, I planned on heading out to Scissors Creek to do some placer mining."

That statement spurred a snort of derision from Van Ostrand. "I can see you need to talk to that dim-witted Mexican packer, Manny Berdugo. He's been sluicing that creek bed for three years and he's still wearing shoes stuffed with newsprint."

Sage figured Van Ostrand was wrong but he wasn't going to argue. Having fought off more than one Yukon claim jumper, Sage was willing to bet Berdugo was about as dim-witted as a wolverine. A smart prospector didn't advertise success—not if he wanted to make it out of the woods alive. And, he wouldn't stay three years along a creek unless it showed yield.

The two sheep ranchers exchanged looks. Thomas reached across the table and said, "Looks like you're hired, Mr. Miner. Can you start today? We've got a passel of bills that need paying." Sage shook the congressman's hand as he accepted their offer. This was an unexpected chance. Hanging around the Rimrock might bring him information from the herders but working for the sheep ranchers was another way to find out whether they had retaliation plans in the works. If there was going to be a two-sided range war, he'd be more apt to get advance warning if he associated with both groups of sheepmen. 'Ole "Charlie" would like that.

Pocketing the men's advance for a new suit of acceptable clothes, Sage returned to his table where he continued to mull over the idea that these two were part of a "plan" to take on the cattlemen. After all, they'd lost a shepherd and a flock of sheep. And the Ochoco dead lines were shrinking what little grazing land they had left.

He also thought about the exchange. The calculating looks between the partners seemed cool, not angry. Still, the dentist's meager smile never reached his eyes. And once, Sage thought he'd seen desperation glittering in those stony depths. Did this mean they were plotting revenge? Nah. If they were desperate, it was probably because they were facing a mountain of unpaid bills. Time will definitely tell, Sage told himself as he signaled for a refill on his coffee, this one without Twill's alcohol enhancement.

ELEVEN

"WELL, SIR. YOU'VE DONE QUITE well for yourself. It's a far easier job sharpening pencils here in town than wading a chill creek looking for gold flakes," commented the barber as his scissors snipped around Sage's ears. "Besides, 'ole Mexican Manny's been panning the Scissors for years and he hasn't got but two nickels to rub together."

Dang, news flashed through Prineville like fire through Hell. He'd told the barber about working for Thomas and Van Ostrand. He'd said nothing about gold prospecting. Earlier in the day, Sage had moved back into the Poindexter Hotel. Now that he had a legitimate job in the sheepmen's ranks, he didn't have to sleep on the floor. Besides, he wanted to keep an eye on Xenobia Brown's house.

The well-equipped barber shop opened off the Poindexter's lobby, its sign announcing proudly, "Shaving, hair cutting, shampooing, with the finest bathing room in the City." Sage had taken advantage of the latter offering. Now he was smoothly shaven and getting a hair trim. He had to admit, the rough clothes and stink of an itinerant worker were not as comfortable as they used to be.

The barber, "call me Walter," was a balding, dapper fellow with precisely trimmed hair and moustache. The shop floor was a clean expanse of red and white diamond tile. Up-to-date hydraulic barber chairs smoothly raised, lowered and twisted. The shop's nickel-plated mountings and green leather upholstery were definitely top of the line. An elegantly carved oak and marble counter, sporting drawers underneath, held all the grooming implements. Above the counter hung two beveled mirrors, each elaborately ornamented with carvings and fluted columns. A carved cup case hung on a side wall, each cell proudly displaying a ceramic shaving mug, the owner's name printed on a neat label below. The display advertised that the barber had plenty of regular customers.

Briskly snipping away, Walter nattered on, sharing what he knew about Sage's employers. "Funny partnership, that one. Everyone likes Newt but hardly anyone likes Van Ostrand. Oh, he's a very good dentist, don't get me wrong. But he's not the friendliest person in town, if you get my meaning."

"Hmm, I did notice the dentist was a brusque man," Sage offered. "What's their sheep business like these days?"

"Oh boy. Your question certainly smashes the nail's head," Walter said, eager to impart additional information. "They've been summering their sheep on the Santiam Military Road allotments for years. Doing pretty well. Matter of fact, just last summer they grew their herd to five thousand. Right after they made that purchase, the road company says they can't lease the grazing land no more. That hurt them plenty. What can you do if you've got no place to graze thousands of sheep? Had to sell a bunch off at a loss."

"Road company? How did a road company get acres of grazing land?" Sage asked, hoping to nudge the barber into more disclosures.

"Well, that there's a damn swindle and shame," the barber said. "Officially it's the Willamette Valley and Cascade Military Road. Most folks call it the Santiam Military Road because it crosses the Cascades through the Santiam Pass at Albany."

"Seems like that's a fair bit from Prineville?"

"That's where the scandal comes in. The road company contracted to build all the way to Fort Boise, just across the Idaho border. Got paid federal money because the military would be using it. They did a fairly passable job over the Cascades. But, Lord, from Prineville east the so-called road was fraud, plain and simple. Some places, they just dug a single twelve-inch wide trench on the upside of a slope for the wagon wheels to roll in." The mirror showed Walter shaking his head. "Tell me, do you wish me to refresh that black dye in your hair? The one covering your blaze?" he asked.

"Umm, yes, please," Sage said embarrassed the barber had noticed this part of his disguise. He quickly changed the topic, "I still don't understand what a military road has to do with grazing land."

"You surely aren't from the plains," Walter said without rancor, clearly relishing the opportunity to further educate. "Every thirty-six-square-mile township is broken into thirty-six, one-square mile sections that are numbered, 1 through 36. The federal government gave the military road builders odd-numbered sections of land along the route. Funny little scheme. Once surveyed, the road builder could pick three odd-numbered, 640 acre sections, for every mile of road built. The picked sections had to be within six miles on either side of the road. That comes to almost two thousand acres for every mile of road."

"Why did the government do that?" Sage wondered aloud.

"The idea was that the company would sell the sections to pay for constructing the next mile of road. Of course, like all good government plans, it never worked that way because the greedy guts always manage to get involved. The rascals spent next to nothing building a non-existent road but still got title to all the sections they picked."

"Sounds like theft," Sage observed. "How many total acres are we talking about?"

"You bet it was theft—over 440,000 acres of theft. And it hurt the homesteaders because sometimes the road company claimed their homesteads. And, because the government had not surveyed the land, the homesteaders couldn't lay claim to it before the road company did. Bunch of them lost their little homesteads when the road company sold the sections to the timber barons. The homesteaders have to pay rent on the land they were the first to tame. Dad-burned scheme sticks in folk's craws, it does."

"So what happened with Thomas and Van Ostrand?"
"Road company decided to lease their grassland sections to the Kepler brothers instead."

"You know, I've heard that name recently, just since I've been in town," Sage said, hoping to learn more about that the miss ing shepherd who had worked for the Keplers.

"That's probably because people are still talking about their sheep barn out in the Ochocos being burnt to the ground. Theirs was the first sheep barn to be torched. People say it was the sheepshooters," he said before returning to Sage's original question. "Your employers' troubles got worse right after they lost the lease because somebody ran a dead line across part of the federal range that Van Ostrand and Thomas were using to run their remaining sheep. Then, just days ago, their shepherd got murdered," Walter told him.

Groomed and suitably dressed, Sage strolled to the dentist's office. He noticed that the newer commercial buildings were more substantial and showed more architectural detail than the older ones. Prineville was here to stay, unlike many western towns that quickly deteriorated into tumbled structures and tumbleweed once their original purpose ceased to exist.

Sage climbed the stairs to Dr. Van Ostrand's office which occupied two rooms above the drug store. The dentist was working in the first room, busy in a woman's mouth, when Sage stepped through the door. Seeing him, Van Ostrand stopped pumping the drill pedal and said to the woman, "One moment madam, I must speak to this gentleman." The patient cast a frantic look toward Sage and abruptly closed her mouth. A blush flamed her neck and face.

Ushering Sage into the second room, Van Ostrand said, "Glad to see that you have the virtue of timeliness, Miner. That desk over there is your workspace." He gestured toward a desk overflowing with papers and unopened envelopes. "You'll need to sort through and figure out what needs paying immediately, what we can wait on and what needs response letters. I do my own book work for the dentistry practice. Everything on your desk should only pertain to our ranching business. Keep a list of your questions. I don't want you interrupting my work again." With that, the dentist left the room, his back "straight as if his hind end rode a pitchfork," as his mother would say.

Fortunately, the office window opened to the north so Sage was spared the blazing sun. That didn't stop the heat from building as the afternoon wore on. Sage finally had to remove his suit coat. He wondered how Van Ostrand was doing in his doctor's smock. Still, it was bearable compared to full sun or the Rimrock's sleeping loft.

He began sorting through the correspondence. There were at least two months' of bills. He found charges for stock pond digging, metal water troughs, tobacco dip and something called 'docking.'" That last was a puzzler.

Van Ostrand came to check on his progress and seemed mildly pleased that much was already tidied. He authorized Sage's suggested payments, and told him to enter the payments in the ledger, write out the checks and leave them for signature on the dentist's desk. He also dictated responses to a few letters once Sage displayed his legible penmanship.

Work over, Sage dined in the Prineville Hotel, reading the *Crook County Journal* and contemplating all he'd learned. Van Ostrand told him to write checks only for those bills that were overdue by at least sixty days. Not a good situation for a business. Those past due bills were an indication of why the partners were tense. Sage sighed as he concluded that, so far, he'd learned nothing that would help Siringo.

The night sky was cloudless, letting moonlight brighten Xenobia Brown's back yard. Sage stepped to the shrub's side, hoping no one was gazing out the hotel's back windows. A boot scuffed on hard packed dirt, causing Sage to retreat further into the shrub. A figure rounded the privy and paused. It was a man wearing a cowboy hat who froze, listened, then shrugged. A match flared and seconds later smoke drifted upward from a cigarette. The man sucked deep and gazed up at the moon. For the first time, Sage saw his face. Siringo.

Sage stepped away from the bush. The Dickensen detective whirled silently around, his hand grabbing at his holster.

"Slow down partner. It's me, John Adair." He heard the other man release held breath before he drawled, "You 'bout got yourself shot, Adair."

"What are you doing here, anyway?" Sage's voice sounded both sullen and challenging to his own ears. If he had only a few minutes to spend with Lucinda, he sure didn't feel like sharing them with this cowboy.

"Well, John," Her voice sounded behind him. "Charlie and you sure can't converse on Main Street, can you? Not after you two brawled publicly. In case you haven't figured it out, people in this town chatter more than magpies. He's heading back out to the range and needed to see you. Besides, the three of us should talk."

Siringo didn't hesitate. "So, Adair, have you managed to meet Asa Rayburn yet? He's the fellow I told you about. Used to work for Bellingham."

"Nope. I haven't. A fellow in the Rimrock said Rayburn went to Farewell Bend the other day but will be returning soon. Maybe it doesn't matter because I've managed to get in with the sheep ranchers. Van Ostrand and Thomas have hired me temporarily to straighten out their book work. "

That brought a grin from the cowboy detective. "Now that's fast work. Already friends with both the shepherds and their bosses. Lucinda said you were darn clever. Have you heard whether the sheepmen are hatching any retaliation plans for the shepherd's death?"

"Don't forget they also killed the shepherd's dog," Sage said. "His name was Felan. Seems that's just as great a sin. Anyway, thanks to our little dust up on Main Street, I'm now fast friends with Twill McGinnis. He seems to be a natural leader of the shepherds. He's that big fellow I sided with during our 'public brawl.'" Sage glanced toward Lucinda who merely raised an unapologetic chin.

He returned to Siringo's question. "Something's up with the shepherds. Some kind of plan is a'brewing according to McGinnis. I'm thinking that's why McGinnis is sticking around. I haven't worked long enough for Van Ostrand and Thomas to get a handle on what the sheep ranchers might be planning. All I can say is their partnership has financial troubles. Mostly because they've lost an important grazing lease, have a dead line across their current grazing land and now have lost both sheep and a shepherd."

"Well, I wish I could say things are calm as dozing cattle out on the range but that'd be a damn lie," said Siringo. "Cattlemen from the Mauer Mountains, southeast of town, plan to move against a sheepherder early tomorrow morning. I came into town on the excuse I had to pick up a delivery from the stage. Thought I'd ride out after our talk, swing by the herder's wagon and give warning."

Lucinda spoke in a low voice, "They're going to launch another attack this soon after that poor Timothy O'Dea's murder?"

"Yup, 'fraid so." Siringo looked grim. "I managed to overhear their plans. They're going to do some sheep shooting, then set a blaze around the meadow."

"Why would they set it on fire?" Sage was puzzled.

"Not fire. They'll carve marks in the tree bark. They only post a few signs. They use tree blazing in between. You know . . . ." Before Siringo could explain further Lucinda interrupted. "Listen fellows, I don't know how long I have. Remember that poor young man who died of the pox? I learned that he also rambled when Frank was taking care of him. He said enough to make me certain he was definitely involved in an attack where someone died."

"Lucinda! Are you all right?" It was a woman's voice, softly calling from the house's back porch

"Yes, Xenobia, I'm fine. Be right there," Lucinda called back.

"That's our signal. Dr. Rosenberg's here to see our patient. He'llwonder where I am. You two wait a few minutes before leaving. And be quiet. He might hear you."

A swish of skirts through dry grass and she was gone. She'd left him with a question he hated to admit having. Had she smiled at him any longer than she'd smiled at Siringo?

TWELVE

THREE HOURS BEFORE DAWN, SIRINGO found the meadow carpeted by still, white forms. His soft cursing ceased once a few sheep stirred sleepily at his quiet approach. He wasn't too late after all.

A black and white dog rose from the grass, its entire body straining toward him, ears pricked alert. As he ambled past, the herd dog caught up, silently pacing right behind horse and rider. The herder's round-top wagon stood next to a solitary pine. The dog barked softly and, seconds later, a light flared within. Siringo pulled his bandana up, covering his lower face. Halting, horse and rider waited about twenty feet from the wagon's back door.

"Who goes there?" called a quavering voice.

Siringo slowly raised both hands as the door's top section swung open. Metal glinted as a rifle barrel slid out the opening. "I am a friend," Siringo called, "here to warn you. Take your wagon, your dog and your sheep and leave immediately. They are coming for you and the sheep in a few hours. Head northwest and you'll be all right."

"Who? Who's coming for me?" asked the man inside the wagon, fear sharpening his voice. In response, the dog stiffened and growled low in his throat.

"You know who. Get moving. You don't have much time."

With that, Siringo turned his horse around and walked it away. His back twitched at the thought of that rifle barrel but he retreated slowly. He didn't want to startle the sheep into bolting. At the hillside's base, he urged his horse upward. Reaching a level bench he halted, slid off and stepped forward to study the meadow below. A man's figure bustled around the wagon. His high whistles spurring the dog into racing around the herd. Using a series of yips and charges, the dog got the sheep up and bunching.

Meanwhile, the man rapidly harnessed his mule to the wagon. Within ten minutes, the entire outfit was on the move, the racing dog running to and fro—not letting a single animal dally. Siringo waited, letting his horse graze and rest, until the meadow below was empty of man and beast.

Wearily remounting, Siringo leaned forward and scratched between the horse's pricked ears. "Come on old fellow, let's head in. We'll take it slow this time," he promised. He straightened, gently squeezed with his knees and worked the reins. The horse began picking his way over the rocky ground between the pines, heading south in the pre-dawn light.

Sage knew something was different the minute he strolled into the Poindexter's dining room. Although three-quarters full, the restaurant was strangely quiet. He made a beeline for a table in the far corner so he could face into the room. A few minutes later he concluded it wasn't his imagination. People were speaking in hushed voices, their gestures subdued. The waiter was placing the breakfast plates onto tables as if they were fragile crystal instead of sturdy, thick porcelain. Normally, the fellow just thumped them down.

Some patrons he recognized as hotel guests. The others appeared to be townspeople or local ranchers, since many nodded to each other as they entered. As he watched, a table of four such locals finished their meals, stood and departed in complete silence. Other mornings, they had lingered and laughed, clearly enjoying each other's company. The waiter arrived at Sage's table with menu and coffee, poker-faced and speaking so softly it was hard to hear him.

Opening the day's *Crook County Journal,* Sage sipped his coffee and studied the room over the paper's top edge. It had to be the stranger sitting near the room's center. The man was studying a variety of documents as he ate. He appeared oblivious to everyone else. Yet, they were clearly aware of him because every person entering the dining room took his measure before sitting down as far away from him as possible. Once seated, the newcomers repeatedly darted looks in his direction.

There was nothing remarkable about the man. He appeared to be in his early sixties—well-dressed but not ostentatious. Thin silver hair, parted in the middle, lay flat against his skull. He wore wire-rimmed glasses and the absent, genial smile of a weary cleric. The man looked familiar but Sage couldn't place him. He wasn't a Mozart's regular. That was a relief. Sage's mustache drooped and dye hid the white streak in his black hair. Still, in his new suit, he resembled Mozart's John Adair a little too closely.

"Who is that fellow studying his papers?" he asked the waiter.

The waiter stiffened and for a pause, Sage thought he was going to ignore the question but he didn't. "That's Frances J. Heney."

The name sent a jolt through Sage. "You mean the U.S. District Attorney that Roosevelt appointed to investigate the timber frauds?" The waiter nodded but volunteered nothing more. "What's he doing here in Prineville? I thought that trial was taking place in Portland."

The waiter shrugged and, again, seemed reluctant to answer because he glanced around the dining room as if seeking a reason to escape. Finally he said, "Well, the land that the senator and the others got in trouble for is in Christmas Valley. That's south of here. They tried to get it turned into a forest reserve so they could work a swindle for those Minnesota timber companies. Maybe Mr. Heney's in town investigating that."

Sage knew firsthand about Senator Hipple's timber swindles on behalf of the Baumhauer Timber Company and others.

But he wasn't about to share that piece of information. Instead he asked, "Do you suppose Heney's here to investigate a new criminal conspiracy? A local one maybe?"

The waiter stiffened and his chin came up. "I am sure I wouldn't know, sir." With that, he turned and glided off.

Arriving for work, Sage found Van Ostrand's office door closed. He heard a murmur of voices, then the word "money" followed by an angry exclamation. As he stepped forward to knock, the door flew open and out stormed a short, fat man. He slammed the door behind him so hard that its glass rattled. The man brushed past Sage, heading briskly toward the stairs. Sage only glimpsed a scowling face beneath a wide forehead, with a dangling curlicue of forelock, before the man disappeared down the wooden stairs.

Meanwhile, raised voices sounded again inside the office. Sage stepped closer but the words were indistinguishable. Once the outer door banged shut, he knocked softly on the glass and waited. An agitated Dr. Van Ostrand snatched the door open. He scowled at Sage before recognizing him.

"Oh, it's you, Miner. Ummm, I'm busy right now. How about you go down to the courthouse? The clerk, J.P. Jones, will help you. Tell him you want to locate all the springs in the Ochocos starting at Wolf Creek and heading east and south to the town of Post. Look at all the sections six miles on either side of the military road. Be sure to note the exact sections that have springs. J.P. will show you how to find the springs and the section numbers."

The dentist didn't wait to see if Sage understood. He stepped back inside the office and shut the door. Sage strained to hear, but the voices behind the glass stayed muted. Ambling toward the courthouse, Sage again admired the majestic verticality of the rimrocks to the north and west and south of town.

A refreshing tang rode air devoid of damp. It smelled nothing like Portland. Unless a brisk wind blew, the city air usually carried the mingled scents of people, horse manure and chimney smoke. And, there was another difference—the absence of loud noise. Instead, the sounds were soft and distant—bird twitters, the rattle of a metal pail on someone's porch, the lowing of a cow at the edge of town. No ear-jarring rumble of drays over cobblestones, no workmen's shouts as they unloaded wagons, no penetrating clang as streetcars clattered by on their steel rails. He breathed deep, savoring both tang and silence. The only thing he'd change was the heat. It was too darn hot.

He raised his hat, wiped his forehead and wondered what had just transpired in that second floor office. What did it mean? Could his new bosses' financial woes be even worse than he thought? The stranger had definitely been upset. But then, slow payments always had that effect on creditors.

The county courthouse was Prineville's tallest structure. It was white, wooden and two stories, sitting atop a stone foundation high enough to hold full-sized windows. Not the impressive brick and stone courthouses common in the Willamette Valley but still, quite respectable for a town on the frontier's edge. Besides, if he gauged the town's spirit right, they'd soon erect a more impressive courthouse.

Inside, he found the smiling, amiable county clerk, Mr. J. P. Jones. "Yes, indeedy, we possess some very fine maps," he assured Sage while pulling sheaf after sheaf from shallow drawers. He said that he would happily show Sage how to identify both section numbers and spring locations on the maps.

"Yes, indeedy. These maps showing the Willamette Valley and Cascade Military Road sections are courtesy of the U.S. government. They're up-to-date accurate. The surveyors came through so the road company could pick their sections. But then the surveyors came back again to re-survey when the government sued the road company."

"Sued the road company?" Sage prompted.

"Oh, yes, indeedy. The federal government sued and lost. No road was built. The government could prove that. But, the scallywags over there in Salem issued a certificate of completion anyway and the road company got sold to another fellow. The judge said that because the second fellow bought the whole she-bang in good faith, the government couldn't take it back. Makes things a real mess."

"A mess?"

"Oh yes, indeedy. Homesteaders have gotten booted off their land and billed for back rent. The to-do drove some of them right out of the area. Darn shame. We need all the industrious folk we can get. Others are still here, though. Either they moved to a different place or they've dug in hoping for some kind of miracle that will let them keep their old place."

Despite the depressing tale he was telling, the clerk's green eyes never stopped twinkling. He was a small man, comfortable in the eyeshade he wore and the office he managed. It was a tidy office, everything stowed in its proper place and staying there.

"Here we go. You might as well start with this map," Jones said, placing a large sheet atop the others. "I notice you neglected to bring pencil and paper. No matter. Let me get you those." After he bustled away, Sage bent over the topmost map. Sure enough, squares comprised the map, with a number anchoring the center of each square. When the clerk returned, Sage pointed, asking, "These numbers are the section numbers?"

"That's right. And, you can see the military road running right there along Veazie Creek." His finger tapped a narrow black line that ran southeast across the map. "Surveyors did a pretty good job of it. The maps shows most of the springs. See them? They're the blue dots with 'spring' written next to them."

"Why are some sections outlined in thicker black? Looks like they're just odd-numbered sections," asked Sage.

"You're a smart fellow, spotting that right away. Makes it look like a crazy checkerboard, doesn't it? Yes, indeedy. Those are the odd number sections claimed by the road company as payment for building the imaginary road." The man's smile never left his face but for once, his eyes had lost their twinkle.

Two hours later, Sage left the courthouse with a list of section numbers and spring locations in hand. He wasn't sure exactly why Van Ostrand wanted the information. When he'd asked about the springs the clerk, whom Sage had come to think of as "Yes Indeedy Jones," explained, "Most of those springs dry up come late summer. But, if there's any water at all on the section, it could be that they plan to dig stock ponds. Yes, indeedy, a fellow can make the water last through the dry spell if he digs deep enough." He'd also informed Sage that it was likely the two sheep ranchers wanted to locate the best sections of unclaimed federal land since that was all they could use for grazing now that the Kepler brothers took over the military road leases.

"Yes, indeedy, that explanation makes sense," Sage told himself. Then all thought of his bosses' intentions vanished. Two people were hurrying straight towards him. One was Dexter Higgenbottom, the stagecoach driver. The other was the older woman passenger from the coach—the homesteader, Mrs. Fromm.

Dexter started talking even before they reached him. "Mister Miner," he hailed, "We've been looking everywhere for you. We need your help. Sheriff Smith's arrested Miz Fromm's husband for murder."

"I don't understand. What do you think I can do? I'm not a lawyer," Sage said to Dexter, as he tipped his hat to the lady.

"You might not be a lawyer but you are a smart fellow who thinks on his feet and you've no ties to anyone here in town. That's a hard combination to find hereabouts," Dexter told him.

"But still, Mr. Fromm needs a lawyer, not a gold panning stranger."

The woman broke in, her kindly face twisting with fear, "That's just it. Everybody's so certain sure my Otto's guilty that nobody is going to look any further. Besides, this town takes care of its own. They won't point their finger at a neighbor."

Mentally, Sage heaved a sigh. No matter where he went, he attracted trouble like a magnet did iron filings. Still, this woman reminded him of, Ida, Mozart's cook who'd been terrified when her nephew had been wrongly accused of murder. He hated to think of Mrs. Fromm suffering like Ida had. How could a single woman with children survive out here? Homestead on her own? Few women tackled that.

Sage rested his hand on the woman's shoulder, "Okay, Mrs. Fromm," he said. "The smallpox quarantine means I'm staying in town for a few more days anyway. I'll do my best to help. Who do they say your husband killed?"

Dexter jumped in, "They say he shot that new guy, Asa Rayburn."

The name hit Sage's ears like a blow. Asa Rayburn. The very fellow Siringo had asked him to meet. The man Siringo thought had information they could use to stop the range war. Had Rayburn been killed because he was friends with the sheepmen? Fear prickled across Sage's scalp. The danger of a range war was building with every passing hour.

THIRTEEN

ALL SAGE COULD DO WAS repeat the name, "Asa Rayburn?" That nudge was enough. Mrs. Fromm's eyes turned searing beneath lowered brows. "That rascal turned our cow loose and tried to burn up our hay mow," she said indignantly.

"I don't understand." None of this was making sense. "I thought that Rayburn was a sheepman. Why would he go after homesteaders up north near Willowdale?"

Puzzlement took over the woman's face, then awareness widened her eyes. "Oh, you thought that we had a homestead up north. No, we live just to the east of here, along the military road. I got off the stagecoach up there because my husband and children wanted to visit my husband's brother. He lives near Willowdale. Once the visit was over, we headed south along Trout Creek and then Foley Creek. It's hard going but doable with a sturdy wagon and two good mules."

For a minute, she was back on that buckboard heading home, unaware of the trouble that awaited her family. Then her face darkened. "We got home only to find that someone had set fire to our stacked hay. We hadn't been there but an hour, when our neighbor turned up. He'd been keeping an eye on our place. He said he watched Asa Rayburn leave out of our lane and got suspicious. Lucky for us. When he got to the house, he found our haystack smoldering and our milk cow about to wander away because the scoundrel had let her out of the barn. Our neighbor doused the fire and took our cow home for safekeeping."

"I still don't understand. Why would Rayburn attack homesteaders?"

Dexter jumped in to answer. "Asa Rayburn was a varmint willing to do anything for money. He's been accused of bad doings in the past but he was always too slick to get caught redhanded. These folks, their place is out along the military road. It has good pasture and year around water. For some time now, that darn road company has been trying to outright steal it from them. Otto Fromm and the missus here, they've been resisting because they filed their claim fair and square. Since it doesn't have a valid legal case, my guess is that the road company men hired Rayburn to drive them out. He probably heard the Fromm family was gone up north and figured to starve them out by getting rid of their feed and cow."

Sage recalled Mr. Yes Indeedy Jones talking about some homesteaders resisting the road company's seizure of their land. So, this lady's family was one of those.

"Why does the sheriff think Mr. Fromm has something to do with Rayburn's death?"

For the first time, Mrs. Fromm hesitated, then told him the worst, "Otto and I came into town this morning. We planned to confront Asa Rayburn and file charges. After we got here, Otto went from place to place looking for the scamp. Otto was pretty hot under his collar and he didn't hide it. He thought he should warn people about Rayburn.

She drew a shaky breath. "Otto carried a revolver—an old Smith and Wesson. Everyone saw it on his hip. What with the rattlers, a gun is a good idea. He killed one just outside town. Then, this afternoon, someone shot Asa Rayburn in the back when he was down fishing the river."

She paused, unable to go on. Dexter patted her arm and said, "Sure as rain falls from thunder clouds, the sheriff heard about Fromm's trouble with Rayburn. So, he finds Fromm, sniffs the gun barrel and next thing Mrs. Fromm knows, her husband's in the hoosegow. She spots me and I get the notion of finding you. Since you're a stranger around here, we were thinking you could nose around, see if you can scare up the fellow who really killed that rascal. People might talk more freely around someone who's just passing through."

The sheepherders inside the Rimrock were a somber bunch. Asa Rayburn was yet another sheepman dead. Angry muttering sounded all over the saloon. Sage took a seat at a table by himself. "I say we burn them out, like they tried to burn the Kepler's out. See how they like it," said one.

"Maybe we should set up some ambushes of our own," said another.

"What about taking on cowboys while they're riding herd on their cattle? Cause a stampede? Lots of them are out by themselves, just like we are," suggested another to somber nods all around.

Then came that stillness that meant they'd alerted to the fact of a stranger in their midst. They shut up. Sage smiled to himself. Dexter was wrong. Folks weren't going to talk freely around a fellow who was just passing through. So, where to start?

He spotted Twill sitting alone and went over to join him. Maybe he needed to learn more about Timothy O'Dea's murder. Twill was willing to talk, his voice low as he described the murder scene to Sage. "Imagine a bright green meadow, grass waving high as your knees. Eagles float overhead and the only sound is three brooks burbling, meeting in a pool. On every side are grassy hills with yellow ponderosa pines straight as God's finger and huge boulders the color of caramel. That's Gray's Prairie. That's the place Timothy and Felan died."

Twill paused to sip his whiskey before continuing, "Timothy lay about thirty feet out from the shack door. Felan . . ." Twill drew in a shaky breath, "Felan had drug himself about twenty feet to reach Timothy. There was a trail of blood. His head lay on Timothy's chest." Twill's eyes filled with tears, his fingers flicking them away before they fell.

Sage said the first thing that came into his head. "I lost my uncle and my cousin some years ago in a mine explosion. I survived the explosion but I couldn't save them." Even all these years later, he again felt the grief and guilt behind the words.

It had been the right thing to say. Guilt was definitely astride the Irishman's heart because he replied, "It's my fault. If only I hadn't stayed in town that night. I wasn't planning to, but the bosses were happy about some deal and they asked me to celebrate with them. It got too late and, to tell the truth, the 'ole legs had already gone to bed by the time I thought of heading back to Gray's Prairie."

"What do you think happened out there?" Sage asked.

Twill sighed heavily, took a deep breath and said, "It looked like one of those cowpokes decided to shoot the bosses' sheep and that Timothy and the dog tried to stop him."

"Just one fellow?"

"Aye, I trailed him back to the main road. After that, I couldn't tell where he went. Probably headed east, deeper into the range." He shook his head. "There was no reason for Timothy to die. Dr. Van Ostrand made us both promise that we'd never try to stop any sheepshooters. He told us more than once to just stay put and let them shoot. Tim promised but he didn't do it. He didn't stay put."

Twill released a clenched hand and he stretched the kinks from his fingers. "It was his dog, Felan," he said. "Timothy loved that dog. We both did. A bonny, bonny dog, he was. If Felan was hurt, Timothy would have run out to save him."

Silence filled the space around them. Sage was glad to hear that the sour-tempered dentist valued human life more than the money he had invested in sheep. Not surprising. More than one man's gruffness concealed compassion.

Clearing his throat, Twill continued, "That shack where we bunked sits in a stand of river bottom pines. They grow taller than hillside pines. The two of us built a stone corral. It was just like one back home in Ireland. We used it to bunch the sheep for tick spraying and docking. It sends them down a narrow chute that turns them out into a bigger square. We'd been having trouble with coyotes. Too many hungry mamas with young ones."

Twill tiredly rubbed his forehead as he said, "So, we decided to pen the ewes and their lambs in the corral. We could do that because there weren't that many, only about thirty sheep. Our bosses had separated the whole flock into smaller ones so they didn't need as much space to graze. Timothy and I were given the smallest number to herd.

"Anyway, just before I left, we penned the ewes. That way, it was easier for Felan to watch over the rest of the flock and Timothy could get some sleep. Usually we took turns staying out with the sheep but that night, the bosses wanted me in town."

Twill swallowed more whiskey, his Adam's apple jumping. "Whoever he was, he just rode along the side of the corral and shot our penned woolies. Maybe when he got there, he didn't see Felan or maybe he didn't care. The dog must have charged the bastard's horse. There was blood on his muzzle. Poor Felan's leg was broke, like he'd been horse-kicked. And there was a bullet in his bonny brave chest."

Twill's eyes filled and he looked away. When he signaled for another shot, the bartender ignored him. Twill took no offense, just shrugged and picked up with his story. "I'm thinking that when Felan yelped, Timothy just grabbed his rifle and ran out. I found his rifle lying right beside his hand, just as if he'd dropped it when he fell. He never got off a shot. Must have been killed right as he came out of the door. Then something must have scared the bastard, because only a few of the penned sheep were shot and he didn't open the gate to scatter the rest. None of the unpenned sheep were hurt although some of them wandered off."

Sage let the silence stretch out a bit before changing the subject. "I heard that dead fellow, somebody 'Rayburn,' was a wrong one. Do you think it could have been him?"

Twill was nodding, even while Sage was still asking. "Asa Rayburn. Aye. He's the sort my sainted mother would not want her second-born son befriending. He'd jolly you up just to pick your pocket. Not that Asa'd do such a low-class crime. He considered himself an elite gentleman of sorts, 'swelling like a turkey-cock' at every opportunity."

The Irishman's genial face turned mulish. "I intend to learn the name of Timothy's killer. Asa Rayburn had it in him to do something like that. He was one of those fellows where the best that can be said about them is, 'when they are not drunk, they are sober'.

"But, no, it wasn't Asa who murdered Timothy. I know it wasn't because he helped us celebrate that night. For all Asa's strutting, he was no match for an Irishman when it came to drinking. He couldn't have stood up, let alone mount a horse and found his way to Gray Prairie in the dark."

Twill looked at Sage, raising one dark eyebrow. "That's two you missed," he observed.

"*Henry V*, Gower talking about Pistol. But I can't name the source of the second quote," admitted Sage though his mind was really elsewhere. A single man, not a posse of sheepshooters, killed Timothy O'Dea. What the hell did that mean?

"None but the master W.B. Yeats himself, ye ignorant laddie," Twill teased for the first time that night.

The Irishman's lightheartedness was short-lived. Twill raised the empty shot glass and shouted, "From this time forth, my thoughts be bloody, or they be without worth."

"Hear, hear," came answering shouts from around the room.

"You look tired," said Lucinda from where she waited beside the shrub. Shadows hid her face so he couldn't tell if the kindness in her voice also softened her eyes. "What's been happening in town?"

Sage told her about the federal district attorney being in the restaurant, the argument in the dentist's office, the courthouse research, Otto Fromm' arrest, the shepherds' dangerous mood and he ended with Twill's story.

She tilted her head to one side, sympathy softening her face. Then she seemed to switch to another thought because she said, "I suspect I'm getting fanciful with having only three people and four walls to talk to. But, it sounds like the whole countryside's busy as an angry anthill. Sheepshooters, homesteaders up in arms, arsonists, murderers. Lordy, it almost makes me glad I'm cooped up in a pesthouse."

He laughed, just as she'd intended. Whenever his worry threatened to boil over, she was the next best thing to his own mother when it came to adding a calming dose of salts.

FOURTEEN

"MR. MINER! MR. MINER!" VIGOROUS knocks accompanied the man's calls. Sage opened one eye as he fumbled for his pocket watch. Six in the morning. He yanked on his pants and opened the door.

Dr. Rosenberg stood in the hallway flashing Sage a wide-awake display of teeth. "Good morning there, sir! Thought I'd catch you before you left for your new job." For a minute, Sage wondered how the doctor knew of the job but then he remembered. He was in Prineville. Standing back, he gestured for the doctor to enter.

"You missed your appointment yesterday," Rosenberg said, putting his doctor satchel on the pine dresser and digging through it. "We need to make sure that inoculation is taking." He turned toward Sage, a small ruler in his hand. "Oh good, your shirt is off. So, if you'll just roll up your undershirt sleeve, I'll take a quick measurement to see how we're doing."

Sage complied, seeing a swollen red patch with two small yellow centers. No wonder it felt uncomfortable. But still, not too bad.

The doctor was smiling and nodding. "Good, good. It's looking very good. But it is important to track it a few more days just to make sure it develops all the way." He laid the ruler alongside the blotch, studied its markings and then stepped back. "Exactly, right. One-half centimeter," he said turning to replace the ruler in the satchel.

"I'm sorry I forgot to check in with you yesterday," Sage said, finally fully awake.

"No problem. What with your new job and all the doings around town it must have been easy to forget. Besides, I was out all afternoon. You heard about the shooting?"

"Asa Rayburn you mean?" asked Sage.

"Good Lord, I hope there weren't two shootings. I'm the only doctor in town because Belknap's off chasing critters through the trees. The sheriff had me examine the body and declare death."

"I heard he was shot."

"He certainly was. Clean through the heart. From the back. I'm a bit surprised at that. Otto Fromm always struck me as a man who'd look a fellow straight in the eye and tell him to go to hell. Maybe he'd shoot a man who'd wronged him but only in an even fight. But a back shot?" The doctor shook his head, "Just doesn't seem like something Otto would do, no matter what the provocation."

"You know Fromm, then?"

"Yes, better than some, not as well as others. I've seen his family here in town and drove my buggy out to his place a few times. Like I said, he's always seemed an upright man—one of those old-school Germans, sober and straight-laced. Only thing I can figure is that almost losing his family's animal and feed unhinged the man. If their hay had burned or if wolves or cougars had killed their milk cow, that could have ended their homesteading. They live that close to the bone. They depend on the milk cow's butter to trade with their neighbors for things they need and don't have."

"What about Asa Rayburn? Was he the kind of man who made enemies?"

"He was a scoundrel through and through. It's probably better for the town that someone shot him. Just wish it had been one of his wastrel friends, instead of Otto Fromm."

"Where was Rayburn staying?" Sage asked.

The doctor cocked an eyebrow. "For a stranger in town, you seem awfully interested in folks' business. That just curiosity?"

Sage looked at this man who'd been nothing but kind to him since the minute he'd stepped foot in Prineville. He found he couldn't lie. "Nope more than curiosity. I met Mrs. Fromm on the stagecoach riding down from Shaniko. I thought her a real nice woman. She says her husband didn't do it. She's asked me to help prove him innocent. I told her I would try."

"Well, Rayburn had been in town just a few months. Got into trouble up north in Wasco County. Some say it related to the sheep business. He high-tailed it down here and wasn't indicted. I'm told he was a small fry and the federal prosecutor is aiming higher. Going after the boss man himself—Bellingham. Some speculate about where Rayburn stood in the mess. But that's all it is—speculation. Here in Prineville, he seemed to have ways of making money. Even invested a bit in the Rimrock, something Daggett, the owner, now regrets. And, I hear Rayburn worked for the road company—evicting and hounding homesteaders for rent."

Why drive them out? Who'd want that land in the middle of nowhere? Sage wondered. Not the sheepmen. They could lease grazing land from the homesteaders. He asked that question and got a ready answer.

"Timber. Doug firs aren't the only money trees. There's demand for our yellow ponderosa pine as well. The Fromm's have a big stand of timber on their land."

Sage switched to another possible motive for the Rayburn murder. "So, maybe the Rimrock's owner might have cause for celebration?"

"Ah, maybe a bit. But Rayburn was more an irritant than a real problem for Daggett. Once Rayburn invested, he thought it gave him right to order Daggett about. That was short lived. Daggett set him straight with the support of all his customers. I hear tell that of late, Rayburn's been avoiding the Rimrock. Besides, Barney Daggett's a decent fellow. Plays in the town band with me. I like him."

"I bet Daggett still owes on Rayburn's investment," Sage mused.

The doctor's glance sharpened as he said thoughtfully, "I'm sure you're right on that account. Between the sheepshooter nonsense and the quarantine, the Rimrock's business has dropped in half. Rayburn took advantage of Daggett's troubles." Rosenberg shook his head. "No, I can't believe Daggett would go to such lengths. He'd walk away first."

As Sage closed the door behind the doctor, he thought it likely that Rosenberg would tell others about Sage investigating the Rayburn murder. Not that it would matter. Hereabouts, gossip flew faster than tumbleweeds in a wind storm. He chuckled at his attempt to come up with a western metaphor. The sun and sage brush must be getting to him.

Still, the doctor's good opinion of Otto Fromm counted. It set Sage's mind more at ease. He'd made the right choice. His promise to Mrs. Fromm hadn't been reckless. Despite Mae Clemens saying too often, "Son, you must have been bent over tying your shoelaces when the good Lord doled out caution."

The horses slowly picked their way southward along a rocky streambed. Only a trickle of water pooled here and there. Soon even that water would disappear in summer's heat. Only the creak of saddle leather, iron shoes ringing on rock and the horses' occasional blowing marked their passage. Charlie Siringo studied the straight backs of the men before him. Despite failing in their primary objective, they were not disappointed. Just the opposite.

His had been a rough ride last night. Dawn was near breaking when he'd finally reached the cowboy's camp. They'd all been wide awake—too fired up to sleep, telling stories, laughing softly, all to stiffen their courage. He'd offered to join them on their foray. After brief hesitation, during which looks were exchanged, Gary Blue had said, "I guess you might as well, seeing as how there's no way we can hide that we're all heading out at first light. We didn't expect you back until tonight. But if you ride along, you must swear to secrecy under pain of death. You willing to do that?"

Siringo responded, with appropriate solemnity, that he was willing to take the secrecy oath. And there was, indeed, an oath. He'd raised his hand just like he had in various courts of law across the West. The deception lay heavily on him. He understood their desperation, He'd grown up on a hardscrabble, Texas Panhandle ranch where a single instance of bad luck meant permanent failure. Here, their livelihood, their way of life was threatened. Like the sheepmen, they were being victimized by men they'd never meet. Men who'd profit from their misery.

Siringo filled a cheek with chaw. "Saving forests for future generations." Hah! Another good idea exploited by greedy, powerful, amoral men and the fawning politicians who did their bidding.

His mental rambling ceased when Gary Blue began laying out the morning's plan. As he learned from earlier eavesdropping, their target was the shepherd and his flock at Little Summit Prairie. Cattle had always grazed there in the summer. Now a band of sheep were stripping it bald. The cowmen figured there'd be nothing left for the cattle. They hoped killing the sheep would cause such financial damage that the sheep rancher would keep the rest of his sheep away. As for the shepherd, well, he'd be tied up, a flour sack covering his head, guarded by two cowboys. He'd come to no harm so long as he cooperated.

Their scheming had come to nothing. Topping the low ridge above Little Summit Prairie they found only an empty meadow, a creek meandering across its expanse. They rode down onto the flat. Tracks and droppings indicated the sheep and their herder had left hours before, heading northwest.

If anything, the sight lightened the men's spirits. To a man, their faces immediately relaxed and soft laughter sounded for the first time. Their relief was a contrast to the forced bravado they'd spouted around the campfire. As they sat atop their horses, they shook their heads and congratulated themselves for having scared the shepherd away.

Their work wasn't over. They intended to encircle Little Summit Prairie with a dead line to keep the sheep out. Spurring their horses northward, they rode into the foothills of Bear

Mountain. There they set to work hacking blazes into tree
trunks. Some hours later they finished. "Another dead line laid
in the Ochocos," Siringo grumbled to himself. "Every new dead
line is a poke in the sheepman's eye."

Siringo mulled over the origins of the dead lines. Before
meeting with the governor, he'd read every newspaper article he
could find about the expanding range war. It had been declared
by a published announcement of the first dead line. He'd read it
more than once, until he had it memorized:

NOTICE

To whom it may concern: The Crook County Cattlemen's
Protective Association have located for its exclusive use the
territory bounded on the north by the summit of Maury
Mountain, on the south by the desert, and extending from
the north fork of Bear Creek on the west to Camp Creek on
the east.

By order of the Executive Committee

Tree trunk blazes and posted signs soon marked the cattlemen's declared boundaries in other parts of the Ochocos.
The crudely fashioned signs marked numerous dead lines that
crisscrossed the range. Siringo rode over the Santiam Pass from
Salem, determined to find and join the Executive Committee.
He'd promised the governor that the threats would stop and
no men or sheep would be killed. He'd failed. That young
Irish sheepherder, his dog, and his sheep had been murdered
on Gray's Prairie, not far from where he'd spied on the sheepshooter meeting.

Today, he'd had to act the sheepshooter as he rode
among the ponderosa pines. Leaning down from his saddle,
Siringo spent hours gouging "X's" into tree trunks with his
hatchet. Overhead, eagles had soared above golden
meadow grass. It pained him to know that his actions would
sow fear and hate across such a beautiful land.

The dead line complete, they'd all trailed south toward the Maury Mounts with Siringo bringing up the rear.

He again studied the men riding trail ahead of him. They were part of a so-called "sheepshooter committee." Their particular little committee lacked organization and seemed to stick close to home. There had to be more than one such group operating in the Ochocos.

If only the shepherds would honor the dead line warnings. Not because the cattlemen were right but because financial adversity was sharpening them into bitter, dangerously determined men. The governor needed more time to find a solution at the state and national level.

Ironically, most cattle ranchers raised sheep themselves. Fleece profits are what kept their cattle ranches on an even keel. Small flocks weren't the problem. For years, even large bands of local sheep weren't a problem. It was the federal government closing the mountain reserves to grazing that created the problem.

"Doggone it," he muttered softly to himself. "These fellows' lives are tough enough." And there was a new worry. They'd be quicker to ride down on the next sheep flock. When that happened, there might not be time to give the herder advance warning. If so, then Charlie Siringo would have no choice but to have them arrested, bringing even greater hardship to these men and their families.

Since the governor had hired him to stop the range war, at least one man, maybe two, had been murdered and hundreds of sheep killed. If these men were responsible, he'd do his duty as an honorable Dickensen detective. Siringo pulled off his cowboy hat, wiped the sweat from his brow and slammed it back onto his head. Yup, he'd do his duty by God —no matter how much he hated doing it.

FIFTEEN

"HOWDY, GREENHORN," CAME THE FRIENDLY voice. Sage started and then felt a flush of irritation. Siringo was again horning in on Sage's nightly visit with Lucinda.

"You try spending a couple of winters in the Klondike before you call me a 'greenhorn.'" Sage snapped back. "What are you doing here, anyway?"

Siringo's voice was mild as he responded, "My cover lets me get around a bit."

"What cover is that?" even to his own ears, Sage sounded cranky as an arthritic old man.

"I'm a horse buyer who's also willing to break horses. Once I broke a few horses that nobody else could break, they accepted my story. Gives me a lot of freedom to move about. Right now, I am supposed to be heading up north toward Wildcat Mountain. Thought I'd better check in with you first. Did you get a chance to talk to Rayburn?"

That question reminded Sage of the other reason he was standing behind Xenobia Brown's privy in the dark of night. "Can't talk to Rayburn," he told Siringo. "The man's dead."

Siringo swore softly before asking, "What the hell happened?"

"Someone shot him in the back this afternoon. They've arrested a homesteader by the name of Otto Fromm," Sage said, adding, "Rayburn had enemies, bunches of them. I don't think Fromm did it."

"Why do folks think a homesteader would shoot a sheepman?"

"That's just it, Rayburn was the kind of fellow who'd do pretty near anything for money. Lately, he's been running off homesteaders for the road company. He got caught trying to set fire to Fromm's hay and turning his cow loose. Fromm came to town to confront him. The wife claims Fromm never found Rayburn. But someone shot the fellow and folks suppose it had to be Fromm. Odd thing though, it seems that Fromm's homestead isn't on road company land. So, why would Rayburn go after Fromm's homestead? Doc Rosenberg thinks it's for the timber."

The two men stood silent, both considering the new turn of events. "Sure is a lot of shooting going on lately," Siringo commented.

"Those fellows you're riding with know anything about Timothy O'Dea and his dog getting killed up at Gray's Prairie?" Sage asked Siringo.

"I don't think they do," the Dickensen detective responded. "Fact is, they seemed alarmed by the killing since it's in their territory. One said he'd met the herder and liked him. Really seemed to regret the death. For all their bluster, I don't think those men have a yen to be murderers."

"Well, I find that hard to believe. Who else would want to kill a bunch of sheep?"

"Oh, they want to kill sheep alright. Provided there is provocation. But I believe that the group I'm riding with had nothing to do with killing that young Irishman."

Sage's bark of laughter was derisive. "Sounds to me like you've formed an attachment to your new cowboy friends," he said.

In the dim light, he saw Siringo's mouth straight line as his eyes narrowed. "You accusing me of not doing my job?" he asked, anger tightening his voice.

Sage stepped back, widened his stance and stood ready. At least with Siringo, he wouldn't have to fight American style. "I'm saying there's maybe a reason why you don't think those cowboys are cold-blooded murderers. Could be you're overlooking the clues that say otherwise."

"And, I'm telling you I'm a professional," Siringo emphasized the last word. He repeated it again with emphasis, "And, in my professional opinion, the men I have been spending time with aren't acting like they've murdered anyone. Maybe shot a few sheep but so far, there's no call to think they stepped over the line and killed that young shepherd."

"His name was Timothy O'Dea. I'd appreciate it if you'd at least use his name, Sage snapped.

Siringo stepped forward quickly, "You damn citified . . ." Sage shifted his weight to his rear leg and raised his hands.Interrupting, he said, "We'll just see who's . . ."

"Stop it!" The command was sharp and female. Both men's heads snapped toward the voice. Lucinda stood there, her hands on her hips, disgust on her face. "The last thing I need to see after the day I've had is two grown men acting like schoolyard fools." Sage moved his feet so he stood normally and dropped his hands. He was aware that Siringo had also abandoned his pugilist stance. Just then, shots sounded in the street on the other side of the hotel. Siringo and Sage exchanged looks.

"Just some cowboys letting off a little steam," Siringo said. "The sheriff will take them in hand if they keep it up."

"More men acting like darned fool boys," Lucinda said but this time her voice held a smile. She stepped toward them. As she did, a shot rang out. A bullet thwacked the privy boards, sending a splinter of wood shooting off. That bullet had passed between himself and Lucinda, missing them by mere inches. Sage dove forward, threw his arms around her and they both hit the ground. As they fell, Siringo jumped between them and the back of the hotel, drawing his gun from its holster. All three froze, waiting for a second shot. It didn't come. Sage thought he heard a distant door softly close. Siringo slipped his gun back into its holster but kept staring at the hotel.

Sage looked down at Lucinda. "Are you all right? I didn't hurt you, did I?"

For one heart stopping moment, her wide eyes simply stared into his. They held the look so long that he became aware of her body warmth beneath his and the satin of remembered places.

She broke the spell. "I'd probably be doing a bit better if you'd set me up on my feet," she told him, her voice shaking just a bit. "You're not exactly a feather, you know," she added dryly but her smile blunted any bite in her words.

He scrambled to his feet, pulling her up with him. Siringo looked at them and said, "Glad the two of you are done rolling around on the ground. We better clear out of here. Whoever fired that shot might decide to come back."

"You think it wasn't just the cowboys letting off steam again?" Sage asked, though he knew the answer. He just wanted to see if Siringo agreed.

Siringo shook his head. "There's no way someone raising cane in front of the hotel could send a bullet shooting all the way through to the back of the hotel and into that privy. Besides, that sounded like a sissy pea shooter. Not a cowboy gun, at all."

Siringo pulled his hat low on his forehead, his eyes narrow glints beneath its wide brim. "Whoever the shooter was, he was aiming at either you or Ms. Lucinda. So, we best get going. Ms. Lucinda, you head for the house. Adair, I'll meet you in half an hour, behind the Prineville Light generator building."

"I've noticed that you've said nothing about the cowboy kid who met with the Dickensen fellow in Portland. Are you thinking now that he's also a real fine fellow?" Those were Sage's first words to Siringo when they met up behind the powerhouse. Behind them, the creek was a silent black ribbon beneath overhanging oaks. From the building, the sounds of a huffing steam boiler and squeaking leather belt meant the dynamo was up and running.

Siringo shoved his hat back on his forehead so Sage could see his face clearly. The cowboy eyed him for a minute, before saying, "Look Adair. I've obviously done something to offend you. I don't know what but, whatever it is, I'm right sorry." The man's expression was earnest, his smooth cowboy assurance gone.

Sage was glad it was dark because hot shame flushed his face. Siringo was right. He'd done nothing to justify Sage's hostility. Heaving a sigh, Sage admitted to himself that his treatment of Siringo was nothing more than jealousy. It wasn't Siringo's fault if Lucinda had taken a fancy to his long, lean cowboy looks. "I'm sorry, Charlie," Sage said and meant it. "You've done nothing to offend me. I'm just out of my element in this situation. Taking it out on you, I guess."

The cowboy nodded understandingly, "That's how I feel when I'm in a city," he told Sage. "I didn't mention the kid because he's not working with fellows I've been riding with. That's one reason why I need to head north. See if that's where the young scoundrel has gone. I've checked all the saloons here in town and he's nowhere to be found. I figure he's somewheres out on the north Ochoco range."

Sage cleared his throat. "Umm, I am also sorry I never had a chance to talk with Rayburn. I know it was important but I just never ran into him. I'm hoping that the sheepherder Irishman I told you about, Twill McGinnis, will do just as well as Rayburn. Maybe better. He worked with the shepherd who was murdered last week. And the other shepherds like him. They didn't like Rayburn." Sage had deliberately not used Timothy O'Dea's name by way of making a subtle apology for his earlier jab.

Siringo noted the effort. "You mean McGinnis herded with Mr. Timothy O'Dea?" he asked, then grinned.

Sage grinned back. It was no wonder Lucinda liked the fellow. When he let himself, he liked the cowboy too. Sage continued, "So, I've also developed a bit of information that might be related. Besides doing their bookkeeping, the sheep ranchers had me research sections deep in the Ochocos. They are definitely focusing on grazing sheep there. I understand that's been cattle country for a long time. Sparks will fly if they move into even more sections, I'm thinking. And, the shepherds' anger is building too. They seem to be nerving themselves up to attack the cowboys. This murder of Rayburn might be the very thing that goads them into acting." Sage went on to tell Siringo the comments he'd overheard in the Rimrock.

Siringo nodded as Sage talked, then said, "Well, I'm not saying a cowboy didn't kill O'Dea. The only ones I can eliminate are the ones running cattle down south near the Maury Mountains. But there's another cattle outfit north of the military road. That's where I'm headed next. Maybe I'll find Tom Meglit there too."

Siringo was silent, pondering the situation. His smile was rueful when he said, "Wahl, there's one good thing. No cattle or cowboys have gone missing or been murdered. So far, at least the sheepmen have kept their heads. What about the sheep ranchers you're working for? Have you learned whether they're planning retaliation for the murder, the sheep shooting and the barn burning?"

Sage took off his derby and ran his fingers through his hair. "Well, I can tell you that they seemed really worried about something. I'll try to find out more tomorrow, just in case. Today, they were fighting and in no mood to talk. I didn't stay in the office. Instead, I spent the day with the courthouse maps locating fresh water springs in the sections along the military road."

"So you don't know what their fight was about? Why they were upset?" Siringo asked, lighting a cigarette after offering one to Sage.

"Well, I saw a guy storm out of Van Ostrand's office. He looked like an angry creditor. And, it was their sheep that O'Dea was guarding. So, the loss of those sheep has to have cost them. And, I presume O'Dea's murder also hit them pretty hard."

"Tell me more about this Twill fellow," Siringo said.

"A likeable Irishmen. Quick to laugh, friendly, has a way with words. A really fine, smart fellow. But he's got a temper, too. You saw him. Like I said, he's the one your friends attacked in the street. Right now, he's bound and determined he's going to find out who killed O'Dea. When he does, I don't think he's planning on turning him over to the law."

"Sure is a lot of anger swirling around this town. Sad thing is, it ain't really these folks' fault. They had a pretty good balance going around here before the federal government decided to change how the federal range land was used," Siringo said. "You'd think they'd remember that. These people used to be friends. They used to help each other out—the sheep and cattle ranchers."

For a while, the two smoked their cigarettes until Sage said quietly, "I promised Mrs. Fromm I'd figure out who shot Rayburn."

Siringo nodded, as if he understood Sage hadn't really had a choice in the matter. "You know, two murders of two sheepmen in less than a week seems a tad coincidental," he said, flipping his cigarette butt into the water.

He turned toward Sage. "Adair, I was thinking on it, riding over here. That shot tonight wasn't a stray or a coincidence. What I can't figure out is whether it was you or Ms. Lucinda who was the intended target. Someone might suspicion that the young fellow who died said more to her than he did."

The shiver that comment sent racing through Sage was far colder than the chilly, dark water flowing past his feet.

SIXTEEN

At seven a.m. there were a few sleepy folks eating breakfast in the Poindexter's dining room. One of them was Congressman Thomas. He sat alone, his face morose. Sage hesitated in the doorway until Thomas saw him and motioned him over.

"Good morning John. I trust you had a decent night's sleep?" the Congressman said, but his greeting sounded listless.

"I can't complain. Once the cowboys stopped their six-shooter celebrating, things get pretty quiet around here," Sage answered before quickly moving on. "You're looking worried this morning," he observed and then stayed silent, hoping Thomas would feel the need to talk.

Thomas heaved a sigh. "I received some bad news late yesterday and I'm trying to figure out what to do."

Sage remained quiet, hoping his face conveyed an open, willing-to-help-in-any-way, look.

It must have, because Thomas kept talking. "You probably heard that we lost our grazing rights along the military road to the Kepler brothers," Thomas said.

Sage nodded. "I figure the work I did at the courthouse yesterday had something to do with that."

"It did. There's a lot of grazing land up there in the Ochocos that the military road builders couldn't claim. We've heard that some entry men are going use the Timber and Stone Act to file claims up there. Once they prove up, we can try buying the parcels from them. In the meantime, we'll try to lease from them. A piece with a spring on it would be the best grazing land for us. Your research tells us which pieces are the most desirable."

"I know about the Homestead Act but how does a Timber and Stone entry man prove up his claim?" Sage asked.

"He only has to say he's going to cut the timber or quarry the stone and publish his claim in the newspaper for sixty days," Thomas said.

That information set Sage to pondering. It meant land grabs by the timber barons would be even easier because proving a claim was dead simple. Homesteaders like the Fromms had to clear the land and live on it full time. And, it took them three or more years of living on that land before they could prove up—not a mere sixty days of publishing a notice in the newspaper.

Sage considered. He hadn't been in the Ochoco Mountains and wondered just how many claimed "timber" acres even had trees on them. Though, for certain, there had to be plenty of stones.

Sage's silence evidently made Thomas uneasy because he changed the subject. "So, Miner, where are you from originally?" he asked.

"Pennsylvania. After that, here and there," Sage answered truthfully. "Did some gold panning up in the Klondike a few years back. I sure didn't like the cold. And, by the time I got there, all the good claims were gone," he added untruthfully.

"Timing is everything," Thomas mused, more to himself than to Sage. Then he straightened and said, "Me, I was raised within forty miles of Prineville. My father was an original settler hereabouts. He began running cattle early on. He's gone now and my older brother is running the ranch. It's a very big ranch." Thomas looked pensive, adding, "I'm not much like my father. I don't like ranching. Dad said I lacked the gumption to make it work. Fact is, being a congressman is the first thing I've accomplished on my own."

"You and Van Ostrand seemed to have made a go of sheep ranching, at least until you lost the grazing lease. "

Thomas shrugged. "It's mostly my money that's being lost. Van Ostrand put in less money, but then, he had a lot less to invest. Still, he's the driving force behind the business. He makes all the decisions, oversees things. I just agree with what he wants. And sometimes, I grease the wheels here and in Washington D.C. For awhile, it looked like we'd succeed but now I don't know." His voice trailed off.

"I take it you just got some bad news," Sage prodded.

"It's that damn Roosevelt," Thomas said, anger in his voice for the first time. "He's so hellbent on making forest reserves that he's blind to the fact he's being manipulated."

"What do you mean?"

"The timber barons want Roosevelt to declare the Ochoco's a reserve and it looks like they're going to get their way. Once that happens, those entry men won't get their claims and we won't get our grazing leases. We'll be out of business."

This time, Sage didn't have to feign ignorance. "I don't understand. How will declaring the Ochocos a reserve end up lining the pockets of the timber barons? Seems like they'd be kept off the land too."

"It's damn complicated," Thomas said, "but I'll try to explain." He leaned forward, his forehead already wrinkling with effort. "Every state is divided into what is known as townships. Each township contains 36 sections and each section contains 640 acres. You saw that when you looked at the maps." Sage nodded.

"When a state is created, all land in that state that is still unclaimed by individuals, belongs to the federal government. The exception is the 16th and the 36th sections of every township. Those two sections belong to the State. The proceeds from that land's sale or taxation, is meant to pay for the education of the State's citizens."

Thomas waited for that information to sink in. Sage nodded his understanding so Thomas continued, "When the federal government creates a forest reserve or an Indian reservation, it takes back the 16th and 36th sections of every township located in that reserve or reservation. In exchange, the federal government lets the State claim an equal amount of federally-owned, unclaimed acreage anywhere else in the State. Those replacement sections are called 'in-lieu-of-lands.' The State can then sell those sections to private individuals—like our friends, the timber companies. There's no need to file claims. It's an outright sale.

Thomas raised a questioning eyebrow. When Sage again nodded he understood, Thomas explained further, "So, what the timber barons do is get the federal government to declare a forest reserve. That's what happened in the Cascades. The minute the federal government declares a reserve, the timber barons' flunkies run to the State land office and pay for unclaimed federal land they've targeted elsewhere in the state. Since they have money in their hot little hands, the State is more than willing to sell. And, at an extremely low price. Of course, because of their Washington D.C. connections, the timber men know in advance when and where to make their move. They always beat everybody else to the best timber land."

The wrinkle in Sage's forehead was genuine. The scheme sounded too complicated.

Thomas saw Sage's confusion. "So, if Roosevelt declares the Ochocos a reserve, then all the open land is withdrawn from public use. That eliminates the open grazing lands now used by homesteaders and ranchers. At the same time, the acres in the 16th and 36th sections become the basis for an equal number in-lieu-of-acres elsewhere in the state. Right now, I guarantee, the timber cruisers know exactly what unclaimed acres they want to buy as in-lieu-of-land when the Ochocos turn into a reserve. The minute that reserve is declared, they will be at the State land office making their purchase.

"So that means that the Ochoco Mountains will be off limits as grazing lands, just like the Cascade Mountains are now?" Sage thought he finally got it. "Jesus, the ranchers around here have already lost the Cascades to the Reserve and some of the high desert to homesteaders. Loss of the Ochoco range lands would be a disaster."

"Yes, that is exactly what it will mean," Thomas said morosely. "As it stands now, there'll be no Ochoco grazing land for sheep or for cattle if they create that reserve. You might not realize it from looking at them," here Thomas swept a hand at the room, "but these men are terrified of losing everything they've worked for. Large ranches like my family's or Hay Creek, have enough acreage to survive, but most of these ranchers, be they into sheep or cattle, won't be able to. Some of these men were lifelong friends before this all happened. Now they've divided up—believing, without question, every self-serving lie they're told or that they tell themselves. Those damn dead lines are running right through decades-long friendships." Thomas sighed, adding, "Sometimes I think my brother has the right idea. It would be comforting just to stay out on the ranch faraway from everyone else and let them tear each other to pieces."

"What happens to the homesteaders, like the Fromm's, who've already proved up their Ochoco claims?" Sage asked.

"Mostly, but not always, they get moved out. Sometimes they are offered other lands in exchange but that won't help this town. Those exchange lands will likely be anywhere but near Prineville. They'll have to start over, losing their neighbors and all the good will they've built up over the years."

"Geez, all this just so some huge corporation in Minnesota can chop down Oregon trees?"

"Yup. And it looks like there's nothing we can do to stop that stupid president of ours from signing away our birthright and wrecking havoc on our community. Havoc not just on sheepmen but on the cattle ranchers and homesteaders as well. And, the fool thinks he's doing the people a favor." Bitterness crackled in Thomas's words.

Sage mulled over the impact faraway Washington D.C. decisions might have on the lives of so many Central Oregonians. "It seems Roosevelt's idea of keeping forests for future generations is a good one. Seems like the problem is that it's being exploited by greedy men who have no moral compasses," he said.

"That's always the way, Miner. Good intentions create a law. At the same time greedy men and their sharpie lawyers figure out how insert and use legal loopholes in the law. I see it every time I'm in Congress. As long as greed is acceptable and obscene wealth laudable, I don't see things changing."

"Is there any possible solution to this grazing mess?" Sage asked.

"Well, there's some talk of loosening the grazing restrictions so that folks can graze their animals in the reserves. But, there's no sign that's going to happen," Thomas answered.

Suddenly the congressman straightened and peered at the street outside. A genuine smile curved his lips for the first time that day. "I do believe it's the Gable brothers," he said. "Right on schedule."

Sage twisted in his chair so he could peer out the window. Coming down the street was a high-sided freight wagon being pulled by two plodding mules. Dingy canvas, stretched over hoops, covered the wagon bed. The contraption looked much like the covered wagons of old. Atop the high wagon seat rode two men, both sporting long gray beards and dusty black suits.

Sage turned back to Thomas, "Gable brothers?" he asked.

Thomas chuckled and then explained, "Those two Jewish traders have been coming to Central Oregon for years. Why, I remember them coming to our ranch when I was just starting to read. 'Course, they were a lot younger then, too."

He leaned forward, seeming happy for the distraction and eager to tell the story. "Early every summer they'd turn up. That wagon they're pulling is loaded with trinkets, candy and all sorts of things that folks out on ranches and homesteads need and want. Back then, lots of folks would raise a few sheep but it was never worth the time for them to drive the sheep all the way to The Dalles. Instead, the Gables would come with their trinkets and trade 'em for fleece. Even today, there's lots of folks who run a few sheep so they can trade the wool for the Gable brother's bits and pieces." Thomas smiled again, clearly taking pleasure in reliving those early days.

"I have to tell you, it was an exciting day when that old wagon rumbled down the hill. All work stopped. Us boys surely loved the hard candy, books and toys in that wagon."

Sage looked at Thomas and saw the once innocent boy inside the jaded, worried man. He felt pity. Thomas was like the man chained to railroad tracks, watching the locomotive's headlight growing bigger.

Outside, the Gable's wagon came to a halt, the mules softly nickering. Across from him, Thomas straightened. He was again peering out the window. "Hmm. Looks like the Gables brought another of their own kind with them this time," he observed. "Wonder what that means? He's an older fellow, too."

Sage twisted back around to see a man clambering over the wagon's backboard. He'd started to turn back toward Thomas when realization hit. Twisting back around for a second look, he felt his chin drop.

He'd never seen Herman Eich wearing a short, neatly trimmed beard. But there was no doubt about it. The man who'd crawled down from the peddlers' wagon bed was none other than Portland's ragpicker poet.

SEVENTEEN

THOMAS NOTED SAGE'S START OF surprise because the congressman's eyebrows rose in inquiry. Sage spoke quickly, hoping to distract the man, "I know about the Kepler brother's barn burning and Twill told me about the murder of Timothy O'Dea but have there been any other moves against sheepmen around here, other than the dead line blazings?"

That question did the trick. "Ahh," Thomas began, then said, "Well, there's that old sheepherder and his dog. They just vanished from a high meadow to the northeast. That was over a month ago. When the rancher took the shepherd supplies, he found the flock scattered, some shot through but most missing. There was no sign of either the shepherd or his dog. Folks figure the missing sheep are dead—prey for bear, coyote, cougar or wolf.

"The missing sheepherder gave rise to quite a bit of speculation. Some folks think he just got tired of being alone and headed out, taking his dog with him. Others, those who knew him better, say the old fellow either got hurt and died somewhere on the range or else there was foul play."

This information focused Sage's mind because a connection suddenly clicked into place. Lucinda said the dead man had felt shame as he raved on about an old man. Was that old man the missing shepherd? Was he the first victim of Oregon's range war? If so, Siringo was right. Lucinda was in danger. Someone could think the dying man had told her about the murder and who was involved.

Thomas tossed his napkin onto the table and rose from his chair saying, "I best be getting on my way. And, I know Dr. Van Ostrand is expecting you about now." The congressman's departing smile and words twinkled with the calculated warmth of a born politician.

Sage tarried a bit longer over his coffee, waiting until he saw Herman Eich enter the hotel and walk up to the front desk. His ragpicker friend went through the registration process like a well-heeled sophisticate. Maybe he once was, Sage mused. He knew little about Eich's origins. Ever since Sage had known him, the ragpicker had lived in a tiny lean-to beside one of Portland's deepest ravines. His meager livelihood came from reselling us-able dustbin items and from repairing delicate porcelains. Twice he'd joined Sage, Mae, Fong and others in an effort to carry out one of St. Alban's missions. Eich's presence in Central Oregon could only mean he was here to help.

Eich received his room key and began climbing the stairs to the second story. Sage stood, slapped coins on the table, crossed the lobby and followed his friend up the stairs.

※ ※ ※

The buckskin reared, its front hooves paddling the air. Between the black pointed ears, Siringo saw a dun-colored hill flash against the blue sky before those hooves crashed down. He loosened the reins and fought to stay centered in the saddle. As the horse's front hooves hit the ground, his rear legs flew skyward giving Siringo a close look at hard-packed earth. Still, the cowboy stayed mounted, hauling on the reins to pull the horse's head to-ward his knee. Unable to buck, the stallion circled first one way and then the other, his turns made in spine-jarring hops.

Siringo heard cheering, saw hats waving and money chang-ing hands—all behind the safely of the corral fence. He'd make money for those few who'd bet he'd stay atop the horse they'd named "Dust Devil." No question, the ride was testing his skills. It was only now, ten minutes into the contest, that the stallion began to tire. Siringo relaxed, his body signaling that the horse was done fighting. He leaned forward to stroke the animal's golden neck, murmuring quiet words into the ear now aimed his direction. After a sedate victory lap around the corral, Siringo dismounted. He stepped slowly to the front of the buckskin, pulled an apple from his pocket and fed the animal, all the while stroking its nose and murmuring words that only the horse could hear.

Siringo exited the corral to the backslaps of the usually taciturn cowboys. One of those doing the congratulating was young Tom Meglit.

"Hey Tony, you rode that bronc right into the ground," the young cowboy crowed. "I knew you'd do it!"

Siringo, who was using the name "Tony Lloyd," flashed Meglit a grin. He'd finally found the young cowpoke. He needed to befriend him quickly.

Despite, their current pleasure in his horse-breaking demonstration, this was an uncomfortable group of cowboys. Unease among them manifested itself in sideways glances and laughs that were cynical rather than easy. He'd been here the whole day, still posing as a horse buyer from down Arizona way. They'd been suspicious and remote. In desperation, Siringo had mounted Dust Devil, promising to be the first to break the dangerous horse. He figured that only a display of superior horsemanship would open their circle to him.

They'd waited until the day's work was done and the heat lessened. Now it was early evening. Golden light washed the land, turning pine needles glistening green against the yellow bark of ancient ponderosa pines. He sat on a stump to roll a smoke. As he'd hoped, the chattering Tom Meglit followed, his glances skittish, his movements choppy. Meglit was one of those lean, twitchy men who made other men uneasy. Siringo offered the cowpoke a tight, hand-rolled cigarette.

Meglit's followers clustered behind him. They were of little note. Just two men, so uncertain of their own worth, so needful of belonging, that they easily became unthinking disciples of anyone who acted confident. For such men, someone like Meglit was both a beacon and a magnet. Siringo had seen it too many times. Sheep weren't the only critters who followed blindly. Sometimes he wondered if unthinking followers weren't mankind's greatest curse.

"Well, that sure was a pretty sight. You brought Dust Devil to his knees," Meglit said, interrupting Siringo's thoughts.

"Nah. We just reached an understanding. Don't underestimate that horse," Siringo cautioned. "He's still full of fight. You get on his bad side and there's no telling where you'll end up."

"I can't argue with that Lloyd, because you're a man who surely knows horses. Brave, too. We need more men like you in this country," Meglit enthused. The other two chimed in like a Greek chorus to underscore their leader's opinion.

"Yup, we need more men like you who ain't afraid and who are willing to stand up and show their bravery. This range is being destroyed and those lily-livered cowboys," here Meglit nodded toward the others who were sitting around a nearby cook fire, "ain't doing nothing." Meglit's words sunk into a momentary silence that had paused all other conversation. The cowboys had heard him.

If Meglit noticed, he gave no outward sign other than his knee started a nervy bouncing. Meglit kept turning the screw, "We've got plenty of problems and not enough brave men to tackle them. Harry Perkins, now, he had the guts but he's dead and gone," he told Siringo. His two buddies nodded eagerly.

Siringo kept his attention fixed on Meglit, even as he felt the other cowboys' anger begin to stir. "What are you talking about, Meglit?" Siringo made a show of looking around, "What problems?" he asked.

"All them damn woolies, they're ruining our grazing land. Not enough real men," he sarcastically emphasized the last two words before continuing, "are around here to take the situation in hand. If you know what I mean."

"What do you mean, take in hand?" Siringo prodded. Out of the corner of his eye he saw the foreman straighten and stare in their direction. Meglit's entourage grinned encouragement even as the other cowboys glowered.

Meglit acted as if he was unaware of the hostility his words were creating. But his smug look betrayed him. He was deliberately goading the men who were within earshot. "Why, I'm saying, the only way we're going to be able to save this here cattle range is to make it damn inhospitable to the sheep and their herders. But, most folks are too chicken-shit to do anything about it."

"That's enough!" The foreman's voice was sharp. He stood and pointed a finger at Meglit. "You either shut up or you pack up. Your choice, Meglit."

The young cowboy smirked but said nothing more. He merely tipped his hat toward Siringo before wandering off, trailed by his two followers. Siringo watched him go, regretting the foreman's intervention.

He looked toward the foreman who was studying him with watchful eyes. "I'd steer clear of that youngster," the man advised. "There's something missing in him. He's more reptile than human. Once we get the cattle moved up to the high pasture, I'm sending him down the trail. This was a tight bunch before he came along."

Siringo merely nodded and the foreman turned away. He happened to agree with the beleaguered foreman but didn't dare let him know it. He had to find out if Meglit had anything to do with the barn burning, the missing shepherd or O'Dea's murder. To do that, Meglit had to believe Siringo was his new best friend. As night fell, Meglit and his two sidekicks moved away from the others to build a separate fire that sent sparks soaring into a starlit sky. Siringo left the bigger campfire to stand among the trees. Central Oregon's clear night skies brought the stars so close that they lit the trails like a full moon. He wandered over toward Meglit's group, a bottle of cheap whiskey tucked under his arm.

"Pull up a chunk, pardner," Meglit said, gesturing toward a log round. Soon they were telling stories, with Siringo adding his share. The whiskey was passed around, each man turning away from the firelight to drink straight from the bottle. It was supposed to be a dry camp.

After an initial burst of exchanges, the group fell silent. Into the silence Meglit asked, "So, where might you stand on our sheep problem?" Then he and his two friends waited, their intent stares belying the casual tone of Meglit's question.

"I don't like sheep," Siringo said. "I don't like to look at them, hear them, smell them or eat them."

The other three looked at each other then laughed heartily as they slapped their knees.

Siringo picked up a stick and poked the coals. "Why do you ask? Are you fixing to turn to shepherding?"

Meglit shook his head. "Nope, I intend to do me some sheep shooting," he answered. That brought a stir of protest from one of the others but Meglit raised a hand to shush him. "Tony here is one of us. He don't like the sheep no more than we do. Ain't that right, Tony?"

Siringo looked each one in the eyes before he said. "This country would be a lot better off if those sheep stayed in Idaho. I know the locals with only one or two of the woolies are no bother. But if you get a thousand, two thousand head moving through and there won't be a lick of grass left."

Meglit looked pleased. "See, I told you he thinks like us."

"'Course," Siringo continued, "it's easy to talk big. Talking is nothing more than lips flapping."

Meglit bristled and rose to the bait. "Listen here Lloyd, You don't have no call to insult me. I ain't just a talker. I bet I've done more than you have about our little sheep problem."

Siringo arched an eyebrow, "Yah, sure, Meglit. So what if you kill yourself a few dozen sheep. That's saved what? An acre of grass?"

That chiding tone gave Meglit the poke he needed because his chest puffed and he said, "That's what you know. There's one less herder and sheepdog in these parts, thanks to me and Harry Perkins. And a whole herd is dead. Maybe a thousand head."

Siringo leaned forward, widening his eyes and raising his eyebrows to show he was impressed. "Tell me about it," he encouraged.

EIGHTEEN

Standing between the branches of the backyard bush, Sage's eyes searched the hotel's dark windows and shadowed rear porch. This time, he'd been careful reaching his place of waiting. He'd slipped out the hotel's rear door hoping that, if someone wanted to shoot him, that person would believe he was still in his room.

If nothing else, the day's events had lessened his worry. He knew now that he was the person someone was trying to shoot, not Lucinda. He fingered the new ache on his chin. It was a painful memento of his peculiar day. First it was Eich, stepping down from the peddler's wagon. Next it was Van Ostrand's disinterest in Sage's report on the springs he'd located, saying only, "That's fine Miner. Go ahead and finish locating the rest. After that, get me a list of the homestead claimants in each of the sections that have springs."

The order was a welcome one. Sage wanted to talk to the imprisoned Otto Fromm so the courthouse was just the right place to be. The jail cell was a solid, one-story masonry addition attached to the building's side. Sage figured t h e s h eriff mi ght let him talk to Fromm, especially if the county clerk, Mr. 'Yes Indeedy' Jones, vouched for him.

That's exactly what happened. Jones had spoken to a deputy, stressing Sage's respectable connection to Van Ostrand and Thomas. Soon, Sage occupied a straight-back chair sitting in the narrow aisle between two iron-barred cells. Fromm occupied one cell, the other was empty. The homesteader sat on the end of an iron cot, facing Sage.

Introductions over, Sage said, "Mr. Fromm, I promised your wife that I'd try to help you. I was hoping you would be able to tell me something of what happened the day before yesterday. The day you spent looking for Rayburn."

Worry had aged the homesteader's face. He was no longer the happy man Sage had seen greeting his wife at the Willowdale station. But Fromm's voice was calm as he answered, "Lisabet, the kids and me reached town about eleven that morning. I went to the sheriff 's office to register a complaint against Rayburn but the office was closed. I decided to confront Rayburn myself. I had to know what we had done to make him try to destroy everything we'd worked so hard to build." Fromm's hands became fists as anger washed across his face. After a second, he continued, "I wanted to know why he'd endangered my family. So I left Lisabet and the kids at Lippman's Furniture Emporium. We planned to meet up later on at the Vienna Café and head back to the farm."

Fromm paused, apparently trying to remember the next sequence of events. "Folks said Rayburn was a drinker so I figured I'd find him in a saloon. I started looking. I don't frequent those places so I wasn't sure which one he'd visit. I first tried the Rimrock because I knew he'd had something to do with sheep. But Rayburn wasn't there. After that, I just started at one end of Main Street and asked at every one until I reached the end."

A brief smile quirked Fromm's lips. "I couldn't find him anywhere. By the time I was done, I had walked off a lot of my mad." Here his middle-aged face turned earnest again and he leaned toward Sage. "I started out ready to punch the fellow the minute I saw him. But, by the time I reached The Reception Room Saloon, I just wanted to know why. You understand?"

Sage nodded and Fromm continued, "At the Reception, one of the fellows said Rayburn had talked about going fishing. So, I headed toward the river." Fromm paused as he remembered the next events. He cleared his throat and continued, his voice tentative with worry, "I crossed the bridge and stumbled through the brush heading upstream. First, I saw a fishing pole, floating in the shallows. Then I saw his boots."

Fromm's voice quieted as he remembered. "He wasn't dead when I found him. I tried to help. I lifted his head but I knew he couldn't make it. Someone had shot him clean through. His whole chest was bloody. It was a god-awful big hole. He tried to tell me something but he was too far gone. Then he died."

"Did you hear the shot that killed him?"

"I think I did. But I was by the river and it was making noise and I was making noise crashing through the brush. If I did, it was just a single shot."

"What happened after that?"

Fromm looked shamefaced. "It's funny how a mind works so fast when it's scared. Once I saw that he was dead, I first thought of going to get the sheriff. But then, I realized everyone would think I'd killed him. I'd told everyone I was looking for him and I'd told them why. Now here he was, dead. So, I left him there."

"And where were you when they found you?"

"I met Lisabet at the café. We sent the kids out to buy candy and I told her about finding Rayburn. Just as she noticed the blood on my sleeve, the sheriff comes in. He asked for my gun, smelled it and arrested me. Here I am." Fromm gestured around the cell which was small, dark but clean. Still, the tin roof overhead radiated the morning sun's gathering heat. By late afternoon, it would be unbearable.

Fromm stepped closer to the bars. "Mr. Miner, God in heaven as my witness, I didn't shoot Asa Rayburn. I might have slugged him a good one if I'd found him," he raised his big fists, knuckles scarred from rough work, "But I sure the hell didn't shoot him in the back. I've been sitting here, trying to think how to prove I didn't kill Rayburn. But, I can think of nothing."

Sage studied Fromm. He was sweating, but so was Sage. Otherwise, the homesteader seemed to be forthright and honest. He could see why Dexter believed that Fromm was innocent. "Well, Mr. Fromm, you're right. The facts look bad. The only chance we have of proving you didn't kill Rayburn, is to figure out who had reason to want him dead."

That observation brought a nod from Fromm. "I've been thinking on that. Rayburn had no call to burn us out unless he was working for someone. It could be the military road owners. They've been trying to chase the homesteaders out but I'm not homesteading in one of their sections. My place has a spring and those are short in supply. But, if the military road owners plan on selling their sections to the timber companies, maybe they want to be able to say there were more sections available. I've been going round and round in my head and that's the only reason I can come up with. Otherwise, I just can't figure why Rayburn was at our place that day. That was going to be my first question to him."

There was no faulting the man's logic. He was right. Sage considered what he'd learned about Rayburn. The man had been in the sheep business up north and associated with the herders at the Rimrock. The owner had given Rayburn a partial interest in the Rimrock only to regret it. The military road owners had been using Rayburn to bully the homesteaders into abandoning their claims. Sage cast his mind over all he'd learned in the six days he'd been in Prineville.

"Tell me," he asked Fromm, "do you know anything about that Morrow County sheep rancher, Bellingham's, trouble with the federal district attorney?"

Fromm looked puzzled then his face cleared as understanding dawned. "Why I know they indicted Bellingham for having his workers file sham homestead claims so that he could tie up open range for his sheep." The homesteader jumped to his feet. "Why, that Rayburn fellow used to work for Bellingham. And, when I was asking after Rayburn at one saloon, a fellow told me that the federal prosecutor was asking after him too. Do you think Rayburn was going to testify against Bellingham? That maybe Bellingham wanted Rayburn dead?" For the first time, eagerness enlivened the homesteader.

Sage raised a cautionary hand. "From what I've heard, Rayburn would do anything for money. Maybe he'd throw his old boss on the fire if given the choice between himself or Bellingham. But, right now, we have no proof that Rayburn was going to betray his former boss. Besides, we still don't know why Rayburn tried to burn you out. That doesn't tie to Bellingham at all."

Fromm dropped down on the bunk and put his face in his hands. After a moment he looked at Sage. "If I'd just held on to my temper. If we'd just stayed home, none of this would have happened. Lisabet can't keep the homestead going all by herself. Whoever sent Rayburn out to burn down our place has won."

※ ※ ※

Sage left the jail without any clear direction but lots of questions. He'd returned to his records search for Van Ostrand. His list of names complied, he headed back to the dentist's office. As he climbed the stairs an attractive woman, with two children in tow, was descending. There was a worry crease between two fine dark eyes. Just as they were about to exit, she told her children, "It looks like we won't be visiting grandma and grandpa this summer. Your father says we can't afford it. We'll find something else fun to do. Maybe go camping in the mountains." The door closed on the children's whines of disappointment.

Heat lay heavy in the upstairs hallway. Sage first looked through the open door of the treatment room. It was empty of both patient and dentist. The office door knob turned under his hand and he pushed it open. Inside, Van Ostrand sat at his desk, head in hands, shoulders hunched.

Sage clearing his throat caused the dentist to turn around. "Oh, it's you," he said without enthusiasm or interest. He took Sage's list but didn't look at it before he tossed it onto the desk. Instead he asked, "Do you have any children, Miner?"

Oddly, the answering "no" stuck in Sage's throat, snagging on the memory of a fantasy he'd once had . . . one of Lucinda and their daughter carrying lunch to where Sage and their son worked clearing an orchard. Those two children had never existed and never would now that Charlie Siringo had staked his claim. Sage cleared his throat. "No. Though, I wouldn't mind having a couple," he answered truthfully.

"Well, the most awful thing a man can do is disappoint his children," the dentist said.

Dr. Van Ostrand abruptly stood and charged into his treatment room where he began cleaning his various instruments. Sage trailed behind to say, "The list I gave you identifies t he springs in each section and shows the homesteaders who own the land around those springs."

"Yes, yes," the man responded, with irritation. "Wait a moment, I have to finish c leaning these i nstruments before the blood dries. Just stand over there by the window and be quiet," he said, then added sharply, "And, don't block the light!"

Sage stood against the wall and studied the room. It was well appointed for a dentist's office located so far from a big city. He gazed about, noting the patients' black leather reclining chair, the white ceramic spit bowl and a drill arm arching over the chair. Following its lines, he saw the well-worn foot peddle Van Ostrand pumped to turn the drill at the end of the apparatus. Ether's pungent smell hung in the room. Sage stepped closer to the open window. The smell was nauseating, maybe because Sage retained a vivid memory of when a killer shoved an ether-soaked rag against his face. He'd come close to a grisly end.

Shaking off that memory, Sage realized that Van Ostrand was muttering as he dried his alcohol-soaked instruments. The dentist seemed to be lecturing himself: "There are three components. Scaling to keep the teeth clean, regulating to avoid crowding and most delicate of all, filling." He put down the instrument and picked up another one, only to repeat the same litany.

Sage shifted uncomfortably. Was the man going barmy? His movement caught the dentist's eye because the man stopped muttering to issue an order. "Go next door, and wait for me in the office." As Sage left the room, Van Ostrand's muttering resumed.

Once in the office, Sage sliced open the sealed correspondence lying on his assigned desk, finding more bills and a handwritten letter from the partners' prior accountant. Sage scanned that last missive, dismayed to read that the man intended to remain in Portland. He'd apparently found himself a job and would not be returning to Prineville. Given Van Ostrand's agitated state of mind, Sage decided to keep that bit of news to himself. He returned the letter to its envelope and lay it on the dentist's desk for him to find.

Van Ostrand had apparently recovered his equilibrium because he was strangely cheerful when he entered the room. "Mr. Miner. I am most pleased with your work. I had lunch with the court clerk, Mr. Jones, and he informed me that you are most diligent in your perusal of the files and maps." Narrowing his eyes, the dentist continued, "Mr. Jones also told me of your visit to that Fromm fellow. A word of friendly caution, Mr. Miner. You are new to this country. You don't know how things are. It would be far safer for you if you minded your own business and stayed out of other people's."

Without giving Sage a chance to respond, Van Ostrand said, "The workday is essentially over so I suggest we call it a day. You may return tomorrow and we'll discuss your next task." With that, the dentist exited the room, leaving Sage to stare at the empty doorway.

NINETEEN

MID AFTERNOON, THE SUN BLAZED in a near-white sky. Inside, the dim light gave the illusion that the Rimrock was cooler. Sage was hoping Twill or someone else would have more specific information about Rayburn and his activities.

The saloon was nearly empty. Only a few older fellows sat here and there, nursing beers in the afternoon heat. Their solitariness reminded him that these were shepherds—men used to, and probably preferring, their own company.

"Where is everyone?" Sage asked the bartender.

The man grimaced. "I expect the ones in town are snoozing somewhere under a shade tree. That damn pox means most of our regular customers are avoiding town. There's just a few that have the pox scar so that they can come and go. It's about killed our business. Barney hasn't paid me in over a month. It ain't his fault, neither."

"Is that why the owner took Rayburn's money?"

The bartender nodded. "I suppose. I know Barney didn't much care for Rayburn. 'Course now, I suppose, he doesn't even have to worry about paying the man's investment back." As if suddenly realizing the implications of that statement, the bartender rushed to add, "Barney was here all that day they found Asa dead, so he had nothing to do with Asa getting shot."

"I guess you know I am trying to help that homesteader, Fromm," said Sage.

"Oh sure, the whole town knew that within an hour of you saying you would. Ain't no way something like that could stay secret. Especially if Mr. Jones is in the know," the man confirmed.

"What do folks think about Fromm shooting Rayburn?"

"I guess they're of different minds. Most folks think Fromm's a hard-working honest fellow—salt of the earth. And lots of them think Rayburn deserved to be shot for trying to burn Fromm out. If Rayburn had succeeded, the Fromm family couldn't have lasted through next winter. They would have died or had to walk away from their homestead."

"So they figure Fromm shot Rayburn?"

The bartender shrugged. "Some do because they say they would have shot Rayburn if they'd been Fromm. Others, the ones that seem to know Fromm best, say he's big and strong and would have thrashed Asa, not shot him. And then, there's the third group who think that while Fromm might have shot Rayburn, he would never back-shoot any man."

"What about Rayburn? What are folks saying about Rayburn?" Sage figured he might as well hear all the gossip since the bartender seemed willing to talk.

The man raised his eyes and looked straight at Sage. "Asa Rayburn was a big-mouth bully who'd do anything for money. That's what people are saying. Nobody much cares that someone decided to relieve the town of his presence. But, no one can figure out who had reason to kill him besides Fromm and maybe Barney. And, Barney's got an iron-clad alibi. That afternoon, me and a dozen shepherds were right here with him."

Sage waited a couple hours but Twill never turned up at the Rimrock. The bartender said Twill's bedroll was upstairs so the shepherd was somewhere in town. Sage finally left, figuring he'd return later that night to meet up with his new friend and ask more questions about Rayburn. As he exited the Rimrock, Sage surveyed those on the street. Thanks to Mr. "Yes Indeedy" Jones the whole town knew Sage was hunting Rayburn's killer. That meant the killer knew it as well.

Sage was to meet Eich near sundown in a thicket of willows and scrub brush, upriver from the bridge—very near the spot where Rayburn was murdered. Sage wanted to examine the area just in case the killer had left some trace of his presence.

That decision to examine the scene of Rayburn's murder had nearly cost Sage his life. Standing in the dark, waiting for Lucinda, Sage fingered his chin again, wincing at the pain. He'd gone searching for a torn scrap of clothing, a cigarette end or something he could use to track the killer. He'd found nothing. Instead, the killer had found him.

Lucinda was late. As he stood in the dark, Sage replayed the afternoon's final event. After seeing no suspicious characters loitering outside the Rimrock, Sage'd headed toward the river. A tingle had kept wriggling up his spine. But, whipping around more than once, he'd seen no cause for his unease. No one had seemed to be following him.

Five blocks later he crossed the wooden bridge to follow the dirt path along the river's western bank. Walking around a willow cluster, he saw trampled wild grass. This was probably where they'd discovered Rayburn's body. He searched the ground in ever-widening circles but found nothing.

Further upstream a man stepped out of the brush to the river's edge. He carried a net in his hands. The dark-skinned fellow had black braids and wore a loose calico shirt over old-fashioned deerskin breeches. Up to that moment Sage had seen no Indians in Prineville, other than the garish wooden one standing guard outside the mercantile store on Main Street.

His searching done, Sage decided to practice his snake and crane movements. He stepped back around the clump of willows so that he was out of the fisherman's sight. Hard packed sand provided a firm footing. Breathing deep, relaxing his shoulders and waist, he raised his hands as Fong's quiet voice in his head murmured, "Raise hands to greet the day."

One hundred and four movements later, Sage felt invigorated by the calm, steady energy Fong called "chi." Standing by the river's edge, he watched its moving surface, realizing that every molecule of water passing him by was new. Like the moments in a life. Would remembering that each moment was unique and unrepeatable change how a man lived? What if he always knew that wasted moments could never be recaptured? What if he always realized that bad choices and put off decisions could never be revisited? Would he act differently?

Sage raised his eyes to gaze at the spare landscape, trying to escape from his regrets. A breeze traveled through, rustling grass stems. Above the river, a trail of slanting sunlight crossed the rimrock, burnishing its ridges and blackening its grooves. Further south, a yellow, grass-covered hill stood bright against a dark and distant, pine-clad ridge.

Sage closed his eyes to concentrate on the sounds. Life was abundant here if one listened. So many birds. Did Central Oregon have more birds? Or, did the noises of the heavily populated Willamette Valley drown them out? As he considered that question, the bird song abruptly stilled. Why?

He opened his eyes and then struggled to make sense of what he saw. He was no longer standing by the river. Instead, he lay on his back staring up at layers of multicolored blankets stretched over a cone-shaped structure formed by long, skinny poles. He was in a tipi. Dim light filtered through the faded blankets. How had the day turned from bright to evening so fast? An intense pain in his jaw overrode thought. His fingers probed his chin. Ow. Had he been in a fight? Did someone slug him in the chin? No. That didn't make sense. He'd been by himself, standing on the river bank, waiting for Eich.

And where was he now? He studied the busy patchwork overhead. Drying plants hung from the supporting poles. Then he recalled seeing the Indian fisherman. Had that man knocked him out? Kidnaped him? But why? It made no sense.

And where was this tipi? He'd seen nothing like this around Prineville. Had he been taken away from town? His fingers told him that he lay on a pallet made of folded blankets atop a deer skin. Sweet-smelling flattened grass, still green and pliable to the touch, formed the tipi's floor. Various packs and small baskets crowded the edges of the enclosed circle. He reached into the nearest basket, his fingers touching something supple and soft. He pulled it out to find a finely stitched deerskin glove.

Murmuring soft voices outside the tipi caught his attention. For the first time, he was aware of smoke. He couldn't see it but, the scent was all around him. Some of it was stale, wafting down from the blankets. But, sweet-smelling, fresh burning wood also scented the air. Thin tendrils of smoke drifted in through a small opening between the blankets. He raised his head, struggled to sit up, groaning when his chin encountered his shoulder.

The blankets parted and Eich stepped inside, a wide smile splitting beard from moustache. "Ah, my boy. I see that you have decided to wake up."

"What happened? Where am I?"

Eich, a sturdy but not gigantic man, stepped closer until he could stand erect beneath the tipi's apex. "In answer to the last question, you are the guest of a small band of Wyam Indians. They are traveling through Prineville on their way to the Willamette Valley where they hope to find work in the hop fields."

"Hop fields," Sage echoed.

"Yes, it is their annual trek. Along the way, they hunt animals for making jerky and harvest edible plants for drying. It is how they prepare for winter." He gestured at the tied bundles overhead. "Let me begin at the beginning. You recall that we were to meet in the cluster of river willows, near where someone shot Rayburn?"

Sage nodded. That much he definitely recalled. "I got there early. Tried to find evidence of the killer. I didn't find anything. I was waiting for you. Looking at the cliffs, watching the water, listening to the birds."

"Yes, exactly," Eich said. "From the bridge, I saw you standing on the river bank. I was making my way toward you when a shot rang out and you dropped to the ground. I ran toward you. I found you face down, unconscious."

The ragpicker's face reflected the anguish he must have felt. "All I could think of was that you, too, had been shot in the back. That I had failed Mae." His voice trailed off and Sage understood how awful it would have been for him to tell Mae that her only child was dead.

Sage wriggled on the blankets. "Funny, I don't feel like a bullet hit me."

Eich laughed. "That's because it didn't. It appears that you knocked yourself out when you dove to the ground. I think your chin encountered a rock."

Another tentative touch of the chin made Sage wince and he said, "Yup. I fear you might be right. It feels like someone landed me a walloping uppercut. Great. Knocked myself out with a rock. I can hear Fong's jokes already."

Then he remembered everything. "Speaking of Fong, I remember now. I was standing there practicing what Fong calls 'ear' awareness. Trying to hear all the different birds and other sounds. There was the water swishing, a breeze rustling willow leaves and a passel of birds singing their hearts out." He looked at Eich. "Have you noticed how many birds live here? They must like the long prairie grasses. I've never heard so many different bird songs."

Eich nodded but said nothing. Sage squinted, trying to capture the memory. "Then the bird song stopped," he said slowly. "That made me listen harder. I thought I heard the swish of legs moving through grass. So I held my breath, fanned out my ears. There was a metallic clink just like a revolver hammer being pulled back to turn the cylinder. I threw myself forward. That must be when I hit the rock."

"And so, the bullet missed you. But it looked like you fell because you'd been hit. The killer probably thinks he shot you."

"So how did I end up here?" Sage gestured at the tipi's interior.

In answer, Eich stood up, went to the opening and called, "Mr. Henry, would you kindly come sit with us?"

There was no sound before a small man with a round, dark face entered the tipi. Sage recognized his form and clothes. It was the fisherman he'd seen at the river. Eich sat down on the flattened grass, as did the newcomer. Sage struggled upright on his pallet. Other than the throb in his chin, he felt fine.

"Mr. Miner, I'd like you to meet Mr. George Henry. It is his hospitality you are receiving.

Sage leaned over and shook the Indian's offered hand. "Thank you very much, sir," he said. The black eyes looked back at him, bright with warmth and curiosity. That look reminded Sage of Fong. With a pang, he realized he missed his friend and teacher.

"Mr. Henry was fishing the river," Eich said. "He heard the shot, then my shout and came to investigate."

Henry nodded. "Yes, I saw you. I wanted fresh fish for our supper. I heard a shot and saw Mr. Eich running. At the same time, I heard another man running away, into the bushes." He looked at Eich who nodded that he should continue. "Once we saw you were not shot, we talked and thought it better to let that man think you were dead. That is why we carried you here instead of taking you into town."

Sage looked at the two men sitting comfortably side-by-side. "How long have I been out?" he asked.

"Oh, about two hours, a little bit more," Eich answered. "We were thinking to hide you away until dark. Then we'll sneak into the hotel, through the back door. After that . . . ." Eich shrugged.

"That's probably the best plan," Sage said. "Maybe when I come back to life, it will shock someone into revealing themselves. By now, he must be wondering why the town isn't in an uproar over my murder. Good, I hope he's feeling real nervous."

"We have at least an hour before dark," Eich observed and turned toward their host. "Do you mind if we stay here, out of sight, until then?"

"My wife, Donna, is frying up the fish. We will eat, drink and talk until darkness comes," answered Henry.

"Mr. Eich tells me that you are heading to the Valley to pick hops," Sage said.

"Yes, every year, we work for a German farmer near Salem. He has grown hops for many years. It is for the beer."

Sage thought of the beer he'd drunk in Silverton, a small Willamette Valley timber mill town near Salem. "Those are some very good hops," he said. "Mr. Eich tells me that your group is of the Wyam tribe? Is that part of the Warm Spring's reservation?" Sage knew little about the Central Oregon Indians. Just that there was a reservation west of Madras called the Warm Springs and another reservation, further east, called the Umatilla.

For some reason, that question made his host grin broadly. Eich cleared his throat and said to Henry, "Correct me if I explain it wrong, sir." Then he turned toward Sage. "First of all, there is no Warm Springs tribe. When the federal government created the reservations after the Civil War, they forced a number of tribes, some of them mortal enemies, all on to that one reservation."

Eich gestured toward their host. "Mr. Henry and his small band are what the government has historically labeled 'renegades.'"

Sage felt his eyebrows raise. The western penny dreadfuls had given him to understand that renegade Indians were murdering outlaws some thirty years or more ago. Like the Apaches in Arizona.

Sage's thoughts must have traveled across his face because Eich hastened to explain. "All that term means is that, back when they told the Indians they had to move onto reservations, some of them refused. The Wyams stayed on the traditional land along the river. In Mr. Henry's case, that meant on the Columbia River at the Celilo Falls. Much later, the government allowed the Indians to actually claim their own land as homesteads. That was in the mid-1870s."

"We Wyams come from more than one tribe," George Henry said, taking up the explanation. "We are people of many tribes living together at the falls. We refused to move onto the reservations. We call ourselves 'people of the river.' Once there were problems between the reservation Indians and us, but now, we meet together at the falls every year to celebrate the return of the salmon."

Henry continued speaking in the low, rich voice common to the other Indians Sage had previously encountered. "We fish for salmon in the spring and fall. In between, we travel to the Valley for the hop harvest. Along the way, we men hunt. Our women collect roots, nuts, berries. They gather half of what we eat during the winter. The women dry the meat, roots and berries."

"Are we still near town?" Sage asked.

"Yes, at the west end of the bridge, across the river. We come here every year to sell deerskin belts, gloves and salmon jerky to townspeople and ranchers. That is one more way we prepare for the winter months. I came ahead to catch fish and my son came to hunt deer and has not returned. The rest of the band arrived just before the man shot at you. Tomorrow we will sell our goods. The next day we will leave."

"It's lucky you were here. Mr. Eich would have had a hard time trying to hide me," Sage said.

Henry studied Sage with an intense gaze. "Do you know why someone tried to kill you?"

Sage looked into dark eyes, bright with polite curiosity. Something told him this man was trustworthy. He glanced at Eich who inclined his head in assent. Sage took a deep breath and told the Indian about the murder of sheepherder Timothy O'Dea, the burning of hay barns and the dead Asa Rayburn.

Sage's story done, Henry pondered for a few minutes before saying, "The grazing problem is everywhere this side of the mountains. Many, many people are angry. If an Indian is willing to lease land, there is more than one sheep or cattle man who wants to use it. Sometimes they cheat. Not all of them are good men."

"Well, it is hard to tell the good from the bad sometimes. If a range war breaks out, many people will be hurt. And, some of them will be good people," Sage said.

"You know," said Henry, "my wife heard something the other day that fits your story. Let me ask her to speak with us." He left the tent. Seconds later, he could be heard saying something in a language containing popping sounds. A woman's soft voice replied in kind.

The opening parted and a small, round woman entered. She looked at them with merry, deep brown eyes. Sage liked her instantly. Henry said, "This is my wife, Donna. On the way down to Prineville we stopped at a sheep rancher's house to sell gloves and other things. The ranch woman was in the house, finding money. The window was open. Many sheep ranchers were inside, talking." Finished with this introduction, Henry looked toward his wife, nodding for her to speak.

"They were very angry. Shouting," she said in a soft but clear voice. "They were talking about their sheep getting killed. Many said they'd had enough and were going to make sure the cattle men knew that they could not hurt others and to expect punishment when they did. Then they talked about a plan."

Sage had little hope that this woman had overheard the details of the "plan." Still he had to ask, "Could you hear what they were planning?"

She shrugged, saying, "I heard the words 'shoot' and 'burn' but they spoke in low voices. One man kept asking them to wait. He talked about a meeting. The other men shouted him down."

This was not good news. Until now, the sheepmen had resisted retaliating. It sounded like the they had decided to move in that direction. Darn. Siringo wasn't going to like it. He became aware that Donna's soft voice wasn't finished.

"One man left sooner than the other men. He spoke to them as he was leaving out the door. I heard him say "I'll meet you all here, eleven days from today."

What did that mean? Were they going to attack the cattle-men in eleven days? But, no. "When was this?" he asked hoping it wasn't days ago.

"Yesterday," she replied.

"Where? Where is the ranch where they are going to meet?"

That question unsettled her because she looked at her husband who returned the look. She shook her head, "No," she said. "This could cause trouble for my people. And, the rancher's wife is a kind woman. Lonely."

Sage nodded his understanding and turned toward George Henry who was gazing into the distance, one hand thoughtfully rubbing his chin. At last Henry said, "We try to stay away from white men's fights. Too many times, we are the ones who suffer," he said, smiling ruefully before adding, "But, we will be camping here and there around Prineville for about one week. We travel to the east and south selling to the ranchers, hunting and gathering. We will keep our eyes and ears open. If we learn more, I will find a way to let Mr. Eich know."

With that, Henry rose and left the tipi. His wife also rose to leave, "I will bring you coffee and food very soon," she said before exiting.

Sage and Eich exchanged a look. "You never know," Sage said. "Maybe they'll hear something we won't."

TWENTY

A BAND OF CLOUDS MOVED in from the west as night fell. He and Eich returned to town along residential streets and slipped between houses to reach the hotel's back door. Sage waited in his darkened hotel room for 10:30 p.m. He used the back door again to reach the pesthouse's rear yard where he'd been waiting for Lucinda for the last half hour. His day reviewed, his ears straining to hear the sound of her arrival, he pondered something Eich had said.

As they had made their roundabout way to the hotel, the ragpicker talked about Sage's mother, Mae Clemens, as he never had before. "After the shot, as I was running to you, all I could think was, 'What am I going to tell Mae'? It felt like that bullet had hit my heart." The ragpicker, put a hand on Sage's forearm, bringing him to a halt. Eich's derby was tilted back, revealing an intense, earnest face. "Your mother, she's one of a kind. Clear as a mountain stream but, also, as hard as the rocks over which it flows. She's a strong woman. But, I'm not sure she could survive losing you," he'd said.

"Clear as a mountain stream, hard as the rocks it flows over." That description suited another woman just as well, Sage thought.

Then she was there. Her face a pale oval in the cloud-dimmed light. He stepped forward and threw his arms around her. His recent brush with death gave his arms a vigor that surprised even him. She froze, then hugged him in return before pushing him away and stepping back.

"Just what do you think you're doing?" The words were harsh, but amusement warmed them. She stepped closer. "What is that you have on your chin?" She reached up to touch the bruise and he quickly jerked away from the pain.

"Ouch! Don't touch. That's a bruise and it hurts like hell."

"Did someone manage to plant a facer on Fong's star pupil?" This time, he didn't need to guess at her reaction. She was grinning.

"No. Someone did not 'plant a facer.' I managed to hit a rock with my chin."

She chortled before cutting it off with a hand over her mouth. Her face turned somber as he went on to explain the events by the river.

"Is someone shooting at you because you're asking questions about the shepherd's murder or because you're asking questions about Rayburn's murder?" she asked.

"I wish I knew. Maybe both. The good news is that it means that he wasn't shooting at you the other night. But, it also means that we have to be extra careful meeting here. Right now, whoever shot at me figures I'm dead, my body carried down river. Once I turn up, alive and kicking, he might come looking here. We'll have to stop meeting."

He was surprised to see her smile and wished he could see her in the daylight. "Well now," she said. "That happens to be the good news that I have. Tomorrow morning, I will be moving into the Poindexter Hotel. Dr. Rosenberg says since there have been no new outbreaks, the quarantine is over. Xenobia is going to go back into business and she'll need my room."

"You'll be staying in the hotel?" Sage asked, even as images flashed into his mind. Him creeping down the hallway, late at night. The two of them entwined on rumpled sheets. He shook himself free of those hopes. He had to because she wanted Siringo, not him. He could hear his mother's chiding voice, "Well, Sage, what did you expect? The way you treated her."

Lucinda was studying him and her tone was a bit testy as she said, "I have no intention of cramping your style."

"No, no. I was thinking of something else," he said, aware his words sounded distracted.

"I hear the back door," she said. And with that, she picked up her skirts and vanished around the privy, leaving him staring after her.

"Huh. I didn't hear a thing," he muttered to himself as he turned toward the hotel, disappointment a heavy lead ball in his gut. But, by the time he was stealthily climbing the hotel's back stairs, his mind was no longer on her. Instead, he was thinking ahead to the morning. John Miner's unexpected resurrection was going to shock someone. He hoped to catch sight of that man's surprised reaction.

Hours later, a slamming door woke him from a restless sleep. Looking out his window, he saw bands of wispy clouds drifting west to east. South of town, two large hawks circled silently, either communing with each other or hunting a critter down below.

The Poindexter's dining room was busy. He paused in the doorway to gaze at each patron and give any would-be assassin ample time to see him. The town regulars were there, a few strangers and his boss, Congressman Newt Thomas. No one twitched in surprise nor showed dismay, although some started showing curiosity at his overlong pause. Thomas signaled to him, his genial face all smiles. Sage sauntered over, meeting various gazes, exchanging nods with a few. Not a hint of guilt in any of them. He felt his shoulders relax. His would-be murderer wasn't here.

"Mr. Miner, please do join me," invited Thomas, gesturing to the chair opposite him. "I am awaiting Dr. Van Ostrand, but I am sure he won't mind your joining us. I understand that you did a bang up job on the map survey and records search." The congressman had not waited for his partner because there was an empty plate before him, knife and fork crossed to signal he'd finished.

Before Sage could respond, he saw Thomas straighten as something behind Sage caught his attention. Sage turned to see Van Ostrand standing in the doorway. The man's face was set in angry lines and there was a thin-lipped bristle about him. Those entering at the same time gave the dentist as wide a berth as the archway allowed. Apparently, the townspeople were familiar with Van Ostrand's moodiness.

"Oh great. Looks like he's cantankerous this morning. Wonder what's set him off this time?" Thomas said more to himself than to Sage.

Sage thought he knew. Van Ostrand had finally learned that the partners were losing their accountant's services for good. Sure enough, that was it.

The dentist yanked out a chair, sat down, waved the waiter over and silently pointed at the empty coffee cup before him. He addressed Thomas, "I suppose Miner has told you that ungrateful wretch of an accountant has decided to remain in Portland? He has the audacity to ask that we arrange for the shipping of his household goods. Hah! I will write that ingrate and inform him that he can make his own damn arrangements!"

Van Ostrand snapped open his napkin, laid it on his lap and instructed the waiter, who was pouring the coffee, to bring an order of biscuits and gravy.

Thomas looked alarmed. "Why no, Harold. Mr. Miner just arrived and said nothing about our accountant not returning. That is bad news indeed." Thomas turned to Sage, "Well, Mr. Miner, since you have proven yourself a capable fellow, how about working for us permanently?"

Out of the corner of his eye, Sage caught the sudden angry flush across Van Ostrand's face and hastened to say, "Thank you for the kind offer, Congressman Thomas, but I'm afraid that I still have a bit of that gold fever. I want to try my luck up there on Scissors Creek."

Thomas started shaking his head even before Sage finished his refusal. "A young educated man like yourself can make something of himself here in Central Oregon. It will be a waste of your time to rush off into the woods. That gold's been tapped out for years. The real gold hereabouts is in timber and ranching."

Van Ostrand interrupted, "Let Miner think for himself. He doesn't want to stay in town, don't try to make him."

Thomas shrugged and changed the subject, addressing Van Ostrand. "Has McGinnis returned to Gray's Prairie and the sheep?"

If anything, Van Ostrand's scowl worsened. "No, the damn fool insists he's staying in town until he figures out who killed O'Dea. A waste of time. The killer's long gone. Besides, that shepherd brought it on himself. I told him not to fight back if the sheepshooters turned up. He chose to ignore my instructions and paid the price."

Sage studied Van Ostrand and admitted to himself that he didn't like the dentist. Up to this moment, he'd excused the man's rudeness and seeming lack of compassion, telling himself that it came from Van Ostrand's financial woes. But, to blame Timothy O'Dea for his own murder was a step too far. "I understand from Twill, that O'Dea was protecting his sheepdog, Felan," he said in mild reproof.

"Only an ignoramus would put a cur's life above his own," was Van Ostrand's surly rejoinder. Thomas looked dismayed.

Sage felt his own brow wrinkle. From what he knew of sheepdogs, a good one possessed great value in its own right. And according to Twill, the murdered Felan was one such dog. It seemed odd that a sheep rancher like Van Ostrand, didn't share that understanding. But then, Van Ostrand struck him as someone who cared only about dollars and cents. Sheep ranching didn't appear to be in his soul. He had neither Twill's appreciation for the land nor Thomas's deep ties to its history.

Silence fell over the trio. Sage cast about in his mind for something to say, finally settling on, "I heard that the government finally let the Indians homestead some land and that they are leasing that to sheep ranchers. Any of that land around here?"

Van Ostrand acted as though he hadn't heard the question, seemingly focused on cutting his biscuit into small bits. Thomas, however, said, "Nope. That would have been a real help to us but most of the Indian homestead land is up closer to the Columbia. Besides, the government is poking its nose into those arrangements. Claims they don't want the Indians taken advantage of. Humph, treats them like they are children."

After shaking his head disgustedly, Thomas drained his coffee cup and stood. "I best be off, Gentlemen. May you have a good day, the both of you," he said as he clapped his bowler onto his head. Without further comment, he meandered his way to the lobby, pausing to shake hands at every table.

Sage twisted in his seat to watch Thomas depart. He realized he liked the man. That thought turned him around to face Van Ostrand. The dentist was staring at him. Sage arched an inquiring eyebrow.

"I am trying to think what we need you to do next. You heard, of course, that Dr. Rosenberg is lifting the quarantine. You're now free to leave Prineville on your wild goose chase."

Sage feigned surprise. "Why no. Now, that's good news! I take it no one else has come down with the pox?"

Van Ostrand nodded and took a deliberate sip of his coffee. Clearly the man was considering what he planned to say next. He cleared his throat, "You've involved yourself in the Rayburn murder. For the second time, let me give you a bit of advice. Newcomers to Prineville can get themselves into a lot of trouble when they intrude into local matters. You're just passing through. I strongly suggest you gather up your equipment and head for Scissors Creek. That's the best way for you to stay out of trouble."

"I wasn't aware people knew I was trying to prove Mr. Fromm's innocence," Sage lied.

"I very much doubt there is anyone in this town who doesn't know that you've promised to help him. That's what I am trying to tell you. In this town you can step on toes without even knowing you're doing it."

"Otto Fromm didn't kill Rayburn. His wife is a fine woman. I promised her that I would help and I intend to honor that pledge," Sage said, his tone emphatic.

Van Ostrand didn't respond to Sage's declaration. Instead, he was staring at someone who'd just entered the dining room, his attention locked on the newcomer. Sage twisted around and saw that it was the U.S. District Attorney, Heney. The man glanced at their table and his eyes narrowed. Van Ostrand's hand twitched, knocking his water glass over. Water flowed and the waiter rushed to mop it up. Van Ostrand paid no attention. Instead, he abruptly stood, threw his napkin onto the spreading pool, dropped a coin onto the table and tossed some folded bills in Sage's direction. He said to Sage, "Do what you please, Miner. But never say I didn't warn you. We have no work for you today. I will contact you if we ever need your services again." His tone told Sage that was highly unlikely.

Sage twisted again to watch Van Ostrand stride out. He glanced toward Heney. The district attorney was scanning the room, his eyes calculating and watchful above the top of his morning paper.

TWENTY ONE

SAGE SWITCHED TO THE CONGRESSMAN'S vacated chair so his back wasn't to the room. Before he got fully settled, bustling in the lobby caught his attention. Lucinda had strolled in and was approaching the hotel desk. She wore neither faded calico nor her hair in straggling wisps. Instead, her honey-colored tresses were elegantly upswept beneath a flowered straw hat. Her dark brown dress suit was the latest style—no doubt a Chicago purchase. Expensive looking, the suit had three rows of copper satin trim around its bottom flounce. The same trim encircled her jacket cuffs and edged the fashionably-wide lapels of her jacket. His breath caught, first at her beauty and then with the realization that the carefully tailored suit hung loose on her body— testament to the long days she'd spent nursing the sick.

He glanced around the room, noting that others were staring in Lucinda's direction, some with admiration and, on a few faces, disapproval. At one table, all six matrons turned to look toward the lobby, even though some had to twist awkwardly to see. These well-dressed, confident women were, undoubtedly, Prineville's aristocrats.

He glanced at Lucinda. She was waiting for the clerk to finish with a sales drummer. Idly gazing around, she appeared oblivious to the attention she'd attracted. An abrupt movement at the ladies' table drew Sage's attention back to them.

His ears caught an angry hiss of words. The women were now leaning toward each other across the table, engaged in a whispered argument.

Abruptly, the most dignified of the six women folded her napkin, laid it carefully on the table and rose to her feet, determination etched in every line of her face. A few of her companions murmured objections, clearly trying to dissuade her from taking her intended action. With a flick of her hand, she silenced their protestations. Fixing her gaze on Lucinda, the woman advanced toward the lobby.

Sage rose too. No way he'd let Lucinda suffer insults or ridicule. Not after all she'd done for this town and its people. She might consort with the town's bawdy house madam but she'd done work that none of those biddies were willing to do. Anger surged and his fists clenched as he strode swiftly across the room, heading for the lobby.

It was as if Lucinda felt his approach. She looked directly at him, her blue eyes widening in surprise and brightening. When she saw his expression, her brow furrowed. The woman was now just a few paces from her. Sage advanced faster.

Then, he halted abruptly because the woman was reaching out a friendly hand. Lucinda first looked startled before smiling and also reaching out. He couldn't see the woman's face but it must have shown kindness because both of the woman's hands now clasped Lucinda's. Sage shied away. She didn't need rescue. His supposition had been wrong. He glanced back at the woman's table to see a mix of scowls and smiles. Obviously Prineville's proper ladies were not of one mind when it came to the town's smallpox nurse. Good. At least some in this town could still make up their own minds and heed their own moral compass.

The matron finished her greeting, giving Lucinda a hug around the shoulders before turning back toward the dining room. As she came towards him, Sage saw the woman's smile fade and her chin lift. There was both determination and pride in the woman's eyes. As she swept past, Sage bowed slightly. She nodded gravely, her back straightening at his signal of approval.

Now in the lobby without an obvious excuse, Sage had no choice but to head for the water closet. Lucinda was busy talking with the clerk so there was no opportunity to exchange looks or words.

Minutes later he exited the small room to a sight that hit his solar plexus like a blow. Charlie Siringo was pushing his way into the lobby, his hands and arms full of traveling bags and cases. The cowboy strode over to Lucinda and piled them around her feet. A young boy immediately stepped forward and began gathering them up.

Sage's teeth clenched and bitterness washed through him. Of course her man friend would help the little lady move. Sage's gut twisted. She was smiling up into Siringo's face, her hand on his forearm. "Stop it," he ordered himself. "You've got no call to be jealous. She was yours and you lost her. It's your own stupid fault. Let her be. Accept it. Wish her well." Still, it took effort to keep his face bland as he passed the two of them on his way back to the dining room.

Once seated, he ordered breakfast and waited, casting casual glances around the room and out into the lobby. For a while, Siringo and Lucinda conversed. At long last, the cowboy raised his hat and headed toward the hotel doors. Lucinda turned to follow the young boy and her luggage up the wide stairs. "At least they're not so brazen that he goes to her room in the sight of everyone," he muttered into his plate.

Breakfast arrived. Unlike previous mornings, the eggs were stale, the toast dry and the coffee bitter.

Freed by Van Ostrand from the need to work, Sage decided to follow up on Rayburn's murder. He hadn't spoken to Twill in a couple of days. Maybe talking to the Shakespeare-quoting Irishman would take his mind off all the damn romantic nonsense he'd been feeling. He sucked in air while counting to four, breathed it out for another four and then held it for another four counts. It seemed to work. He felt calmer, more in control. Yet another of Fong's helpful lessons in the art of copng.

The Rimrock was half full but conversation was desultory. Most were silently eating or staring into the distance. Twill stood with his forearms resting on the bar, shoulders rounded and head drooping. He didn't look up when Sage stopped beside him.

"Hey there, Irishman, why the long face?" Sage asked as he clapped his hand onto his friend's shoulder. He noticed that shoulder seemed stiff and the face Twill turned toward him lacked its usual good humor.

"I figured you'd turn up here some time or the other," Twill said. "Van Ostrand told me that you'd finished most of the work he had for you. Said you did a good job and thanked me for the recommendation." Despite the positive words, the sheepherder's voice was toneless, almost mechanical in its lack of expression.

What had made the sheepherder so down-hearted, Sage wondered. "Twill, it sounds like you've lost another friend. Has something else happened?"

That question triggered a morose nod of the head and heavy sigh. "Ah, there you have it. One friend murdered, another one proved false," he responded before quoting, "My heart is drowned with grief."

"Gloucester, *King Henry the VI.*" Sage automatically supplied the citation. "I am sorry to hear of your friend's betrayal."

Twill raised his head and looked at Sage. "Some that smile have in their hearts, I fear, millions of mischiefs."

The Irishman's face was so bleak that Sage was left with nothing to say. "Can I get you anything, mister?" the bartender's voice broke the silence.

After ordering coffee, Sage turned back to Twill. The Irishman seemed to have snapped back into his normal self because he stood erect.

"What are you plans for today?" he asked.

"Well, Van Ostrand told me there was no more work, so I thought I'd get my gear together and head out to Scissors Creek. Now that the quarantine has lifted, I'm free to leave town. Before

I do that, I thought I'd go visit that group of Indians camped across the river. They did me a favor. I'd like to thank them. Maybe buy a few of their trade goods."

Twill snorted and said a bit portentously, "Yes, it is important to return favors, keeps the world in balance."

Ignoring the man's foul mood Sage asked, "You want to come along? Keep me company in my wanderings? I could use some cheering up."

After a hesitation the Irishman said, "Well, it is not as if I am finding myself busy at the present. So, I may as well be keeping you company."

They walked to the Indian encampment, Twill providing a running commentary on all the new construction along the way. A flurry of activity was underway on the far side of the bridge. The small group of Wyams was dismantling their tipis and piling their belongings atop calm ponies. Sage found his host, George Henry, and thanked him again for his hospitality.

The man acknowledged Sage's gratitude with a smile and dip of his head, but it was clear he was eager to finish packing and get his small troop on its way.

"When I was here before, I noticed a basket of beautiful deer skin gloves. I was wondering whether your wife was selling any of those?" Sage asked.

Henry spoke to his wife in a low tone. She picked up a woven basket and stepped toward them. He greeted her, smiling as he said, "I also want to thank you very much. I know that you cooked that fine dinner and made that perfect coffee last night."

She smiled in return, saying, "You are welcome. It is not often our tipi is visited by white men with such good manners." She held the basket out and Sage took it.

"I would like to buy a number of pairs if you don't mind. These are so finely sewn and the deer skin is velvet soft. I have friends who will prize them."

His praise brought forth more smiles and the transaction was completed. Six pairs of gloves became his. This included two pair of women's gloves with delicately stitched flowers decorating the cuffs. One pair was for his mother, the other for

Lucinda. He chose that second pair at the last minute, even as a ridiculing voice in his head noted that it was not his place to buy gifts for another man's woman.

During most of the exchange, Twill stood silent, watching. At the last moment he stepped forward and purchased a thick pair of heavy work gloves for himself.

As they crossed the bridge back to town, Twill made a pointed observation. "Six pairs are a lot to buy. You don't seem to be shy in the pockets, I'm thinking."

For a moment, Sage didn't know what to say so he lied, "Van Ostrand paid me off. And I brought a bit of money along because I knew I'd have to purchase various items to complete my prospecting outfit."

Twill grunted, then asked. "You been out Scissors Creek way yet?"

That question was mystifying because the Irishman knew that Dr. Rosenberg had quarantined Sage the minute he'd stepped off the Shaniko stagecoach. Thinking that maybe the Irishman had forgotten, Sage told him again.

After that exchange, they walked in silence up Prineville's main street. Twill apparently decided he wanted no part of Sage's provisioning activities because he abruptly said, "I best head out. I've got me some unfinished business to attend to that I just remembered."

Sage doubted that Twill had any "unfinished business" but he made no protest. After the morning he'd had, the last thing he needed was a down-hearted Irishman piling gloom onto his afternoon.

TWENTY TWO

SAGE RETURNED TO THE POINDEXTER with prospecting provisions tucked under his arm. He hoped that was the only ruse he'd need. He didn't want to squat in Scissors Creek, to dig and sluice bed sand. Not only was it backbreaking work, but it was also guaranteed to be fruitless. He'd find no gold in Scissors Creek. Maybe only Manny, the old Mexican prospector, knew where to find it. Once again, Sage questioned whether Prineville folks were being fooled by Manny's apparent poverty. Safety lay in keeping gold discoveries secret. Sage had figured that out early on. It was the reason he'd left the Klondike a very rich man with no one the wiser.

'Anyways,' as his Ma would say, creek panning was usually a bust. In the Klondike, the gold lay beneath abandoned stream beds. Winter months, it meant setting a fire atop the permafrost to melt it. That was followed by hand digging down to bedrock. Each pail of dirt and rock had to be winched up and dumped. Come spring, that same dirt went into a rocker where shaking separated out the gold. His muscles still twitched with remembered cold and pain. Though prospecting had made him wealthy, he'd vowed to never lift another spade of dirt in search of glitter.

Yet, here he was, readying to make a show of doing it again. Not for the first time, he wondered why he always ended up doing the very thing he'd vowed never to do. That was the last question in his mind as the heat sent him down into a late afternoon nap.

Sometime later, his eyes snapped open. Every sinew of his body was on alert and his heart pounded like he'd just raced up a mountain. What had startled him awake? Through the window came the rich, fluting warbles and chirps of the western meadowlark. It sounded like a whole flock of them were having a party. Maybe that was what woke him.

Then an insistent knock sounded on his door. Sage rolled off the bed, remembering that he had planned to meet Herman. He grabbed for his pocket watch. He was an hour late.

Sure enough, Portland's ragpicker poet stood in the hallway looking pleased and relieved all at the same time. "I see you decided to slumber away this fine afternoon," he said.

"Aw, Mr. Eich. I'm sorry. I just lay down for a minute and, the next thing I know, you're waking me up."

"No matter, my boy," Eich said as he stepped inside so Sage could close the door. "I'm rather tardy for our appointment myself."

That piqued Sage's interest. Had Eich learned something? The ragpicker raised a hand as if reading Sage's mind, "I uncovered little bits and pieces of information but nothing solid. Of necessity, I must travel south toward Farewell Bend right away."

"Why? What's down there that can help us?"

Eich's dark brown eyes twinkled and he smoothed his beard before leaning forward to say in a conspiratorial tone, "A band of Gypsies." Then he laughed at the astonishment on Sage's face. "No, really," Eich said, his face turning serious. "A band of Gypsies passed by Prineville this week. Some of the town's leading ladies, all of them vaccinated of course, met them at the west end of the bridge."

Seeing Sage's incredulous look, he laughed again. "No, it was not a social occasion. The Gypsy women make intricate lace and the Gypsy men are masters when it comes to creating and fixing tin pots and such. I've encountered such bands elsewhere in the West."

Sage had seen Gypsies in the East. Even one or two in Portland. But it had never occurred to him that they'd also roamed the western prairies, far from any city.

Eich continued with his explanation. "My friends, the Gable brothers, tell me the group had planned to stay longer but something happened to make them pack up and leave. The brothers encountered them over west, on the road heading to Farewell Bend."

"When did the Gypsies leave?"

"That is what I find interesting. They left in the night, on the very day Asa Rayburn was murdered. When they encountered the Gables on the road, they warned them that it wasn't safe to stay around Prineville. Said the Virgin Mary told them so in a vision."

"Why did they say that? Did the Gable brothers ask why?"

"Seems the band traveled up through the Ochocos on the military road about the time that young shepherd and his dog were killed. When they reached Prineville they found that it was still under quarantine. So, they circled their wagons outside of town and did a bit of selling to the local housewives. Next day, they learned of O'Dea's murder out in the Ochocos. Next they apparently heard the shot that killed Rayburn. Historically, whenever there's trouble, the Gypsies tend to get blamed. I suspect that was really why they decided to leave."

"So you doubt it was a religious vision?" Sage asked.

Eich chuckled. "Saying it's the Virgin Mary who told them to leave serves two purposes. It lets everyone know they're Christian and that they can keep secrets close to themselves. I plan to locate their little band and learn whether they know anything about the shepherd's or Rayburn's murders."

❅ ❅ ❅

Eich departed, hoping to find a horse for his journey to Farewell Bend. His information left Sage too keyed up to stay in his room. Besides, the bird twitters and the warm air streaming through the window made him want to be outside. He ambled downstairs and ordered a coffee. Taking it in hand, he climbed back up the stairs and went down the hallway to where an outside door opened onto the veranda roof. This time of day, it was shaded by the building's high false front. Finding a wooden table and chairs, he sat with outstretched legs. From this vantage point, he could gaze up and down Main Street while a breeze dried his sweat.

He wondered whether Lucinda was in her room just steps away. Or, maybe, Siringo was showing her the town. She probably hadn't had any chance to see it before she went into the pesthouse. A pang hit his chest followed by a dark emptiness. "Stop," he chided himself. "You have Otto Fromm to save and a range war to stop. Mooning about like one of Shakespeare's lovesick swains is ridiculous."

He gazed over the town. Prineville was nothing like he'd expected. Sure he'd envisioned the ranchers and cowboys, herders, and homesteaders—all sunbaked and hard-muscled. Unexpected, though, were the Gypsy lace makers, renegade Indians, a prospecting Mexican, traveling Jewish traders, homesteading Germans and shepherding Irishmen.

Noise filled the air. Below him, two overloaded freight wagons rumbled slowly down the street, hitched one behind the other. Eight horses were tiredly pulling the entire train. Dexter had said such wagons took three days to reach Prineville from the Shaniko railhead. Looking at those heavy wagons, he could believe it.

In the distance, hammers pounded nails into lumber. Nearby, voices drifted upward, some from open shop doors, others from folks on the veranda below.

Sage looked toward the intersection of Main and Third just as Ed Harbin trudged past. The piled bits of his little stand filled a rickety hand cart. The hero of Prineville had fulfilled his mission and dismantled his station.

Sage raised his coffee cup in silent salute to the oblivious Harbin. Then he raised his eyes to gaze at the shimmering Crooked River, surrounding bluffs and far distant piney wood hills. It was a sweet location—protected and watched over by the rimrock's grandeur. If only it wasn't so hot.

Enough idleness, he chastised himself. The important thing was to save Fromm from the noose and stop the budding range war. Fromm first. Tracing the homesteader's activity in Prineville had yielded a dead end. All he'd discovered was that Fromm could have been Rayburn's murderer. There was no one who could say different.

Maybe he needed to work backwards. Why did Rayburn set fire to the homesteader's hay and let his cow loose? From what he'd learned of Rayburn, the man was not given to idle mischief. Nor could it have been a personal vendetta. Fromm said that he'd never talked to Rayburn. Didn't even know him. The first Fromm learned of him was when the neighbor had named him as the arsonist.

That meant Rayburn was at Fromm's homestead not to make mischief but, instead, for a purpose that was neither idle nor personal. Surely, Rayburn himself had absolutely nothing to gain from harming Fromm. So, Rayburn had to be acting on someone else's instructions. Whose? Who would gain if the Fromm family died or fled? He'd have to visit Fromm in jail again. Maybe the homesteader could answer that question.

He turned to the problem of the range war on the brink of igniting. Of course, now that Lucinda was safe and could leave, he really didn't have to help Siringo. But "gosh-nabbit" as Dexter would say, he'd promised Siringo and a promise was a promise. Sage heaved a sigh. Cattlemen and cowboys, sheep ranchers and herders, homesteaders and fences, forest reserves and timber barons. It was a complicated situation with way too many players.

He reviewed what he'd been told. Thomas was right. That Forest Reserve Act was at the heart of the problems. It was driving sheep and cattle out of the mountains to crowd the same scarce prairie land. The new Shaniko railroad head was attracting sheep by the thousands—some from as far away as Idaho and Klamath Falls. Those animals grazed the land down to dirt, leaving the range cattle to starve. Cattlemen, trying to recover from a slew of cattle-killing winters, were seeing once-lush meadows destroyed.

Adding to the volatility were homesteaders, like the Fromms, desperately trying to "prove up" their land by plowing and fencing. Mixed into the whole mess were Indian allotments and military road land that the cattle and sheep ranchers were eager to lease. These might look like wide open, empty spaces but, to Sage's way of thinking, the forces at work were just as brutal as any he might find in Portland. And, what was U.S. District Attorney Heney doing in Prineville? He was already prosecuting timber frauds committed under the Forest Reserve Act. Were the same kind of frauds happening in Central Oregon's Ochoco Mountains?

A dry chuckle tickled his throat. In his teen years, he'd devoured the penny dreadfuls with their heroic tales of cowboys and Indians in the wide open West. Those thrilling tales had spurred his trek to the Klondike after his Princeton graduation.

His Klondike experience had set him straight. Up there, he found the same mix of good and bad people. Hardworking, hopeful humanity living side-by-side with those lacking any moral standard—driven only a burning desire to get rich quick and easy. And always, there were the already wealthy, relentlessly twisting the law and politicians, as they plotted to keep and expand their wealth. It differed little from what happened in the dense urban cities of the East. The same dynamic at play. Ravenous greed running amok and resisting all attempts at restraint.

So this place would have that same mix. Many decent folk for the most part and most times. But these weren't most times. People were taking sides and letting hatred build. Still, he'd met no one who seemed like a killer.

Maybe if he considered the sequence of events he could discern a motive. First, threatening dead lines were blazed across the open range. Next the Kepler brother's old shepherd and his dog disappear. Then their barn is burned. Then someone murders the young shepherd, Timothy O'Dea, killing his dog and sheep. After that, Rayburn tries to burn homesteader Fromm's hay only to be murdered himself a few days later. Finally, the U.S. District Attorney arrives in Prineville. He was certain these things were related. But how?

TWENTY THREE

"How you doing there, Partner?" Siringo called over his shoulder. His chuckle, when he faced forward again, was loud enough to be heard over horse clop and leather creak.

Sage didn't bother to answer. Instead he imagined how things would have been different if only he hadn't opened his hotel room door.

He'd been lying wide-eyed on his bed, wishing for sleep, when three soft knocks sounded. "Lucinda!" had been his first thought. Jumping up, he'd hurried to the door and flung it open.

Siringo stood there, taking in Sage's expression as it transformed from expectant to disappointed. The Dickensen man didn't comment, but his sardonic smile said he'd noticed.

Sage heaved a sigh and gestured the man into the room. Sitting in the chair by the window, Siringo gazed out toward Xenobia Brown's house. He looked lost in thought. When he turned toward Sage, his face was grim.

"Sorry to knock on your door so late, but I need your help. I found the body of the old shepherd. I need you to bring him into town."

Sage stiffened at the thought of what Siringo wanted him to do. "How long ago was he killed?"

"I'm thinking three to four weeks. He's buried in a shallow grave with rocks piled on top so the animals haven't gotten to him yet." Siringo's tone was matter-of-fact but sadness filled his face.

"I'm sorry you had to find him," was all Sage could think to say.

Siringo turned to gaze again out the window. "Everyone says he was a friendly old fellow. Never bothered anyone. Always had a kind word and a smile."

Sage said nothing. Someone needed to mourn the old sheepherder and, evidently, Siringo was shouldering that task for now.

"If he was buried, how did you find him?" Sage asked.

"His name was Paddy Campbell," Siringo said. Then he sighed heavily. "I was up breaking and buying horses south of Steins Pillar. Remember, I told you about that young fellow I suspected of causing trouble, name of Tom Meglit?"

He waited for Sage to nod and then continued. "The trail boss runs a dry camp but I snuck in a couple bottles of liquor. From what I'd heard of Meglit, his tongue loosens when he gets drunk. So's after everyone bedded down, I took him aside and we went off into the trees to drink. By the time I opened the second bottle, he'd told me about him and another fellow killing the old man. Told me where they'd buried the body. I managed to get him to be pretty specific. It took all of today, but I finally located the remains."

"So, you brought the body to town?"

Siringo shook his head. "Nope, couldn't do that. I'm here gathering information the Governor needs to prevent a range war. If I brought that body in, Meglit would know right away I'm no horse trader. He was drunk, but not so drunk he wouldn't remember telling me where to find Campbell's body. He gets to talking, every cowboy in the area will distrust me. I've spent months building that trust. They'd never suspect that you and I are in cahoots since you've been working for the sheepmen and I planted that facer on you."

"I guess that means that I'll be hauling Paddy Campbell's dead body into town." Sage said.

"Well, unless you can think of a better idea, it seems the logical thing to do."

"I don't suppose that we could just leave him where he lies?" asked Sage, only to feel shame at his words.

"He's got a sister back East. She's been writing about him," Siringo responded.

"Won't folks think it odd that a stranger in these parts just happens to stumble on a buried body?" Sage asked, though he knew Siringo's answer would not change the course of events. He was going to do it. He was going to bring the poor old shepherd's body back to town.

"That's the beauty of it," Siringo said, a faint smile lifting the corners of his razor straight lips. "You been telling everyone who'd listen that you plan to prospect on Scissors Creek. Just so happens, that's where the body's buried. You can just say you stumbled upon the body. You weren't around when Campbell disappeared so no one will suspect you of being involved."

Siringo's plan made perfect sense. People would believe that story. Sage ran a hand through his hair before saying, "Okay, I'll set out first thing in the morning. How am I going to find the old fellow?"

Siringo stood, clapping his hat back on, invigorated now that he'd convinced Sage to help. "I'm heading out now. Make your way eastward on the military road that runs along Ochoco Creek. Once you start climbing into the mountains, out of the ranch valley, I'll be waiting. I'll lead you right to him."

The cowboy nodded at Sage. "Thank you for doing this, Adair. You don't have to. It isn't part of our deal." He stretched out his hand and they shook. Siringo strolled toward the door. Just before he opened it, he turned and said the words Sage didn't want to hear.

"You'll need to rent two horses. One to ride and one to carry." That said, the Dickensen agent opened the door and was gone.

❀ ❀ ❀

Dawn's red radiance brightened the eastern range just as Sage reached the livery stable. A grizzled old man moved about inside, tobacco chaw bulging his cheek as he murmured to the animals he was feeding. Nickering from one of the animals made the fellow turn.

"Why, howdy there, mister. Can I help you this fine morning?" He sounded full of good cheer despite the early hour.

"I want to rent two horses for a few weeks of prospecting up around Scissors Creek. I need one to ride and one to carry," Sage answered.

"Oh, you must be that fellow I've been hearing about," the man said, his voice still friendly. "I'd be happy to provide you with two fine animals." He paused, clearly debating whether to say his next words. Compassion won. "But, much as I'd like to take your money, there ain't no gold in Scissors Creek. It's been all panned out. Only that old Mexican packer, Manuel Berdugo, believes there's gold. Everybody thinks he's a bit tetched in the head."

Sage grinned, appreciating the fellow's honesty. "Yah, I know," he admitted. "That's what folks keep telling me. But, I'm a guy who needs to prove it to himself."

The old fellow stepped forward, offering a hand as he said, "Wahl, okay then, if that's how you feel. Howdy Mr. Miner, my name's Samuel Hamilton."

"You know my name already?" Sage asked as he shook the firm, calloused hand.

"Wahl sure. Dexter Higginbottom's an old pal of mine. Puts up here in the stable most nights when he's in Prineville. He told me how you saved him and the runaway stagecoach coming down Cow Canyon."

The man turned and gestured toward an animal inside the nearby stall. "This here is a fine horse. His name's Twister. He's a mite frisky, but as long as he knows you're the boss, he does right fine."

Sage eyed the big gray horse, noting that his nose seemed overly long and narrow. The one gleaming eye he could see looked crazed. "Umm, how's Twister do with barking dogs?" he asked.

Hamilton wrinkled his forehead. "Wahl, this here is a cow pony. He's probably worked around more ranch dogs than you'll ever come across. I don't think he's much afraid of them."

"And does he have anything against barbed wire? I once ended up on the neck of a horse that was afraid of barbed wire."

Hamilton didn't bother to hide his grin. "On the neck, hmm? Don't think Twister would like that much—you landing on his neck. Just may take exception." He turned to look at the horse who curled a lip, displaying huge yellow teeth before stamping on the floor with a heavy hoof and sidling backward in the stall.

"I understand there are a lot of rattlesnakes out in the mountains. Does Twister know what to do if he sees one?"

This last question seemed to make up Hamilton's mind about something because he sent a long arc of brown spit out the open door, put down the feed bucket and walked briskly toward the farthest stalls leaving Sage to trail behind.

Hamilton stopped at the last stall. Inside was a swayback horse, who seemed to be sleeping because his eyes were closed and his head drooped.

"This here's Rocky, he's kinda old but he still can do a day's work. A tad pokey, but very dependable. Nothing seems to upset Rocky, maybe because he's partly blind in one eye and can't see as many disturbing things." Hamilton chuckled to himself so Sage couldn't tell if the stableman words were truth or a tale.

Sage stepped forward and studied the old horse. Rocky's eyelids opened, long black lashes framing the liquid brown eyes that stared calmly at Sage.

"Rocky's got a horse that he likes in particular when it comes to traveling," Hamilton said before giving another one of his private little chuckles. "That horse's called Gasper. He won't tolerate no rider but he'll haul your stuff all day long without complaint. If he's with Rocky, he does just fine."

"Rocky and his friend, Gasper, it is then," Sage said, relieved that he'd be spared the failure of showing Twister who was the boss. Hands down, that horse would have won.

"Yup," said Hamilton, "that's what I figured you'd say."

The man's eyes twinkled but Sage couldn't take offense. He'd never liked horses much. Thus far, that dislike seemed to be mutual with just a few exceptions. It was why he was hoping the new horseless carriages would take hold. "Horseless" was the selling point as far as he was concerned.

After paying Hamilton in advance, he led the two horses to the hotel where he tied his prospecting kit onto Gasper's back. After that, the three of them had headed east, moseying down the wagon track that ran alongside Ochoco Creek. Since their speed never exceeded a sedate walk, he had time to admire the rich green grasses of the creek bottom, the cloudless expanse overhead and the symmetrical pine trees dotting the low hillsides. Here and there a ranch house sheltered from the blazing sun under huge shade trees.

The open space let his mind stretch and wander. Which of those cattlemen were shooting sheep and murdering shepherds? Siringo was having a devil of a time finding that out. In eight-days, according to Mrs. Henry, the sheep ranchers were going on the attack. From what he'd overheard at the Rimrock, the shepherds were also plotting to do the same. Who could blame them, really? Two shepherds murdered, sheep slaughtered, dead lines springing up everywhere and a sheriff they couldn't trust because his sympathies lay with the cattlemen.

A thought struck him. Maybe Twill was the go-between. Maybe the shepherds and the sheep ranchers were coordinating their counterattack against cowboys and cattle. That would explain Twill's odd behavior. Still, the Irishman might resort to fisticuffs but would he murder cowboys? No, Sage refused to believe that. And what about Van Ostrand and Thomas? Did they plan to join the other ranchers in seeking revenge? Since both men were very tense, maybe they did. All of which meant that he and Siringo had less than eight days to prevent the sheepmen's retaliation and the start of a full-fledged range war. To do that, they had to discover who killed O'Dea and Rayburn. Then bring Meglit and the other killers to justice—removing the need for revenge. It was a deadline of a different sort than the dead lines blazed on trees. But, in one sense it was the same. If they ignored it, death could follow.

By the time they'd started to climb into the mountains, Sage's nether region was signaling it had enough of Rocky's wide back and jarring steps. "A man's legs aren't meant to wrap around anything this big. No wonder some cowboys walk like they're holding a small barrel between their knees," Sage mused aloud.

Rocky stopped. Looking forward, Sage saw no reason for him to stop. "Come on, old fellow. Just a bit more to go. Don't stop now." Sage's boots nudged the horse's side without effect. He glanced behind him. Old Gasper was already nibbling the trail side grass.

Sage turned forward and nudged Rocky's sides more firmly with his heels. It made the horse's ears twitch but still, the old horse stepped back, not forward. Sage sighed. He would have to dismount and lead the animal. He pulled one foot out of the stirrup and began to lift his leg over the saddle. Rocky nickered and stepped back again quickly—so quickly that Gasper snorted in irritation. Rocky had bumped into him. Sage grabbed the saddle horn as his unanchored foot flailed for the stirrup it had just abandoned.

A calm voice called from his right side. "Don't do anything but hang on. Let the horse be in control. There's a rattler beside the trail."

Sage looked to his side. Siringo sat up slope in the shade of a tall pine, high atop a huge black horse. Sage looked forward and he saw it. Just five feet from Rocky's right leg. The biggest snake Sage'd ever seen lay coiled beside the trail, head and tail raised, its rattle silent. Time seemed to freeze as snake, horse, and man studied each other. Then the snake lowered its head and glided away like water down a smooth channel.

Sage's hand shook when he leaned forward to pat Rocky's neck. "Sorry, old boy," he said. "I won't make that mistake again." That had been over two hours ago. With Siringo leading, their little cavalcade had continued along the trail, climbing ever upward into the mountains. Sage's backside and legs were beyond aching and sweat had glued his shirt to his torso.

Turning in his saddle, Siringo called, "We're nearly there." "Thank the Lord," Sage responded under his breath only to hear the other's snicker drift back through the hot air.

TWENTY FOUR

"At last," Sage muttered as Siringo's horse stepped off the trail and into a clearing. They'd reached the camp. Rocky apparently felt the same relief because his head raised and his pace quickened. The jostling gait worsened the aches but Sage didn't care. The dependable old horse was as eager to get the human off his back as the human was eager to be off.

The camp looked well-used with a packed-earth clearing, blackened fire pit and a hitching rail rigged between two trees. Downslope, a creek burbled over a rocky bottom.

Sage dismounted, staggering when his feet hit the ground. He untied the line between the horses and led them to the creek where Siringo's huge steed was already drinking.

"This here is Scissors Creek," Siringo said, gesturing at the rocky creek bed. "Our old fellow lies in a small meadow about a quarter mile upstream. Pretty place. He probably wouldn't mind staying there," the cowboy added.

"Are we going to go get him once the horses finish drinking?" Sage asked, though dreading the answer. It was the last thing he wanted to do. To unearth a moldering corpse, after a day of horseback riding, would be a special kind of hell. "My, my," he chided himself. "Getting a little soft, are we?" It was a gibe Sage had given himself more than once over the past year.

At thirty-three he was no longer the lively young fellow who'd climbed over Chilkoot Pass on his way into the Klondike.

Siringo interrupted these thoughts by saying, "Wahl, Adair. Aren't you the eager beaver?" with that hint of a chuckle. "But no, we'll leave him be for now. The horses have to rest and we sure don't need to be sleeping around a body. Especially one that old. We'll dig him up tomorrow morning, load him onto your ancient pack horse and you can head out. You should make town before dark tomorrow."

"His name's 'Gasper'," Sage said more to himself than to Siringo. He wondered how a horse, who refused to be ridden, would react to having a decaying corpse slung across his back.

"Who's 'Gasper'?" Siringo asked.

Good grief, the cowboy must have the ears of an elephant. Maybe it was from spending so much time in the quiet back of beyond, Sage thought, but answered, "Gasper's the horse that's going to be carrying the old shepherd's body back to town." Hearing his name, the horse raised his head from the water to eye them. Sage grabbed Gasper's lead rope and Rocky's reins and led them to the hitching rail. Once they were tied up, he quickly removed Rocky's saddle and Gasper's light load of prospecting equipment. Digging into his pack, he extracted a brush and began to brush Rocky. He felt Siringo's eyes on his back.

"You're spoiling them animals. They're working cow ponies. Water 'em, give 'em a handful of hay, hobble 'em, let 'em graze and they're happy enough," he told Sage.

Sage finished brushing Rocky and moved toward Gasper. "Well, I'd be the last to say that I'm a horse lover but I figure these animals deserve special treatment. Rocky saved me from getting snake bit today. Old Gasper's got a rough day ahead of him tomorrow."

Siringo said nothing, just shook his head and began gathering dried sticks. The two men busied themselves. Siringo building a fire, Sage piling hay he'd brought at the feet of all three horses. Rocky nickered his thanks and Siringo's black horse tossed his mane before dropping his head to munch.

An hour later, Siringo lay back against his saddle, his legs stretched out on the ground. "Adair, you might not know much about horses, but you sure are handy around a cook fire. I never expected such a fine meal."

"It's hard to go wrong with steak," Sage said, though the meal had been pretty darn good. "The saving grace was the ice. The clerk tells me the Crooked River freezes every winter, keeping the town's cellars full. That's why the meat tasted so fresh."

Siringo nodded, took another swallow of coffee and said, "I guess we better get to figuring exactly what we know about the doings hereabouts."

"You've solved the mystery of the missing shepherd. So, that's one thing done. Do you think Meglit also murdered the other sheepherder, Timothy O'Dea and his dog, Felan?

Siringo heaved a sigh. "Nope, that's one thing I'm certain sure Meglit didn't do."

"How come you're so sure?"

The cowboy leaned forward. "Wahl, first of all, he didn't brag about doing it. If he had done it, he would have bragged. Once he decided I was a hard case like him, he couldn't wait to boast about how darn bad he was." Siringo grabbed a small rock and forcefully threw it against a pine tree before adding, "Sooner we get that sorry critter locked up, the sooner everyone will be safer."

Sage gazed at the widely spaced trees and sparse grass between them. No knee-high tangle of fern, vine and shrub. It was possible to see far. A much easier place to travel cross-country than the rain forest side of the Cascades.

He poked the fire with a stick. "So, we still have to solve the O'Dea murder, the Rayburn murder and the Kepler brother's barn burning. You sure those cowboys with Meglit didn't do any of that?"

"Yup, their foreman keeps a tight rein on his crew and Meglit is not popular with most of them. Besides, they were up north herding cattle when O'Dea was killed. And, not a one of them was in Prineville when Asa Rayburn got shot. Maybe they could have burnt the Keplers' barn but I'm thinking not."

"Why?" Sage asked.

"No one's bragging about it. And, near as I can tell, Meglit's been with that outfit for over a month. If they'd had anything to do with barn burning, he would have been involved. Besides, that foreman's a straight shooter. I can't see him condoning a barn burning. He'd be more likely to go at a man bare-knuckled."

"Well, somebody's making it hard for the sheepmen. I 've seen Van Ostrand's and Thomas's outstanding debts. They're in financial trouble. And, Van Ostrand's acting 'jumpy as water on a hot griddle,' as my mother would say. Maybe Thomas and Van Ostrand have decided to join the other sheep ranchers in a retaliation scheme. The one I told you about last night. That could explain why he's so surly acting."

Siringo leaned forward, using his own stick to poke the embers. Sparks wheeled upward and blinked out. "Could be that's it," he said. "For sure Van Ostrand, Thomas and the Kepler brothers have it particular hard since their ranches depend on grazing land out here in the Ochocos."

Siringo was silent for awhile. When he spoke, his words were subdued. "The sheepshooters down south of Post, they definitely want to drive the sheep out. Sad part is, those fellows aren't bad men, just desperate. They might kill sheep hereabouts but, Adair, I can't see any one of them murdering that young shepherd.

"Matter of fact, when they went on their little raid, they carried a burlap bag to pull over the herder's head. And they smudged their faces with soot and planned to cover their chins with kerchiefs. Those aren't the acts of men ready to kill easily. And, every one of those men seemed relieved when we found the shepherd and his sheep gone."

"Maybe, you're right. But Twill said there were signs that O'Dea and his dog resisted."

Siringo's forehead wrinkled. "I heard that. But I'm willing to swear on a Bible that it can't be either of the two cattle outfits I've been riding with. With the exception of Meglit, I'm just not seeing murderers. Sheepshooters, maybe. Murderers, nope." His eyes narrowed thoughtfully.

"What's been happening in town? Maybe that's where we should be looking," he said.

Sage dropped his poking stick onto the embers. "You might be right about our killer being a town man. Someone's shot at me twice, right in Prineville. And, so far, the only snooping I've done was into Rayburn's murder. He was thought to be an unsavory fellow. Nobody seems to have liked him. He held a minor financial stake in the Rimrock. In fact, the fellow who disliked him the most was his partner in that saloon. But, for sure, that fellow didn't shoot him. He has too many witnesses saying he was at the saloon all that day."

Siringo had been stirring the coals as Sage talked. He tossed his own stick into the fire and said, "Wahl, Rayburn was involved in the sheep business. I suppose you heard he used to work for that sheep baron, Bellingham, up north? You heard what he was doing up there?"

"Not really. I've speculated that maybe Rayburn was somehow involved in Bellingham's land fraud scheme. I talked with Fromm about it. We wondered if Bellingham might have wanted him dead." Sage said.

Siringo nodded, "Could be that he did. Rayburn rounded up entry men to lay false claims on grazing land and then made arrangements for Bellingham to take over that land once the entry men took title. It was how Bellingham planned to secure permanent grazing for his sheep."

"So, maybe he helped Bellingham commit land fraud? You know that for certain?" Sage was familiar with land fraud involving timber but this idea of land fraud to obtain grazing land was a new twist.

Siringo held up his hand to halt Sage's train of thought. "That ain't the most important part. Rayburn was going to testify against Bellingham. Before I headed back here, I visited with Mr. Heney in Portland. He asked the Dickensen Agency to keep an eye on Rayburn. He was afraid Rayburn would run or that Bellingham would figure out Rayburn was a turncoat." Siringo's face turned morose as he added, "I surely failed in that job."

"Heney's in Prineville, did you know that?"

Siringo's eyes widened. "Why no. I ducked in and out of town trying not to be too conspicuous. Stayed away from the usual watering holes." His brow lowered as if working through the implications of the federal district attorney's presence in Prineville. "You know," he said slowly, "If he's on this side of the Cascades because of the Bellingham trial, he'd have no call to be straying this far south. That trial's happening in Portland. Rayburn was the only person in Prineville was involved. He was here avoiding Bellingham until the trial. So, it makes no sense that Heney would expose Rayburn by traveling out here to meet with him. Arrangements were already in place for Rayburn to leave for Portland next week."

Silence fell. Sage picked up a new stick and began poking the fire alive. Despite the heat of the day, a breeze through the trees was driving warmth from the air. "I got fired by Van Ostrand," he told Siringo. "Remember, they've lost their grazing lease along the military road. The Kepler brothers got it instead. Apparently, they bought a bunch of sheep before learning they weren't going to get the lease again. Anyway, Van Ostrand had me looking at survey maps of the Ochocos. My task was to locate sections with watering holes."

"Mmm," was Siringo's only answer before he clambered to his feet and headed toward the hobbled horses peacefully grazing among the trees. "We'd best tie the beasts closer to the fire. I saw the tracks of an old cougar hereabouts. The older they get, the more desperate they get. Could even take on a hobbled horse—probably one of your two. They're a bit long in the tooth to put up a good fight."

When Siringo came back from tying up the horses he'd obviously reached a decision of some sort because his stride was purposeful. "I'm thinking I'll follow you back into town. It sounds like you might need some help and I want to hook up with Heney and find out why he's here. Maybe it has something to do with our mission. I also have to take my lumps for not protecting Rayburn."

"It'd be good to have you around," Sage said. "Much as I don't like making myself a target, the only thing we have to go on right now is the fact that somebody's trying to stop me from investigating Rayburn's and, maybe O'Dea's, murder. Why did Rayburn agree to cooperate with Heney, anyway?"

That question twisted Siringo's lips. "Stupid fool put his name on papers associated with the phony entry men's filings," he said. "Heney had him stretched tight over the barrel. It was either testify or go to jail."

The log at their feet collapsed into the fire. "We best turn in," Siringo said, stretching out flat on his blanket pad. "Tomorrow's going to come soon enough. It'll be a long day." With that, the cowboy pulled a blanket up to cover his shoulders. Just as Sage began settling into sleep, Siringo made a statement that jerked Sage wide awake.

"I've been thinking about giving up this life. It's looking more and more like my paychecks are coming from a bunch of low-down, money-hungry scalawags. Maybe I'll settle down on a ranch somewhere nearby, get married. This is mighty fine country." The cowboy detective heaved a sigh and was soon snoring lightly.

The embers blackened as Sage lay staring upwards at the vastness with its glittering points of light. He tried to picture the elegant Lucinda living on a remote ranch. Maybe, Siringo hadn't asked her yet. Maybe, there was still hope.

TWENTY FIVE

PADDY CAMPBELL LAY BURIED BESIDE the creek in a small glen where stately pine trees stood guard over lush grass gleaming in the sunlight. They dismounted, leaving the horses to graze.

The stone mound was conspicuous, out of place. Its rocks must have been carried from the stream because they were water-rounded. Sage wondered why a murderer would have gone to the trouble of burying the body in such a lovely spot, let alone make such an effort to cover him.

When he asked that question, Siringo ruefully shook his head saying, "We humans are funny animals. I've seen the worst of us show great kindness. Almost as though a remaining smidgen of humanity must break out now and again. Who knows? Maybe Meglit has it in him to feel guilt and picking this beautiful spot was his way to atone. Or, maybe the fellow who helped him insisted on it."

Sage remembered the dying man and the guilt he'd expressed to Lucinda. Could be he was the one who'd insisted that the old shepherd's body be treated with respect.

They walked over to the mound of stones. Its length and width suggested what lay beneath. Without saying anything both men began tossing the rocks aside. After a bit, Sage asked, "They did a good job covering up the body. What am I going to tell people about finding it?"

"The simplest story is best, I think," said Siringo. "Just say you saw buzzards circling. Got curious and saw something beneath rocks wild animals had shifted. You moved the rocks and found a body. You discovered he'd been shot and figured the sheriff needed to know."

As they uncovered the body, only their labored breathing, the thunk of tossed rocks and the echoing croak of ravens disturbed the quiet. At last the body lay exposed to the morning sunlight. It wasn't a pretty sight. Meglit's bullet had taken away part of Campbell's skull. Time and insects destroyed even more of him. Sage was glad he'd skipped breakfast. He took the tarpaulin he'd bought to rig up a tent and spread it out. They lifted the dead shepherd onto the heavy canvas, rolled him up, then used hemp rope to secure it at each end and in the middle.

Sage took everything off Gaspar before covering the horse's back with a thick blanket. He smoothed the white stripe running down the horse's face. Looking into the animal's huge brown eyes he said, "Sorry old boy, I know you don't much like people on your back but this is an old fellow, just like you. We need to take him home."

Sage looked around, expecting to find Siringo smirking at such sentimentality. Instead, the cowboy detective stood beside the wrapped body, hat in hand and head bowed as if in prayer. Sage led Gaspar over and the two of them lifted the body onto the horse. Siringo silently anchored the bundle and, once done, the five of them left the glade with Rocky carrying both Sage and the prospecting equipment. A docile Gaspar plodded steadily along behind.

Reaching the road into town, Siringo halted. "I'll follow an hour behind. Let's meet around ten tonight behind the power plant, like before."

The journey west had been slow. The day was very hot so every once and awhile, Sage reined the procession to one side. There he dismounted to give the horses a rest and a drink of water from the canvas bucket. The sun was three finger-widths above the western rimrocks when they trailed into Prineville. Sage headed for the sheriff's office near the courthouse.

He'd seen Sheriff C. Sam Smith at Twill's street fight. Smith's round face and receding chin gave him a boyish look. A bushy mustache extending beyond a small mouth did little to add maturity. As Sage dismounted, the lawman was stepping out the door, key in hand. Probably heading home to his supper. Seeing Sage he paused, then his eyes widened at the sight of Gasper's burden. "Is that a dead body you got there, Mr. Miner?" he asked.

Sage wasn't surprised that the sheriff already knew his alias. By now, he'd accepted the idea that, in Prineville, everyone knew everything within minutes of it happening.

"I heard tell that the Kepler brothers are missing a shepherd," Sage began, nodding in the direction of the body, "I suspect that the old fellow on Gasper might be him. He was shot and buried beside Scissors Creek."

"I heard tell you were heading up that way. Left just yesterday, didn't you?" Suspicion showed in the man's face and slowed his words.

"Yes, that's right. I headed out yesterday, got there last evening and found the poor fellow early this morning. Thought I should bring him in. If you take a look, you'll see he's been dead quite awhile," he added, hoping that would allay the suspicion. It didn't quite.

"Well now, I guess we'll let Doc Belknap decide when Mr. Paddy Campbell met his Maker. Let's mosey on over to the brewery. We'll keep the body cool until the doc gets a chance to examine him." With that, Sheriff Smith took up Gasper's rope and started walking down the street. Sage grabbed Rocky's reins and followed.

"You planning on heading right back out again?" the sheriff asked.

That note of suspicion remained. "Nope, I found this a bit unsettling, a bad omen. I'm thinking I might stay in town for awhile."

"Good." The sheriff walked a few more steps before saying, "So, I understand you been talking to that homesteader, Fromm. He tell you where to find the body?"

Sage paused in surprise. He hadn't expected the sheriff to make that connection. The sheriff stopped and turned to stare at him. "Good Lord, no!" Sage said, genuinely shocked at the thought. It had never occurred to him that anyone would think Fromm had anything to do with the old shepherd's murder.

The sheriff seemed satisfied. "So, tell me how did you come to find a body, straightaway, in all that vastness?" he asked, gesturing toward the dark slopes of the distant Ochocos.

"Well, like I said, I got an early start this morning. I trailed up Scissors Creek, looking for a likely spot to start panning. Hadn't got very far when I noticed three buzzard's circling down low. I went to look. Someone had made a big pile of creek rocks. The pile was shaped just like a body. When I got closer, I saw that an animal had rolled away a few of the rocks. From the paw tracks, it looked like coyote. Anyways, I saw a cloth shirt and the shape of a man's shoulder. It didn't look like a proper burial. So, I just threw aside some rocks to get a better look-see. That's when I saw the bullet hole." Sage took care to keep his voice matter-offact, letting just a tinge of excitement give it heft.

"Bullet hole?"

"Someone shot him in the head. Actually made a big hole. I figured it wasn't a natural death and you needed to see him. So, here we are."

The summons soon brought Dr. Belknap to the brewery. He took one look and cleared Sage of any involvement. "Looks like the poor fellow's been dead for weeks," he told the sheriff.

With that, the sheriff said Sage was free to "go about his business, but stick around town." So, Sage walked his tired horses to their stable. The sight of them dismayed the stable owner. "What, you returning Rocky and Gasper already? They cause trouble? I tell you, I don't have any milder animals than those two old fellows," he said, clearly agitated at the idea of losing the rent Sage had already paid.

"Rocky and Gasper are fine animals. I've got no complaints," Sage assured the stableman. "And I don't want a refund." Then he told him the reason for his brief trip out to the mountains and back.

"I sure don't like all them sheep ruining the range," Hamilton said. A splat of tobacco juice onto the dirt emphasized his disgust. "But, killing a man, especially a harmless old man, I can't agree with at all."

Sage could only nod. The toil and strain of the last two days had finally hit him. All he wanted to do was check back into the Poindexter, have a bath and a meal and go to sleep for a few hours.

After Hamilton said he'd be willing to store the prospecting gear, Sage gave the fellow coins for an extra measure of oats and patted each horse goodbye. Reaching the hotel, he paused in the dining room archway just long enough to scan the room. Lucinda was nowhere in sight. A low growl of frustration tickled his throat.

❁ ❁ ❁

A clean body, full stomach and a few hours of sleep put an alert Sage back on the street. He had two hours to kill before it would be time to meet Siringo. He headed toward the Rimrock, hoping to find Twill there and in a better mood than the last time he'd seen him.

"Are my eyes deceiving me or has our prospector returned from the hills after being absent but less than two days? You already strike it rich?" the Irishman greeted, raising his glass in apparent friendliness. Sage cautiously edged up to Twill, again sensing that inexplicable shift in his attitude.

"How've you been?" Sage asked. If Twill was part of the group planning retaliation against the cattlemen, this change in him made sense. That must be it.

"Fair to middling. Can't complain. Nobody'd listen," came the response.

Well, that was a less than revealing answer, Sage thought. He ordered a beer and drank deeply. It felt like he'd been gone for at least a week, instead of just forty-eight hours. "Hear any more about Rayburn's murder?" he asked.

"Folks are pretty certain that homesteader sent Rayburn off to meet his Maker. I've not heard a whisper of anything different."

Sage cleared his throat. Might as well give things a poke. "You know, with the killing of Timothy O'Dea, the barn burning and the sheep shooting that's been going on, it's surprising that the sheep ranchers and herders haven't retaliated," he commented before swallowing more of his beer.

"Ha," Twill snorted in derision. "Gutless, that's what they are. Keep thinking talking's going to help. Bunch of gobdaws, every one of them. I'm damn tired of talking to 'em." Seeing Sage's quizzical look, Twill added, "'Gobdaw' is Irishspeak for a 'foolish idiot.'"

They drank in silence after that—Sage sad with the realization Twill no longer trusted him. With his own ears he'd heard the shepherds talking. They were definitely preparing to move beyond talking. And so were the sheep ranchers. Oh, well. The Irishman might not trust him, but Twill was a good man. Sage and Siringo had to catch the murderers before Twill and the other shepherds got themselves into serious trouble.

Twill ordered another beer and a shot of whiskey. "We hear tell you didn't return to town by yourself," the Irishman commented loudly and fixed Sage with a discomforting stare.

Around them the saloon fell completely silent. Sage repeated the same story he'd given Sheriff Smith. Twill's face stayed expressionless during the telling.

His story told, the men in the saloon turned surly with a strong dose of boast. "Ain't nobody going to shoot me, my dog or my sheep and get away with it!" came a shout that garnered loud whoops of support. "Only a damnable coward would kill an old man!" brought another burst of angry agreement.

"You still working for Van Ostrand and Thomas?" Sage finally asked, wondering why the Irish shepherd still remained in Prineville.

"Oh, that be the case all right. They have me doing a special little job right here in town."

When Twill didn't elaborate, Sage prodded. "Special job?"

"Van Ostrand thinks Timothy's killer might be around town. So, I've been checking into things."

"Wonder why he thinks that?" Sage was interested. Did the surly dentist have some information that might lead to O'Dea's killer?

"Well, now. Van Ostrand's a smart man. He's been doing some figuring, asking some questions. Even sent a telegram or two. He's waiting on some confirming information from out of town," Twill said, leaning forward in an exaggerated show of confidentiality. Then Twill straightened and there was a challenging glint in his eye. "Enough of my business. You planning on heading back out tomorrow?"

"Nah, the sheriff wants me to hang around town for a bit," Sage said.

That information only seemed to increase the Irishman's morose mood. "People think they can kill us shepherds and escape the consequences because this here is cattle country." Twill leaned toward Sage, his hot breath a mix of beer, whiskey and free saloon sausage. "There'll be consequences," he promised. "Just like there is for betrayal."

Sage's head reared back. He tried to make sense of the Irishman's somewhat menacing response. Of course, Twill was pretty drunk and that could explain the drama behind his threatening tone. Still, Sage felt the need to probe, parroting, "Betrayal?"

"Whomever put the 'dangerous stone a-rolling' will find it falling on himself," paraphrased the Irishman, heavy portent weighing his words.

"*Henry the VIII*, Duke of Suffolk," Sage responded automatically, before tossing down the last of his beer. It was time to meet Siringo. Besides, he was in no mood to put up with Twill's dramatics. Sage felt uneasy at the absence of the Irishman's prior friendliness.

Still, now wasn't the time to ponder on the change in Twill. It had been a long, hard day, starting with the senseless death of a harmless old man. Sage hadn't known the shepherd but that didn't stop his outrage at the cowardly taking of an inoffensive life. He said goodbye to Twill and headed for the door.

Once outside, he paused. Behind him, he heard the murmurs and intermittent shouts of the saloon's drunken patrons. But beyond the Rimrock, a lowering sky made the way darker than usual. Hands shoved in his trousers, Sage turned toward the power plant. Away from the saloon, the night sounds quieted. Neighboring houses were dark. He passed before a residence under construction, wondering what it would be like to live in such a small town. Next, he paused before a darkened storefront—a candy shop He used to take Lucinda candy and flowers. She liked the flowers best of all. "Stop it," he ordered himself. Dwelling on memories only made it worse.

Stepping off the boardwalk onto the street, he heard a scuffling sound and the heavy breathing of a man moving quickly. He started to whirl around only to find himself falling forward as a sharp blow to his back knocked the wind out of him.

"Hey!" came a distant shout. "Drop it or I'll shoot!" It was Siringo's voice from at least a block ahead. This was followed by the sound of a stout board being dropped to the ground and the thudding boots of someone fleeing.

Sage pushed himself up onto his knees. Siringo's hand appeared before his face and he gratefully grabbed hold so the cowboy could haul him up.

"Did you see who it was?" Sage gasped. It hurt to breathe. Gingerly reaching back to feel his ribs, he winced when his fingers encountered a tender spot.

"Nope, I was too far away and it's too dark. Big fellow is the best I can tell you. You gonna be okay?" he asked.

Sage cautiously took a deep breath, wincing again at the pain. Still, the ache was already easing. He looked down at the board. A short length of two-by-four. His attacker probably snatched it up back there at the construction site. "Lucky for me he hit me with the flat side, instead of the edge. I'm going to hurt for a while but it's nothing I can't handle." He bent over to retrieve his hat and immediately wished he hadn't.

Siringo didn't spend any time conveying sympathy. "I suspect it feels like getting bronc-tossed onto a fence rail. Let's get off the street. Too many people might see us together and wonder."

Once they'd found seats on the power plant's cordwood stacks, Siringo asked, "What happened with Sheriff Smith?"

"At first, he was suspicious. Then he seemed to think Fromm told me where to find the body. I fed him our story and he backed away from those ideas, especially once the doc said the shepherd had been dead for some time."

During this explanation, Siringo had been nodding. "I doubt that Smith is going to be very concerned about tracking down Campbell's killer."

"Why?" Sage would have thought a murder would spur the sheriff into acting.

"Tonight, I downed a few beers in a cowboy saloon," Siringo said. "I learned that Smith's not just sympathetic to the cattlemen, he's a member of the cattlemen's association that's running those dead lines everywhere. In fact, he's one of their leaders. He has a powerful hatred of sheep. And, he's also none too fond of homesteaders, either."

That's not good news, Sage thought. "I guess that was why he was so quick to blame Fromm for Rayburn's murder," he said. "And, why he won't make much of an effort to find justice for the old shepherd." Siringo sounded weary and resigned. Sage looked at the detective surprised to hear defeat in his voice. He'd have thought Siringo was someone well used to such disappointment.

Siringo got hold of his feelings because his voice was more emphatic when he continued, "It's still up to us get the information the Governor needs. We can't do that until we clear up who murdered O'Dea and Rayburn because we now have a seven-day deadline for preventing an all-out range war. Things are heating up on the cattle side as well. Lots of sheep shooting talk in the saloons. 'Course, generally speaking, the more a man talks, the less likely he'll ever do anything. Still, someone's stirring things up. And, it can't all be Meglit. A Silver Lake sheep flock was slaughtered a few days ago. A cowboy gang tied up the herder and then shot, clubbed and drove the critters off a cliff."

"Where's Silver Lake?" Sage asked, wondering how men could be driven to such wanton cruelty against defenseless animals.

"About a hundred miles south. Not likely any of the folks up around here did it. Still, there's too many folks celebrating the news to let me rest easy. People are winding themselves up. I don't like it."

"Well, my bringing in Campbell's body definitely got the shepherds upset. They're mad and fearful. That's a dangerous combination. And, Twill's acting really strange."

Siringo's lips tightened and he sounded angry as he said, "So, in seven days all hell is going to break loose." Both of them contemplated the war that was about to rip apart the town and sweep across the countryside.

"There is a bit of good news," Siringo at last said. "A coded telegram was waiting for me when I got into town. Chamberlain says he's hopeful that the Secretary of the Interior will agree to intervene. But, Adair, it will be too late to talk if the sheepmen retaliate first because we'll be in a full-fledged war. It'd be nearly impossible for folks to back down once it starts up."

Sage shifted position, winced, and said, "Then we better 'get to cracking' as my mother would say. The shepherds are going to start carrying guns and defending their flocks instead of running away. They're bitter. Maybe the shepherds and ranchers are planning to launch a combined offensive."

Siringo tilted his hat so that his eyes glittered in the faint light. "Wahl, one thing's for double-darn sure," he drawled, satisfaction in his voice, "We got it figured right. Somehow this range war mess is a'brewing right here in town because someone living here is a damn murderer. This will be where we're going to find the answers. We can stop the range war only if we find O'Dea's and Rayburn's killer. "

With that pronouncement, they proceeded to lay plans for trapping the killer. Once the plans were set, Siringo's face turned grim once again. "Did it cross your mind that maybe two different men are trying to kill you?" he asked.

Sage started. "What makes you think that?"

"One fellow uses a gun. The other uses a club. You better be mighty careful from here on out. That fella could have smacked you dead with that big stick of his. Next time, I might not be around to save your hide." With that, Siringo flashed his teeth, tapped a finger to his hat brim and strode away.

TWENTY SIX

WITH EVERY TURN, STABBING PAIN jerked him awake. A sure sign of rib damage. The morning's frustration deepened his already glum mood. He dawdled over coffee in the hotel dining room but Lucinda never appeared. For all he knew, she was already on the stage heading toward the Shaniko railhead. Once she reached it, which direction would she go? Back East? Portland? Or was she out strolling Prineville's streets with Siringo? Had the Dickensen agent asked her to settle down with him on a ranch somewhere? Did she accept?

Sage decided it was time to shake himself loose from such fruitless thoughts. He opened the *Crook County Journal.* The legislature had finally passed a child labor law making education compulsory for children under fourteen. He smiled grimly. Of course, to learn, children needed food in their bellies. There'd been no legislation on that, he noted.

There was one interesting thing about the newspaper stories. Despite Prineville being a cattle town, there was an upbeat report on the sheep business. The story projected profits would be higher than usual. That good news was attributed to floods killing both Australian and South African sheep, a sharp rise in the purchase of woolen cloth, and the extraordinarily thick coats on this year's sheep. The latter two circumstances, he read, were due to "colder weather worldwide."

Herman Eich entered the dining room, interrupting Sage's fruitless vigil. Sage gestured for the Jewish man to a take a seat. At this point, Sage didn't care whether Prineville's collective eyebrows shot skyward at the sight of them in friendly conversation. "Any news? Did the Gypsies know anything, see anything?" he asked Eich as soon as the waiter left them alone.

Eich sipped coffee as his brows knit. "Well, I'm not sure. You remember the night that young shepherd was murdered? Twill's friend? It seems two Gypsy men were hunting that night. They'd killed an elk but, after dressing it out, they decided it was too far and too dangerous to pack it back to their camp in the dark. They'd seen big cat tracks and heard cougar screams. So, they stayed put. Turns out, they hunkered down close to that military road. Just before dawn, they heard a horse trotting down the road. They couldn't see who was riding, just his shape."

"Oh darn," Sage interjected. "Just one man though?"

"Yes, just one man. Thing is, they said they were certain he was a town man, not a cowboy. They said he wore a suit and derby and rode stiff on the horse. And, they said that the horse carried no saddle bags or bedroll."

"Well, that is somewhat helpful," Sage acknowledged. "Seems suspicious that there'd be a town man riding in the middle of nowhere in the middle of the night."

Eich nodded in agreement and his eyes were twinkling as he leaned forward. "Thing is, Sage, I also ran into Mr. Henry, our Indian friend. You remember he said his son was away hunting deer when we were at their camp in Prineville? He returned and told his father that as he climbed out of the valley, he heard a shot and looked down. He didn't see Rayburn getting hit or anything but he did observe a man, dressed in a suit and wearing a derby, rushing away from the river—heading toward town."

Sage straightened. "So, it does sound like maybe the same man killed both O'Dea and Rayburn. What Henry's son saw proves the homesteader had nothing to do with Rayburn's murder. Fromm came to town wearing a plaid shirt, wide-brimmed hat and leather jacket. And, I know for a fact that he was up near Willowdale when O'Dea was killed. I saw him there. He was meeting the stagecoach. I doubt he even knew O'Dea."

Then the excitement drained out of him. "This just isn't making any sense. Sure O'Dea and Rayburn were sheepmen. It's logical that the killer is someone who doesn't like sheep. But, near as I can tell, they had nothing to do with each other. Rayburn wasn't even working in the sheep business when he got murdered. And, O'Dea was planning on starting his own homestead. If someone was deliberately trying to incite a range war, they'd maybe kill O'Dea but not Rayburn too."

Eich's lips twisted as he thought. "Seems like a range war would take place out on the range. Not in town like Rayburn's murder. But, I do agree with you. Our Gypsy and Indian friends both describe a man dressed in suit and derby—a town man. It sounds like the fellow who killed O'Dea is the same fellow who shot Rayburn. And, that means that the murderer could be someone who lives here in town."

Sage softly hit the table with his fist in frustration. "I agree. So does Charlie Siringo. He doubts that a cowboy killed O'Dea. But why would a townsman in a derby and suit ride all the way out to Gray's Prairie to kill a sheepherder and then return to murder the town layabout? Ever since I got to Prineville, nothing has made sense," he said, thinking that included Twill's recent strange behavior and Lucinda's baffling absence as well.

Sage heaved a sigh, his eyes staring unseeingly at the table cloth. When he looked up, he saw that Eich was studying him, his dark eyes curious.

"Something else is troubling you, isn't it Sage?" Eich said. The unexpectedly perceptive observation threw Sage into momentary confusion and he shifted to gaze out the window while he debated on how to respond. Should he confide in Eich? How silly would that sound? "Mr. Eich, I think I love the parlor house madam who is going to marry the Dickensen detective—a man I should hate but instead find myself liking?" Nah, he couldn't say that. So, he said nothing.

thing he wanted was pity but still, he asked, "How does a man go about letting go of feelings he shouldn't have?"

Eich responded thoughtfully, "I think that is impossible. We cannot control our feelings, only our actions." Changing the subject he asked, "Does that Siringo fellow have any ideas about what we should do next?" Before Sage could answer, another thought occurred to Eich, "And does he know about me?"

Back on safe ground Sage leaned forward. "Oh yes, I had to tell him about you. We have a plan and we need your help."

Caution narrowed Eich's eyes and stilled his face. He said, "You know, as I boarded the train in Portland, your mother told me that I should watch your left eyebrow."

"My left eyebrow?" Sage parroted back, mystified. Eich smiled, "Yes, she said that whenever one of your schemes was going to expose you to danger, your left eyebrow would raise a fraction of an inch."

Sage laughed. That sounded just like Mae Clemens. "Oh, really," he said derisively. "Sometimes Mother is a little crazy where I'm concerned."

One side of Eich's lip twitched upward. "Well, that remains to be seen. Your left eyebrow shot skyward when you mentioned having a 'plan.' Are you going to tell me there's absolutely no danger attached to this scheme you and Siringo cooked up?"

Distant coyote yips weren't the only reason Sage's shoulders tried to crawl up to meet his ears. To be honest, if only to himself, the dismissal he'd given Mae's concerns was more bluff than fact. Of course, this was dangerous and his whole body knew it. The plan was simple. Once it grew dark, Sage was to visit various saloons to be seen by all and sundry. They wanted his attacker to make his move in those empty dark stretches between the cowboys' watering holes. Siringo and Eich planned to shadow his every move and pounce on any attacker. It was exactly the type of plan certain to make Mae Clemens anxious. "Good thing she's not here," Sage muttered to himself, as he darted furtive looks into gaps between buildings. "She'd probably be sneakily trailing all three of us."

So far, nothing had happened. His congenial conversations with saloon customers ranged from his discovering Paddy Campbell's body to the likelihood of finding gold in the Ochocos. He'd strolled from one drinking establishment after another without incident. The Rimrock was his last port of call. Since this was the sheepmen's hangout, he wouldn't be in danger here. They'd just have to try again tomorrow night.

Inside, hesitation slowed his steps when he saw Twill lounging against the bar in his customary place. Given the Irishman's peculiar behavior of late, Sage wondered whether he should even approach the shepherd. Then Twill saw him and waved an arm. As Sage reached the long bar, the Irishman shouted, "Hey barkeep! Whiskey for my friend here."

The glass was set before Sage, he raised it and swallowed, saying nothing as burn flowed into belly. Then he asked, "You still working on Van Ostrand's little project?"

Twill laughed, his blue eyes glittering. "That I am, boyo. I expect that little job will soon be wrapped up tight as butcher's twine around a rib roast."

"Well, that's good to hear. You plan on heading out to herd once you're done?"

This question sent a sober look washing over the Irishman's face. He downed the last of his whiskey before answering vaguely, "I guess that depends. It just depends."

Sage cocked an inquiring eyebrow but Twill changed the subject. "So, will you be heading out soon to pan the Scissors? Hey, I don't suppose you found Paddy Campbell's dog?"

Sage took another sip, the image of that sunlit glade filling his mind. The sun, the sound, the colors, all bright. "Nope, no dog. And, like I said, the sheriff ordered me to stay in town. That's okay. I need to follow up on the Rayburn murder because I promised the homesteader's wife I'd help. I didn't get to talk to the Fromm's neighbor about Rayburn while I was up in the Ochocos. Finding Paddy Campbell's body put a kibosh on that idea. So, I'm staying here for a few more days until Smith says I'm free to leave. Then I plan on going back to talk to the neighbor."

A crafty look crossed the Irishman's face as he looked around the room. Although the saloon was crowded, nobody seemed to be giving them notice. "I might know a wee bit about the Rayburn murder but I'm a tad shy about mentioning it here. How about we mosey on out back like we're going to relieve ourselves?"

Sage put his glass on the bar. How wonderfully ironic if Twill had heard something useful. Maybe some fact that would help them identify the twice-seen, derby-wearing man in the suit. Sage straightened and looked at Twill. "I think that'd be a fine idea," he said, clapping a hand on the Irishman's rock-hard shoulder.

Twill tossed a few coins on the counter before staggering toward the back door. Sage trailed behind, knowing he was deviating from the agreement that he'd never exit out the rear of a saloon. Having such a large companion by his side would surely discourage any would-be attacker. Besides, since it was the sheepmen who were the murder victims, the shepherds themselves posed no threat.

Once outside, the Irishman turned cautious and less drunk. He stayed within the building's shadow, leading them away from the privy and toward the Rimrock's farthest corner. At last he halted beneath the outside stairs to the second floor. There, he turned around to face Sage. It was dark under the staircase, but not so dark that Sage missed seeing the pistol barrel's silver glint aimed at his belly.

"This is the end of the trail for you, you lying bastard," snarled Twill.

Shock paralyzed Sage. His frantic mind found no answers—just the realization that Twill's Shakespeare quotes about betrayal had been aimed at him. "Why?" spurted from Sage's mouth even before he'd framed the question in his mind.

"Why?" the word coming from Twill's throat sparked with outrage. "Why?" the Irishman repeated before answering his own question. "Because you killed Timothy and Felan. Because Timothy was a good man, and Felan was a fine dog. Because neither one of those dear creatures ever hurt a single soul in their entire life."

"I killed Timothy O'Dea?" Sage repeated, stalling for time as his mind scrabbled for an explanation. "But Twill, I wasn't anywhere near Prineville when he was killed," he protested.

"Yah, I figured a lying bastard like you would say something like that. You don't even have the guts to tell the truth before I send you straight to Hell. Get your god damned hands up in the air. Now!" That last word was a snarl.

Sage raised his hands. He had to keep the Irishman talking until he could spot an opening. He needed just one chance to either launch himself at Twill or run away.

His frantic brain settled on the obvious question. "I don't understand. Why do you think I was in Prineville when O'Dea died?" Sage asked, stepping back in favor of the run away plan.

Twill shook his head saying, "You killed O'Dea, you sorry excuse for a human being. You stood there, giving me sympathy, drinking my whiskey—all the time knowing you'd killed my friend. It's going to be damn fine pleasure to permanently shut your lying mouth." Twill raised his gun. The metallic cocking of the pistol sounded loud in the windless night.

Sage opened his mouth to protest, knowing it was too late. Though they stood in deep gloom, he could see hatred blazing in the Irishman's eyes. Between that hate and the many drinks, there'd be no diverting Twilleran Parnell McGinnis from his determination to end John Miner's life. Right there and then.

As the gun barrel steadied, Sage frantically calculated whether he could throw himself to one side and avoid the bullet about to explode from that black hole. Too late and he'd be dead. Too soon and that barrel would follow his path and still find his heart. Once on the ground, how could he avoid a second shot?

Sudden movement flashed behind the Irishman just before he made an "uh" sound. Then his knees buckled and the gun dropped from his limp fingers. Sage sprang forward and snatched up the gun. Then he turned toward his rescuer who still held a stout stick aloft, ready to strike again.

What Sage saw made no sense. It wasn't Siringo's tall rangy figure. Nor was it the solid shape of Herman Eich. Instead, it was a short, slender man. Sage stepped closer to peer down into the face shadowed by the wide-brimmed cowboy hat.

What he saw made him step back in surprise. "Lucinda!" he gasped. Sure enough, she stood there, legs encased in trousers, a loose coat concealing those unmistakable curves.

"What?" was the only word that escaped his lips.

She let the stick fall to the ground. Her voice was soft as she explained, "I was helping Xenobia with cleaning her house when Siringo told me what you two had planned. I figured Mae would never forgive me if anything happened to you. While Siringo and that other fellow waited out front, I hid behind every saloon you entered. Just in case something like this happened. Why'd you come out here with him anyway?"

Still stunned Sage could only say, "I thought he was my friend. He said he had helpful information."

She laughed but her voice was breathless as she said, "I didn't know if I could hit him soon enough or hard enough to stop him. I kept looking around the corner, screwing up my courage. When he cocked the gun . . ." her voice trailed off and she glanced down at the stick she'd dropped. She swayed but by then he'd reached for her. Wrapping his arms around her shaking body, he squeezed tight, knocking the hat off her head. Her loose hair fell around her shoulders.

"Thank you, Lucinda," he said into that silken hair. "You saved my life. But when I get my hands on Siringo, he's going to get a lesson for involving you in this. You could have been shot."

She stiffened in his arms and drew back. "He didn't know I was trailing you," she said, irritation making her voice tart. "No way I was going to tell him. He's as pig-headed as you are!"

Before Sage could answer, a groan sounded down near his boot. Lucinda picked up the hat and stuffed her hair back into its crown.

"I'll go get Charlie," she whispered before disappearing around the corner.

Sage stepped back from his would-be killer even as a hot flare of jealousy swept through him. "That damn 'Charlie' again," he muttered bitterly, as his boot gently toed the moaning Twill.

TWENTY SEVEN

TWILL WAS SITTING ON THE ground, fingers gingerly exploring his head, when the rangy shape of Charlie Siringo slipped around the building's corner.

"I didn't know what she planned to do," Siringo said by way of greeting. "Still, she's a plucky filly, that one. Lucky for you."

Sage smiled at the "plucky filly" then remembered she was Siringo's plucky filly. "Yup, I'm darn lucky," was all he said.

"I should have known you're teamed up with another scoundrel," Twill mumbled from where he sat at their feet.

Siringo and Sage looked at each other. "Wahl," drawled the cowboy. "Now that we trapped us a crazed coyote, what are we going to do with him?"

Twill snorted like an angry horse before offering an answer. "Kill me of course. Just like you killed Timothy and Asa. 'All the perfumes in Arabia will not sweeten your little hands.'"

"Lady Macbeth," Sage answered automatically. Where the hell had Twill come up with such ideas?

"I didn't kill either one of them," he told the Irishman.

"Oh yea. And, me Mam raised me to always make the same mistake twice," was Twill's bitter response.

"Look, Twill. I wasn't anywhere near in Prineville when Timothy O'Dea was murdered. That was the morning I rode the train out to Shaniko from Portland."

"Stop with the lies. Witnesses saw you, man," Twill insisted before grabbing his head with both hands. "Oh, my head. What in Mary Joseph's name did that woman crack me noggin with?"

Siringo and Sage exchanged a look of consternation, with Sage thinking, "Darn, he must have heard Lucinda's voice. Twill now knows a woman is involved." What Sage said, however, was, "What 'witnesses'?" Those so-called witnesses just might be the killers.

"Hah. There's another of your lies—bald as Caesar's pate. People saw you out in the Ochocos the day before Timothy died. You were working with a bunch of cowboys, running a dead line. Just so those bleeding sheepshooters will have another excuse to murder more shepherds. You can't deny your partner here is on the cowboys' side, he planted a facer on you the other day. Fine show of theater that was. Had me fooled for a bit," he said bitterly.

"What witnesses?" Sage repeated.

"Of yes, as if I am going to give you and your partner here the names of more people to murder," Twill said. "Just get it over with. It'll be a relief from this aching noggin," he mumbled from beneath the two hands still holding his head.

Just then, the rear door of the Rimrock swung open, letting the saloon's hubbub waft out into the silent night. A man stepped out, his fingers already fumbling with his trouser buttons. He didn't try to reach the privy. Instead, he turned his back and stared north toward a patch of dry brush that stood between the saloon and its nearest neighbor. They heard the patter of liquid hitting the hard earth. Seconds later the man re-entered the saloon.

Siringo cleared his throat. "Maybe this isn't the best place to have a little talk with our friend." He gestured at the Irishman.

"Wait here," Sage said, shoving Twill's gun into his own waistband. He ran lightly up the outside stairs and entered the attic. The room was empty. Flipping aside the blanket doors over the cubicle openings, he confirmed that no one was inside.

Back out on the stair landing, Sage whispered down to Siringo, "Bring him on up. No one's up here." In response, he heard Siringo's quiet murmur and the scuffle of boots in the dirt. Siringo and Twill mounted the stairs, the Irishman in front. Siringo strong-armed him into a moonlit patch, slung a ladder-back chair into position and none too gently pushed the shepherd down onto its seat. Then he lit a kerosene lantern and turned the flame high.

"Look here, Mr. McGinnis, me and Mr. Miner are working with the law, not against it," Siringo said with authority.

Sage smirked. Right, as if Twill was going to believe him.

"I'm supposed to believe those words coming from between your lips?" Twill responded. "I've heard enough around town to know you're a cowpoke who's been around the Ochocos for months. Now, it turns out you're Miner's partner." He spoke Sage's alias with contempt.

"That's just an act," Siringo said. Sage smirked again.

"Obviously, just like everything else the two of you have been up to," Twill responded.

"Look here. I'm a Dickensen agent and Miner here," Siringo gestured to Sage, "He's helping me. We're trying to stop the range war before it starts."

"I'm supposed to believe that malarkey?" Twill's voice was incredulous. "You're an even bigger liar than he is, by God." The Irishman clamped his lips shut and crossed his arms over his chest.

Siringo fished around inside his trousers. He pulled out a white card and shoved it toward the Irishman. "Here, read this. It's my Dickensen identification."

Sage smirked yet again. Twill didn't take the card. Why would he, if he couldn't read?

Sage stepped closer to the two men. This wasn't getting them anywhere, Twill wasn't going to tell them anything. He was stubborn as a Klondike mule eyeing a swinging bridge.

"Okay, Twill. I know you're not going to tell us the names of your witnesses. So, I'm going to tell you a thing or two. Yesterday was the first time in my life that I was ever in the Ochoco Mountains. Siringo and I had a meet up out there. Siringo's the one who found the shepherd's body—not me. He also found the old shepherd's killer."

"Who?" Twill demanded. For the first time, contempt was absent from his voice.

"Kid by the name of Tom Miglet," Siringo answered. "Problem is, he didn't kill your friend Timothy or Asa Rayburn. He was nowhere near when they were killed. And, I can't find any evidence that a cowboy killed either one of them."

"Who you working for, the cattlemen?" Twill snapped, suspicion thick in his voice.

"Nope. I work for Governor Chamberlain." Siringo's response was matter-of-fact."

Twill snorted in disbelief. "The governor? Sure you don't want to aim higher? Like maybe the President? Or, how about the man in the damned moon?"

Siringo ignored the ridicule and kept talking, "Governor Chamberlain believes we're about to have a range war in Central Oregon. He sent me out here to try and stop it. He's ordered me to find out who is instigating the conflict and, also, what legitimate concerns might be beneath it all."

"What's your name anyway?" Twill asked.

"People hereabouts know me as Tony Lloyd. My real name is Charles Siringo," came the forthright answer.

"I've heard that name—Tony Lloyd." Suspicion was back in the flat delivery of Twill's statement. "You've been out with the cowpokes running dead lines all through the mountains."

Siringo nodded. "That's right, I've been riding with every cowboy outfit I can find. My job was to infiltrate the cattle outfits. Miner here was supposed to do the same on the sheep side."

"Right, boyo. And me, I swam here from yon Emerald Isle carrying a wee four-leaf clover tenderly between my teeth."

Siringo sighed and stepped back, raising his hands in the air. "I give up. Maybe you can have better luck," he said to Sage.

Sage shook his head. "He's got 'witnesses,' he's not going to believe me either. Can't say I blame him. I know the witnesses are lying but why?"

Looking at Twill's face, Sage saw that their tussle had cleared the alcohol from the Irishman's mind. For the first time, he looked to be considering what they had said.

Then Siringo misstepped. "Maybe we should just give him a few thumps to jar those names loose."

Anger filled Twill's face confirming the damage was done. "You can thump me all the way to hell and back. I'll not be giving names to two murdering liars," Twill shouted.

"Oh, shut your damn pie-hole," Siringo commanded and stepped forward. Sage also stepped forward but before he could say anything, a scuffling sounded right outside the door, followed by boots hurriedly clomping down the outside stairs.

Seconds later there was shouting below followed by a flurry of activity.

Siringo and Sage exchanged looks. "Oh-oh," was Siringo's only comment before running feet charged up the stairs. The door was flung open so hard it bounced off the wall. A group of eight or more men crowded into the attic. None of them had guns but likely all carried knives and one, for sure, carried Lucinda's stout stick.

"Are you all right, Twill?" called one of the men.

"Right as rain on a May day," returned Twill as he glanced at his captors, stood up and walked toward the men. "I thank you kindly for coming to my undeserving aid with such alacrity. As the blessed bard says, 'I am wealthy in my friends.'"

"*Pericles, Prince of Tyre*, Timon," Sage identified the quote's source in a quiet voice.

Twill heard him because he turned and met Sage's steady gaze before giving the slightest of nods and turning away.

Siringo also looked at Sage saying, "Mister Miner, quoting poetry in the midst of a stampede seems right crazy, if you'll pardon the criticism."

That stirred a grumble from the men at the door who pressed forward.

Sage glanced at the window opening behind them. It offered their only possible escape. He wondered whether he'd break just one or, both of his legs, when they hit the hard ground outside.

The slither of a gun leaving its leather holster broke the momentary silence. A glance told him Siringo's gun was out but aimed at the floor.

"First hombre that takes a step forward is going to get a bullet in his leg," the cowboy drawled.

There was a rustle behind the packed men and the crowd parted. The saloonkeeper stepped forward, the twin holes of his double-barreled shotgun aimed at Siringo's middle.

"I expect," the saloon keeper drawled back, imitating Siringo, "Mister, you might want to drop that weapon of yours on the floorboards and then give it a nudge in our direction with the toe of your pointy little cowboy boot. If you don't, I'm afraid 'ole Bessie here will make a mess of my nice clean attic."

Sage tried to ignore the blood rushing into his ears. He looked at Siringo, saw calculation narrow the man's eyes and his lips tighten. A dead line. Sage considered stepping back, away from Siringo. Shotguns had a wide shot pattern. At this close range, if the saloonkeeper pulled the triggers, buckshot would hit them both.

Sage stepped in front of the Dickensen man. Just one thought had seized hold—inevitable as the Klondike's winter snow, "She loves him. I like him. So I have to protect him."

A growl rolled across the small open space between them and the angry men standing behind the saloonkeeper.

"Are these the fellers who murdered Timothy O'Dea?" asked a quiet voice from in their midst. "What about Asa Rayburn? They kill him too?" came another voice. The growl grew louder, ominous as the rumble of an approaching thunder storm. Every face stared at them, the fury building. The saloon-keeper's finger tightened on the shotgun's twin triggers as its barrels lifted and steadied.

TWENTY EIGHT

A BOOT SCUFFED ACROSS THE floorboards and Twill stepped in front of the shotgun. He faced the shepherds, his hands raised in a placating gesture. "Now, let's not be acting hasty," he cautioned. "I'm starting to think this to-do might be a big misunderstanding."

He looked over his shoulder at Siringo. "How about you holster that weapon, mister?" he suggested.

Siringo hesitated, then nodded and the pistol slid back into leather.

The saloonkeeper's shotgun barrels dropped so that the twin holes pointed down. Relief relaxed the deep lines on his weathered face.

Twill began explaining in his soft brogue. "You see, I thought these two had killed Tim and Asa. We were arguing about it when you all came to my rescue."

"I heard that cowboy threaten you," came a voice from the back of the group.

Twill nodded. "For certain you did. But, he was just trying to scare me into telling why I thought they were killers. Except for right at the start, they haven't laid a finger on me." He raised a hand to gingerly touch the sore spot where Lucinda's stick had hit his head. "And, I am thinking a thump on the head is a cheap price to pay for stopping me from doing something I would have regretted the rest of my life."

Twill took a deep breath and then let it out before saying, "Fellows, I am more than grateful that you came to my aid. I will not forget it. You are true friends." He turned to stare intently into Sage's face. "And, it just may be that I misjudged my other friend here."

Sage said nothing, just stared back, glad that Twill had decided to take a chance on believing him but wondering what had brought about the change.

"You fellows go on back downstairs. The drinks are on me," Twill told the group of men.

"You real sure Twill, that you'll be all right?" asked one of the men even as the group began shuffling toward the door.

"Safe as a wee lamb in the middle of the flock on a bright sunny day," Twill responded.

The attic emptied, followed by the sound of descending boots and the clap of the saloon's back door closing. Twill turned to face them.

"What made you decide to believe us?" Sage had to ask.

The Irishman gave him a lopsided grin. "Why, it was you stepping toward your friend there, rather than away. That isn't a scoundrel's choice. Second," here he paused and looked embarrassed. "You kept my secret. Your friend doesn't know that I can't read. If he did, he wouldn't have shown me that card." Then the grin became full and easy, "Besides, I can't help myself. I flat out like you. It sore pained my heart to think you false."

Sage returned the Irishman's grin. "I like you too," he said.

"Afore the two of you decide to take up hugging and kissing, I suggest we figure out how to catch us a killer," Siringo drawled, though the relief was evident in his voice.

Siringo decided it wasn't safe to continue their discussion in the Rimrock's attic. After they followed him down the stairs, he led them to the power plant. It turned midnight as they reached the plant's wood lot because one of its operating generators suddenly fell silent. Like many electric plants, Prineville's ran at full capacity only until midnight. That's when the town's homes went dark. Only saloons and hotels continued to draw electricity but that draw required just a single generator.

They waited, concealed by high cords of slab wood, for the silenced generator's fire stoker to exit the plant for home. Then three men moved to the banks of Ochoco Creek. Once there, they sat on low stacks of slab wood rounds.

"Mr. McGinnis, I appreciate your stepping forward to prevent a ruckus back there at the Rimrock," Siringo began, removing his hat to continue earnestly, "We really are in Prineville to prevent the sheepmen from being harmed. I know that the cattlemen have done some sheep shooting and maybe tied up a shepherd or two. But, except for Miglet killing that old shepherd, I don't think they've have killed anyone, yet."

Sage jumped in. "Twill, we think the person who killed Timothy O'Dea also killed Asa Rayburn. A man was seen on the military road the night O'Dea was murdered. But it was dark and he was seen from a distance. Still, the witnesses all say he was a town man, not a cowboy. That's what is so strange. A town man killing Rayburn might make some sense. But why would a town man ride all the way out to Gray's Prairie to kill O'Dea and his dog?"

Siringo cleared his throat before saying, "And there's the burning of the Kepler brothers' barn. How can that be related? I'm thinking it's related because no cowboy is taking credit for the fire. Believe me, I've tipped more than a few beers with them and spent many hours around the campfire when there's nothing to do but tell stories. If any of them burned down the barn, he would have bragged. At least, there'd be gossip. There isn't. Instead, all they do is speculate on who might have done it."

"And, don't forget Rayburn was up to mischief at the Fromm's homestead," Sage added.

Twill's brow knitted in concentration. "Rayburn, Timothy, Kepler brothers' barn, Fromm's homestead," he muttered almost to himself. He looked at them, puzzlement creasing his face.

"Sheep, darn it. That's what they all have in common. That's why it has to be the cattlemen."

Sage was shaking his head. "Or someone wants us to think that. Twill, we have to trust that Charlie has done a thorough investigation where the cowboys are concerned. That means we've got to look beyond the obvious. Besides, why do you think the Fromms have something to do with sheep? I thought they were homesteaders with just a cow and a chicken or two."

"For sure, they're typical homesteaders but their place is out along the military road."

Now it was Siringo and Sage who looked puzzled. "What does their place being along the military road have to do with sheep?" Sage asked.

"The military road investors have leased all their sections to the Kepler brothers for grazing. That means, the other sheep ranchers have to find new grazing land. If homesteaders like Fromm abandon their claims, then that land opens up for grazing until somebody else claims it," Twill explained. "I've heard that their land has a year-around stream on it so that makes it especially valuable."

"Hmm," Sage said as a vague idea began percolating to the surface. He tried to reason it out, "Well, I know having water is crucial. Van Ostrand had me researching survey maps of that area. He wanted me to identify which sections had springs and streams. I guess he's hoping to find somewhere to move his flocks," Sage commented. Then the idea hit full force and with clarity. A rush of excitement flooded through him.

He jumped to his feet and said to the Irishman, "Say, didn't you tell me that O'Dea was talking about starting his own homestead?"

"Aye, he said he'd filed a claim and would be working it by the end of the summer."

"Don't you need to put down money when you file a claim? Somewhere around $450?" Sage asked.

Twill nodded but said nothing.

Sage pushed on, "So, where did O'Dea get the money to file a claim? Was he a great saver or did he inherit some money?"

Twill shook his head, his brow furrowing once again. "Yah know, I wondered on that at the time. Timothy lived a sober life. Every payday, he'd mail off a bank check to his mother in Ireland. There's twelve brothers and sisters and his da is dead. The whole family is dirt poor. Timothy kept nothing back but a wee bit to pay for thus and such."

There was no suppressing the excitement now. Sage glanced toward Siringo who was staring intently at Twill.

Sage asked his next question gently, knowing it might cause anger as well as pain. "Twill, do you think O'Dea got involved in a false land claim scheme?"

Sure enough the question brought a scowl to the Irishman's face and a quick response. "Timothy O'Dea was a good Catholic boy! He was honest as a summer day is long!"

"But what if he got involved, didn't know it was crooked and found out later? Would he have stayed quiet?"

Twill didn't answer but instead said, "I'm unfamiliar with this false land claim stuff. Every blade of Irish grass is already owned. Has been for hundreds of years," he said to Sage. "That's why I'm here."

This declaration sobered them. After a bit, Sage said, "Well, what I know is mostly about the timber barons. They pay people to file claims on forest land and then to lie—saying they've lived on it and worked it. Once they're given title, they hand it over to the timber barons. They've been running that scheme in the Cascades for years. Lately, I learned that a sheep rancher up in Morrow County by the name of Bellingham, tried to use the same deceit in order to acquire grazing land."

Twill looked puzzled, his fingers worrying his stubbled chin.

Sage raise his hands in exasperation. "Don't you see? Maybe the same game is being played for grazing land in the Ochocos. Once a claim's been filed, the claimant can lease out the land for grazing until he's proved it up. Then he can sell it."

"But there's no way Timothy would have agreed to a lying scheme like that," Twill protested.

Sage interrupted, "But, Twill, where'd he get the money to file on a homestead claim?" Before those words were out of his mouth, another thought struck Sage.

"Heney! U. S. District Attorney Heney's here in Prineville. What if someone here in Prineville did the same thing as Bellingham?" Sage stood and started pacing.

He whirled to face Twill. "Let say you're right and O'Dea didn't know he was part of a land fraud. What would he do if he found out about it later? After he'd filed? What if the man who loaned him the filing fee later told O'Dea he'd have to give up the land for sheep grazing?"

Comprehension widened Twill's eyes. "Yah know, something was bothering Timothy, now that I think on it. That last time I saw him, he was glum as he'd ever been."

"What happened?" Siringo asked.

"He'd left for town, happy. Like air was flowing beneath his feet. I stayed behind with Felan and the sheep for company. But when Timothy came back, he acted like his heart was 'all mad with misery.' He wouldn't tell me what happened. Just talked about maybe going home to Ireland." That remembered last conversation sent sorrow washing across Twill's face.

Sage held up a hand, index finger raised. "All right. Let's assume that, while in town, Timothy learned he'd been used to defraud the government. You knew the man. You say he wouldn't be a part of such a scheme. So, what would he do?"

The Irishman was silent, studying the toe of his worn boot before he looked up to say slowly, "Timothy was the kind of man who thought before he acted. Patient. He'd think things over before doing anything that could not be undone."

Siringo picked up on Sage's direction, "So, let's say O'Dea learned that someone in town had made him part of an illegal scheme. Let's also say that he was upset when he found out. That he confronted the man or maybe his reaction was easy to read. What then?"

That question brought Twill scooting forward on his stack of rounds. "You're right!" he exclaimed. "Timmy's face told you exactly what he was thinking. He said that's why he never tried to play poker or tell lies."

"Okay. Now the next question is what about Rayburn? Did he know O'Dea?"

Sage's question brought a swift head shake from Twill who said, "Nope. Timothy barely knew Rayburn. And, he would have steered clear of him. Most of us did."

"Rayburn sounds like he was an amoral scoundrel. Maybe he was involved in the land fraud," Siringo said. "If O'Dea was tricked into filing a false claim, maybe Rayburn was involved."

"I wouldn't put it past him," Twill said. "But I know for a fact Rayburn was in town the night someone murdered Timothy and Felan. I told you," he said, turning to Sage, "I was drinking with Rayburn that night."

"Wait a minute," Siringo interrupted, his tone a bit suspicious. "I thought you just said you steered clear of Rayburn. Why'd you spend the night drinking with him?"

Twill took no offense. "That night, it wasn't my choice. Like I told John here, Dr. Van Ostrand and Newt Thomas insisted they treat us to dinner at the Poindexter. Afterwards, we went to the Reception Saloon and started drinking. The bosses were buying and well, we just kept on drinking."

"Now just hold up a minute, something's not making sense. I understand why Van Ostrand and Thomas would want your company but why would they want Rayburn's?" Sage asked.

"You know, at first, I wondered that too. But after awhile, with the drink and all, I just stopped thinking about it. Maybe they had some kind of business deal."

Something else clicked into place for Sage as he paced back and forth before his two companions. "Siringo, you told me that Rayburn was going to testify for the prosecution against Bellingham. You said he was involved in Bellingham's land fraud scheme."

"He was, on both counts," Siringo affirmed.

"And," here Sage paused in his pacing, "what if Rayburn got involved in another scheme here in Prineville? What if Heney came to town to talk to Rayburn about a second land fraud case—one involving Prineville men?"

Twill was nodding. "Until just a few days ago. No one here in Prineville knew that Rayburn was going to maybe testify against Bellingham."

Siringo jumped in, having gotten the point. "Say you had an illegal land fraud scheme underway. Then you found out one of your co-schemers had already agreed to cooperate with the federal prosecutor in a similar land fraud trial. You'd be a fool to trust him. Especially once Prosecutor Heney showed up in town."

"So, when did Heney get to Prineville?" Sage asked.

"The exact same day Rayburn was murdered." Siringo's answer made them stare at each other.

Sage started pacing again, "So, let's say we have Timothy who was tricked into defrauding the government over a land deal. We have Rayburn up to his ears in land fraud up north and ready to tell all to the federal prosecutor. And, we have Heney coming to town even though his star witness is already scheduled to travel to Portland in just a few days." The ensuing silence firmly set the connections in their minds.

Sage said it aloud, "That's the link between O'Dea and Rayburn. I bet you dollars to dumplings they were both caught up in the same land fraud scheme. And I bet you Heney is in town investigating it," he finished with satisfaction.

"But, who's behind it? Who tricked Timothy into filing a false claim? Who would be using Rayburn?" Twill asked, clearly struggling to put the pieces together.

Another realization smacked into Sage's mind. "You know, Twill, I never saw Rayburn. What did the fellow look like?"

Siringo spoke to derail what he thought was a sidetrack but stopped when Sage raised a hand. "No, this is important, Charlie. Twill, what did Rayburn look like?" he asked again.

"He was stout. Short, maybe only five foot six."

"Did he have black hair?"

"Aye. Black, usually greasy," Twill answered.

"Did a hank of it sometimes curl down onto his forehead?" Sage asked, only becoming aware he'd been holding his breath when it whooshed out at Twill's slow nod.

Twill and Siringo watched, puzzled, as Sage gave a yip of triumph, raised his fists like a prize fighter and kicked his boots out in an impromptu dance. Finally finished, Sage turned to Twill to ask, "Did you ever consider that maybe McGee died because he knew the shooter?"

Thoughtfully, Twill tilted his head to one side before straightening to shake it.

"I bet you were never given the opportunity to talk to any of those witnesses against me, were you?"

Again, Twill shook his head.

TWENTY NINE

THE SWEET SMELL OF NEWLY mown hay drifted through the stable. Not a forest mix of fir needles and wild berries—but still, it was pleasant. Sage missed the rain forest. But there was allure here too, he admitted. There was something uplifting in the sight of pure white clouds silently drifting above chiseled rimrock, golden hills and grassy valleys.

Sage studied his dusty town shoes. In the far stalls, Rocky and Gasper were contentedly munching. He'd greeted the old horses with pats on their long noses, happy to see them. Maybe he didn't dislike all horses—just the ones who wanted to toss him tail over teakettle, as his mother would say.

Mae Clemens. If she were here, she'd insist there must be a safer way to trap the killers. But she wasn't here. And, this plan should work. The loft's trapdoor was closed but the padlock hung free of the hasp. When the time came, they could yank it open from above.

Federal Prosecutor Heney, Siringo and the stable's owner waited up there. The shuffle and thud of the horses' hooves on the planks would cover any noise they might make. The sheriff was not present. Siringo was adamant that Smith was untrustworthy since he was too friendly with the sheepshooters. Haney had reluctantly agreed.

Sage wondered about the outcome of their efforts. If they captured O'Dea and Rayburn's killers today, how would that affect the range war? The shepherds and sheep ranchers might rest easier but it might fire up the sheepshooters. Maybe the irony of the situation would stun both sides into inaction.

Samuel Hamilton's helpfulness had been a surprise. The livery stable trap had been Heney's idea. Apparently it was the stable owner, not Rayburn, who had spurred Heney into visiting Prineville. When he and Siringo turned up at Heney's hotel room early that morning, Hamilton was already there with Heney. The stableman explained, shamefacedly, that he'd been a willing dummy claimant until his wife had "raised the roof" upon learning of the fraud. His letter detailing the false claim scheme hit Heney's desk the same day as another letter. The wife of The Dalles' Chief Land Agent was signatory to this second letter. Her keen accounting eye caught a surge in claims along the military road in the Ochocos. She started checking and found that the same man had signed every bank draft covering the claim fees. That signer was the same man they now believed played a role in the killing of O'Dea and Rayburn.

The crack between the stable doors widened. Sage stood slowly, his hands relaxed and ready at his side. Twill slipped into the stable. "The Judas sheep has done his work. They're both coming," he said.

"Judas sheep?" Sage asked.

"That'd be a sheep trained up from a lamb to lead the other sheep down a chute," Twill said as he pulled a length of hemp from his pocket and advanced on Sage. "You want to be sitting or standing?" he asked.

"I think sitting. That way I can loosen my feet fast," Sage answered and promptly sat down, his back against the stall wall, facing the stable doors.

Twill bent over him. "I'll be tying you with a half hitch knot. Keep tension on it until you need to drop it off. Otherwise, you'll untie yourself before we're ready."

Outside a boot scuffed the boardwalk. Next came the hiss of two men in a whispered argument.

Twill looked at Sage. "I think that's them," he said, pulling a revolver from his waistband and pointing it at Sage. Seconds later, the stable door swung open and two figures slipped inside.

"I don't know why we had to meet you here," Van Ostrand began in a querulous voice only to end with, "Oh," when he caught sight of the trussed up John Miner.

Newt Thomas stepped forward to peer closely at Sage. "What's this about, man?" he asked Twill.

Before the Irishman could respond Van Ostrand said angrily, "You should never have asked us to come here, McGinnis. You've made the situation impossible. You know what to do. You didn't need us!"

Van Ostrand turned toward Thomas, grabbing his upper arm and steering him toward the door saying, "Come on. There's been a mistake. This is none of our business."

"Just a minute, Dr. Van Ostrand. To my mind, it 'tis very much in the nature of your business. It's you who convinced me that Miner here killed Timothy O'Dea. You've been saying he should feel the 'blade of justice'," Twill declared.

Thomas looked flummoxed even as Van Ostrand radiated anger hot as a roaring stove. For the first time, Sage studied the congressman. It appeared that he might not know what his partner had done.

"You don't need us here to deal with Miner," Van Ostrand snapped. "Surely you've fired a gun before. Just shoot him!" He again grabbed Thomas's arm and began pushing the man toward the door, saying over his shoulder, "Just give us a few minutes to get on down the street."

"No!" Twill responded. For the first time, anger colored his voice. "I'll not be shooting him. I've never taken a life and I'll not be starting now. You want Miner dead, you pull the trigger."

"But he killed your friend O'Dea!" argued Van Ostrand. "You said you wanted revenge."

Twill looked at Sage who'd remained silent the entire time. "Did you kill O'Dea?" he asked.

"No, sir. I did not kill O'Dea," Sage said in a steady voice.

"He's lying. He's nothing but a lying drifter. I told you, I had-someone check into him. He wasn't in Portland. They saw him here, out near Gray's Prairie. On the very day Timothy O'Dea was murdered. He deserves to die. Shoot him, shoot him now!" Van Ostrand shrilled as Thomas began to squeak in protest.

Van Ostrand whirled on him, "Shut the hell up! I'm tired of your weak ways. It's time you got some backbone. Miner here could bring everything down on our heads. You want that Thomas?"

Twill, meanwhile, was shaking his head. "The problem to my mind is that I didn't talk to your witnesses. I don't know them from Adam or Banquo's ghost. But I did drink with this man, had some laughs with him. So, I am not going to kill him in cold blood. You want him dead, you shoot him." With that Twill tossed his revolver into a pile of hay near Van Ostrand's feet.

"Get out!" the dentist ordered through clenched teeth. "I'm surrounded by a passel of cowards and fools," he declaimed to no one in particular.

Twill and Sage exchanged a look. This wasn't what they'd planned. Twill was supposed to remain in the stable, near Sage. Because Siringo and Heney figured Van Ostrand and Thomas might search the ground floor, they'd decided to hide in the loft, ready to rush down when called.

Van Ostrand scooped up Twill's gun and pointed it at the Irishman. "Get out, I said. And you better forget you were here. Head out to Gray's Prairie. I'll meet you out there tonight," he ordered.

Spying Sage's minuscule nod, Twill shrugged before heading toward the door. Once the shepherd had passed outside, Van Ostrand barked at Thomas, "Bar that damn door."

Thomas complied with alacrity, though his faced showed stunned confusion. Once the wooden bar had dropped into the brackets, Van Ostrand gestured Thomas toward the back of the stable. "Go back there and make sure all the other doors are barred. Check the stalls to see that no one is hiding in them."

Sage felt a momentarily fizz of satisfaction that they'd accurately predicted Van Ostrand's paranoia. Thomas would find no one. Then he noticed Van Ostrand staring at the planks above their heads. The dentist pulled back the hammer on Twill's gun and aimed it up. Sage froze, knowing that the three men in the hayloft could not know that a bullet might soon smash through the floor beneath their feet.

He gathered a breath and was about to shout a warning when Thomas returned. "Every door is locked. No one is back there. Just two old, dozy horses," he said. "Richard, what in the world are you planning to do?" Sage could tell the Congressman was fighting to sound calm. He'd been gone long enough to realize that his partner had turned rattlesnake dangerous.

"I'm going to do what I've been trying to do for the past week," Van Ostrand said. He pointed the revolver toward the loft's trapdoor. "Climb up there and snap that padlock shut," he ordered Thomas. When Thomas hesitated, Van Ostrand gestured angrily with the gun. "I said, get up that ladder and lock that damn padlock!"

Thomas did as he was told. Seconds later, the padlock shut with a metallic snick, ending any hope of rescue from above. Sage sighed and said to Van Ostrand. "I'm beginning to think that you're the fellow who killed both O'Dea and Rayburn."

Thomas gasped at Sage's declaration. Obviously, the accusation surprised the Congressman. "You, you killed Asa and Timothy? My God in heaven! Why? O'Dea was such a fine young man," he stammered.

The dentist pulled a small pistol from inside his suit coat. Van Ostrand waggled the gun's barrel at Thomas. "Go stand over there by Miner," he instructed.

"You know Thomas," he said, his voice dripping with contempt. "I've regretted every minute we were partners. You lack vision and gumption. How the hell did you think we were going to save our investment and stay out of jail now that the federal prosecutor, Heney, is on our trail?"

Van Ostrand's voice turned patient, as if he were talking to a three-year old. "Rayburn helped round up our dummy claimants. You knew that. So, your hands are just as dirty as mine. But Rayburn had other damaging information. He burned the

Kepler's barn under my orders. And, the snake watched me ride back into town the night I killed O'Dea. That's why he was in the office demanding money."

Van Ostrand shook his head, ruefully. "You're so stupid, Thomas. You thought he was talking about money I owed him for finding the false claimants. If you ever bothered to examine our books, you'd know we'd already paid him for that little deed. The bastard was there trying to blackmail me over O'Dea."

It seemed that Van Ostrand welcomed the opportunity to finally detail his actions—probably because he knew his words would never be repeated. The dentist continued his telling of all, "But Rayburn was a liability for another reason. Heney came waltzing into Prineville. That same day, I spoke to Bellingham's lawyer who was stopping at the Prineville Hotel. He said Rayburn was a turncoat. That he was going to testify against Bellingham in that land fraud case up north. He'd have done the same thing against us. The man lacked loyalty." Van Ostrand finished with a sad shake of his head.

"But, we're going to be okay. Nobody's turned any land over to us," Thomas stammered. "We stopped most of them from trying to prove up their claim. We've decided to keep only the claims on sections that have year-around water," Thomas protested. "I can't see how a few claims, spread apart, are going to implicate us in any land fraud deal."

Hmm, thought Sage. So that's what they had me doing. Helping them figure out which land claims they should keep and which ones to abandon. Sage cleared his throat, drawing both men's attention toward him. "So, Van Ostrand, why'd you kill O'Dea and his dog?" he asked.

"The damn dog charged at me. It was like he knew I was there to kill O'Dea." Van Ostrand said, no regret in his voice.

"But why O'Dea?" Sage asked again.

"I rode out to reason with him. To tell him he could keep the claim he filed on. He came out of the cabin to talk. Said his 'conscience' wouldn't let him," Van Ostrand's voice was scornful. "Here, I told him he could keep the $450 filing fee and he was still going to turn me in. So, I shot him." This last declaration was said matter-of-factly, with not a smidgen of guilt.

Van Ostrand's words sent a shiver traveling up Sage's spine. There'd be no talking him out of another murder. Sage glanced up at the padlocked trapdoor and then at the barred stable entrance. He would need to rescue himself all by his lonesome. Slowly he brought both his hands and his feet together, releasing the tension on the cords so that he could whip free of them.

Van Ostrand had used the brief lull to come up with a plausible plan of action. He looked at Thomas and said in a slow, sad voice, "It is truly a tragedy that my brave partner decided to confront O'Dea's and Rayburn's killer all on his own. I begged him to wait until I'd fetched the sheriff but Congressman Thomas was so upset, so determined to prevent Miner's escape that he raced off to the stable. Unfortunately, the sheriff and I will arrive too late. Our congressman got his man but, unfortunately," here Van Ostrand shook his head in mock sadness, "the killer managed to squeeze off a fatal shot before he died. Such a terrible loss for our dear congressman's family and the citizens of Prineville."

Thomas looked at Sage, terror twisting his face. Sage switched his own gaze back to Van Ostrand who raised both guns until each targeted a beating heart.

THIRTY

FAINT SHUFFLING SOUNDED ABOVE. SAGE tried to cover it by scraping his heels across the plank floor. They must know that Van Ostrand wouldn't hesitate to shoot up into the loft. Given the padlock, there was nothing they could do anyway.

Van Ostrand cocked his head. He'd heard the sound as well. He glanced upward, his body tense as a coon hound's. "Quiet," he snarled at Sage.

Just then the stable door rattled against the bar. Someone was trying to push it open.

That new noise did the trick. Van Ostrand's attention snapped away from the loft and toward the door. Those inside the stable turned dead silent, as if each of them was holding his breath. Sage looked at Van Ostrand. The dentist's pocket pistol was aimed at the door. His fingers tightened and sweat trickled down the side of his face. Determination stiffened every line of his face.

The rattle came again. This time followed by a pounding fist. The door boards shook beneath the blows. Van Ostrand's eyes snapped back toward Thomas and Sage as if he'd suddenly remembered their presence. "Go away," he shouted. "We're closed!"

"We need horses fast!" came a frantic voice. "My mother's sick. Dr. Rosenberg is already headed out to the ranch. My father and I have to get there. She's really sick! Please open up the door so we can get the horses!" The voice was female and pure music to Sage's ears. Lucinda was trying to save him.

"Go away!" Van Ostrand yelled again. "There aren't any horses left. We've rented all of them out."

"Please mister, I know there are at least the two old fellows still in there." Lucinda's voice was now pleading.

"My daughter's right. We just talked to the stable boy and he told us you have at least two horses in there for rent," said Herman Eich's calm, deep voice.

Van Ostrand's face flushed red. He gestured to Thomas. "Get over here, open the door and tell those people to step inside here. I have to shut them up before they draw people's attention with all their shouting. If you try anything tricky, Newt, I'll shoot you in the back the same time I shoot Miner here."

Van Ostrand had moved to the side. He pointed Twill's revolver at Thomas while turning his smaller gun toward Sage. His hands were steady as he kept both weapons level. Rooting around in people's mouths likely kept the man's hands and wrists strong Sage irrelevantly mused even as his muscles tensed, readying to spring.

Newt Thomas lifted the bar from the door and carefully set it to one side. Van Ostrand turned his head to watch Thomas ease the door open. Strong sunlight illuminated Lucinda. She stood in the bright light with her bonnet, sporting a jaunty red silk flower, shading her face. A rush of love filled Sage as he stared at her. Then he noticed Eich standing beside her, wearing his traveling suit, his gnarled hand on her elbow. He opened his mouth to shout a warning.

Suddenly, Thomas flung the door wide and rushed out, his hands in front of him. He shoved Lucinda and Eich to one side, away from the door. "Run!" he shouted, grabbing Lucinda and pulling her even further away from the door. "He's got a gun!"

The dentist pulled the trigger of Twill's gun. There was only the snapping sound of a firing pin hitting on an empty chamber. There came a second snap and then a third. Exactly as Twill had planned. All but the last cylinder was empty. Meanwhile, all three people disappeared from view. Van Ostrand roared in frustration and flung the revolver to the floor where it bounced out of sight into a mound of loose hay.

All of that registered on Sage even as he moved to take advantage of Van Ostrand's momentarily distraction. Whipping the cords loose from hands and feet, he leapt up from the floor and then to one side. When the dentist swung his remaining gun in Sage's direction, his prisoner had already moved. Not away, as one would expect but closer and to one side. Before Van Ostrand could adjust to the change, Sage's left hand grabbed the dentist's gun hand at the same time he also stepped forward and swung the back of his right wrist upward to connect with Van Ostrand's chin. The gun fired harmlessly into the floor as the dentist stumbled backward. Sage felt momentary gratitude that the bullet's trajectory was away from the two horses, though they started squealing and kicking in their stalls.

Before Van Ostrand could raise the gun for another try, Sage stepped closer, his left wrist rising again, this time to hook Van Ostrand's gun hand aside. At the same time the heel of Sage's right hand drove into the man's diaphragm. This hit sent the gun spinning out of Van Ostrand's nerveless fingers as he staggered backward, gasping for breath. Before Sage could launch a third attack, a huge figure charged through the open door. Twill. With a wild yell, the Irishman flew through the air and hit Van Ostrand, taking him to the floor. Sage stepped back and did nothing as Twill straddled Van Ostrand and landed two very stiff blows on the dentist's face. The sight was gratifying. After all, McGinnis had lost a good friend to this man's greed. Van Ostrand deserved worse than a few blows to the nose.

Shouts sounded above their heads as Lucinda and Eich rushed into the stable. A timid Thomas hung back.

It took a few minutes to find the padlock key but soon everyone stood around Van Ostrand's supine figure. Thomas had finally re-entered the stable. He was tugging at Heney's sleeve and whining "I didn't know all that he was doing. I really, really didn't know."

Heney turned to Thomas. "Get a grip on yourself, man. It's clear what you did and did not know. I'll be seeing you in court over the land fraud unless you use your God-given good sense and plead guilty. Maybe help me with this scoundrel's conviction. At that, Heney toed the unconscious dentist with a dusty shoe, "Though it's more likely that this rascal will dangle from the end of a rope long before any trial for land fraud."

Then the prosecutor's stern face softened. "That was a brave thing you did at the end there, Congressman Thomas. We could see through a crack in the floor that you pushed the woman to safety. If there'd been bullets in that gun, you would have died." After saying this, the federal prosecutor began picking straw bits from his suit coat and pant legs. Tidying finished, he straightened up to look Thomas in the eye. "To my mind, that action brought you some ways back toward redemption. I won't forget it."

Sage heard all this but mostly his awareness was focused on Lucinda's arms. They were wrapped around him, gripping him tightly, her face buried in his chest. He held her close, whispering assurances into her hair, feeling the sweat that dampened the back of her dress. In a single moment of clarity, he remembered when only sweat lay between his hands and her naked back. He cleared his throat, saying again, "There, there. Everyone is fine. You did it Lucinda, you and Herman saved us." Over her shoulder, he caught sight of Siringo's face. The cowboy stood in the stable's gloom, staring at them, one sardonic eyebrow raised.

Sage's heart hit the ground with a thud. He sighed. No way was he going to cause problems between Siringo and this woman. There was no reason to think that Lucinda's reaction was anything more than relief that the danger was over. Sage let loose and gently pushed her away, telling himself that Siringo was a proven friend, that the cowboy was good enough for her and that was what mattered. That realization brought acceptance and released something inside him that had been coiled tight as a watch spring. An unexpected ease filled him and the understanding that, caught up in longing and jealousy, he lost his footing. He'd regained it, finally. He didn't like how things had turned out but he could live with it.

He was lost in this thought when Twill sidled next to him, nudging his big shoulder against Sage's like a friendly dog. Nodding toward Van Ostrand, who was beginning to stir, the Irishman quoted softly, "He did the deed, 'which both our tongues held vile to name.'"

"Ah, the words of that traitor, King James. In this case, all treachery is his and none of ours," Sage said, watching Van Ostrand struggle into a sitting position on the stable floor, his fingers trembling as he probed his bloodied face.

A rustle of skirt and squeak of hinge made Sage look toward the stable door. He watched them slip away. First Lucinda, then Eich.

THIRTY ONE

"Miner," Sage became aware of his alias being spoken and somehow realized it wasn't the first time the prosecutor had tried to get his attention. He turned toward the man. "Yes, Mr. Heney?" he answered.

"I asked whether you'll be staying in Prineville or heading back to Portland."

"Umm, I guess I'm going to be heading back to Portland." A Portland without Lucinda, Sage thought, then forced himself to consider whether Siringo needed him to hang around. Probably not. His work was done. Between them, Heney and Siringo could finish things up. The murders had been solved. He doubted the sheep ranchers would carry out their plan to retaliate against the cattlemen once they discovered it was one of their own who'd done the killing and burning.

He looked down at the dentist who was glaring at Twill. "You didn't have to slug me in the mouth, I think you broke a goddamn tooth."

"Hah, that's not the only part of you that God has damned. Besides, you're not going to be on this earth that much longer to need it," responded the Irishman, his voice fierce with anger. Twill's fists clenched and he stepped toward the cowering dentist.

Sage interrupted what was sure to be an escalating exchange. "Dr. Van Ostrand, I understand that you needed range land for your sheep. Losing your lease along the military road left you with a big flock and no place to graze them."

"Those bastard Kepler brothers, they snuck in and bribed the agent. After years of no problems we suddenly had no place to graze the damn animals. It was a disaster. We stood to lose all of the money we invested, all of the sheep. I'd mortgaged my home. I was going to lose everything."

Van Ostrand pointed at Heney, "Then this man comes to town. He was going to take everything we'd worked for, even our freedom."

"You didn't have to kill Rayburn. I had you dead to rights on the land claim deal without him. Why'd you think no one would notice that you'd paid for all the claim fees?" Heney asked.

"Nothing says I can't loan money to my neighbors," this time the dentist sounded smug. Evidently, Van Ostrand already had thought through his defense in the event their scheme was discovered.

"That weren't no loan you gave to me," came a dry voice from the rear stalls where Samuel Hamilton had gone to calm Rocky and Gasper. Now Hamilton stepped forward and spoke directly to Van Ostrand. "The deal was I lay claim, let you graze and once I prove up, I was supposed to sell the land to you for a minimal fee. In exchange, you gave me a hundred dollars up front and paid the filing fees. And, that's exactly what I'll say when Mr. Heney puts me on the witness stand."

"That wasn't me that told you that!" snapped the dentist. "I wasn't even around when you got the papers and filed them. Rayburn did all that."

That accusation spurred Thomas into speaking. "Oh really, Richard! When I get up and tell the truth, you're going to be right in the thick of it. Besides, like Mr. Heney said," he added with a twist of his lips, "you signed all those checks that went in with the filings."

"You'd betray me? After all my efforts to make you rich?" Van Ostrand was outraged.

Thomas's face flushed, "You tried to shoot me in the back. You involved me in murder. Any claim to loyalty you might have had is long gone, my friend." Before anyone could stop him, his fist landed a solid hit on the dentist's jaw.

"Hey, hey," Heney interjected as he pulled Thomas away.

Sage couldn't resist the opportunity to land his own blow—this one verbal. "You might try to wiggle your way out of a fraud conviction, Van Ostrand." Sage leaned closer to the dentist to add, "But you have no hope at all when it comes to your murdering O'Dea and Rayburn."

Van Ostrand slyly peered up at them and said, "You don't have any evidence that I murdered anyone. You can't prove it."

Heney barked a laugh. "Man, you are not thinking clearly. We were in the loft. We heard every word you said. So did Thomas and Miner here. Bottom line, you admitted to killing both men. There's nothing more to say. I'll watch you mount the scaffold, Van Ostrand."

Sage didn't want to let it go. He needed to know what had driven this man to murder and mayhem. So, he asked, "Dr. Van Ostrand, how did this all happen?"

The dentist shook his head and clambered to his feet. Stepping over to a bound hay bale, he sat down, hands hanging between his knees, head bowed. Heney's words had dealt a fatal blow to the dentist's bravado. At last, he felt the weight of certain defeat. When he spoke, his voice was low, "It didn't start like this. We bought the flock. We had plenty of land. When we lost the lease, I thought if I had Rayburn set fire to the Kepler's Ochoco barn, that they'd decide the sheepshooters were making the Ochoco's too dangerous. I thought they'd abandon the lease they stole from us."

"You thought they'd blame the cattle ranchers—the sheepshooters?" Sage asked.

"Sure. Who else would they blame? The sheepshooters have been taking out flocks. Heck, they left a shepherd tied up with a sack over his head. Told him to leave Crook County or else next time they'd kill him. Another one disappeared until you found his body the other day. Burning the Kepler's sheep barn fit right in with what the sheepshooters were doing."

Sage was nodding encouragingly. "And the fire at the Fromm's homestead?" he prodded.

"Because the missus also put in a claim, the Fromms have a large piece, double the size of most homesteads. And, it has year around water. If we ran them off, we could step in and maybe buy it. Or, at least graze it as open range for a while."

"Didn't you realize that your actions were going to goad the sheepmen into attacking the cattlemen? That you were going to trigger a range war?"

Van Ostrand shrugged. "That's their lookout. I had my family to consider."

Sage glanced toward Siringo, who'd been leaning against the wall, chewing on a piece of straw. "Do you think his confession will be enough to make the sheepmen abandon their retaliation plans?"

Siringo straightened, tossed away the straw and grinned. "It'll help. Also, I got another coded telegram early this morning. It's for sure the federal government is going to intervene. The Secretary of the Interior's local man is supposed to meet with both sides to find a solution. That news ought to cool them all down."

"The governor succeeded?" Sage glanced toward Twill, who was looking mystified, so Sage explained, "Governor Chamberlain has been trying to get the President and the Secretary of the Interior to take responsibility for the mess they've created and to fix it. He finally did it." Turning back to Siringo, Sage asked, "So, what's the federal government planning to do?"

"Wahl," began Siringo, "they are going to meet with both sides. The plan is to talk about opening up the mountain forest reserves for grazing and deciding the fairest way to divvy it up between cattle and sheep. If they're successful, everybody should be happy." He turned toward Twill, "Do you think you can calm the shepherds down now that we know who killed Timothy O'Dea and Paddy Campbell?"

Twill smiled. "Oh yea. Me mates weren't looking forward to going into battle. For one thing, those cowpokes are some pretty hard fellows. Truth be told, us shepherds would much rather 'fight with gentle words.'"

Van Ostrand's moan reminded them that he still sat on the hay bale. He spoke from behind hands over his face, "It was all for nothing? We were going to get access anyway?"

Siringo and Sage exchanged a look. Neither wanted Van Ostrand to know that it was his bad acts that had given Chamberlain the leverage he needed with the folks in Washington D. C.

"Yup, that's right, Van Ostrand. You burned down a barn, murdered two men and a champion sheepdog for no-good reason," Siringo told him. "You dwell on that in the few days you have left to live."

THIRTY TWO

"LOOK PARTNER, I KNOW YOU want to head back to Portland, but we need your help to do this one thing," Siringo said as Heney nodded agreement. The three of them were in Heney's hotel room. Siringo and Heney were trying to convince Sage to go with Sheriff Smith to arrest Tom Meglit for the murder of Paddy Campbell.

"But, I already did what needed doing. The range war isn't going to happen. Charlie, why can't you arrest him?" Sage protested.

"Because, I still have work to do here in Central Oregon. I take part in the arrest, everyone will know I'm a Dickinsen man. I promised the governor I'd keep an eye on the situation until the feds have their meeting and things settle down."

"Well, if the U.S. Attorney can't make Sheriff Smith conduct a proper arrest, how can I?"

"You are exactly right," said Heney who crossed over to a desk. His room was more spacious than Sage's. He picked up a pen and began writing something on a sheet of paper. Once finished, he set down the pen, and waved the paper through the air to dry the ink. "That's why you are now an officially-appointed investigator for the U.S. District Attorney's office," he said as he rose to hand Sage the paper.

Sage stared at the paper before reluctantly taking hold of it. "So, I am supposed to waltz into his office, announce, 'Ha-ha, fooled you. I am really a federal investigator and I know who killed Paddy Campbell'?"

After giving his wide, slow smile, Siringo answered, "Yup, that's exactly what you will do, though I'd leave out the 'ha-ha.' Smith probably won't condone Meglit's actions. The sheriff might shoot a few sheep, but I doubt he's a murderer by nature."

"And exactly how is it I know Meglit is the murderer? I've been in town less than two weeks."

"That's what makes this perfect," Heney interjected. "I'll tell him that I came to town because a witness I interviewed in Portland said Meglit was the murderer and told where to find Campbell's body. I sent you out in advance to verify the truth of that claim. You couldn't do it right away because of the smallpox quarantine. I followed along to officially obtain Smith's cooperation. That way, nothing is said about the range war and Mr. Siringo can keep playing the cowboy."

"Hey! There's no playing. I am a cowboy," Siringo protested, though he clearly hadn't taken offense.

"Well, how about talking to Smith and getting his agreement to bring Meglit back to town?" Sage asked, still trying to find a way to stay in town, meet one last time with Lucinda to say goodbye and leave the next day.

"Nah, that won't work. We don't have a guarantee that Smith wouldn't figure out a way to let Meglit escape. We need a witness," Siringo said.

"Well then, Mr. Heney, why don't you go with Smith?" Before the words were completely out of Sage's mouth, the prosecutor was shaking his head. "I, ah, have a certain physical condition that prevents me from sitting very long on a horse," he said.

So, in the end, it was Heney and Sage who stepped into the Prineville sheriff's office. When Sheriff Smith learned John Miner was a federal investigator, his face flushed with anger. "You should have come straight to me and identified yourself instead of slinking around town fooling everyone," he sputtered.

Heney showed his skill as a conciliator, "Now, Sheriff Smith. I wasn't confident the witness was reliable. You had enough to do, with this range war brewing and the smallpox epidemic. It didn't seem proper to waste your time if my witness turned out to be a liar."

That explanation somewhat mollified Smith, but it was clear his anger still simmered because on their long ride out to the cowboy camp, he said little to Sage and when he did, his only words were curt instructions.

Late in the day, they reached the tree trunk sporting Siringo's blazed "S." Both men dismounted, Sage tying Rocky's reins to a shrub and giving the old horse a pat. Smith was to allow Sage half an hour to work his way up the slope and over the shoulder of the small hill. Once there, he was to position himself close behind the cowboy camp. Then, Smith would ride into camp and attempt to arrest Meglit. If all went well, they wouldn't need Sage. If it didn't, Sage would be positioned to cut off Meglit's escape, should the young killer take to his heels. Siringo would be there too since he'd left town a good hour before the sheriff and Sage. If Siringo had to, he'd intervene as well, but only as a last resort.

Sage climbed through the widely-spaced trees, his boots crunching the dried pine needles and slipping on loose rocks. Overhead, gray clouds had sealed up the sky, a stiff breeze lifted dust and a distant rumble signaled an approaching thunder-storm. Topping the ridge, Sage hid behind a tree while he studied the camp below.

There was a flurry of activity in advance of the storm. A huge cookfire leapt wildly before the stiffening breeze. The cook was hurriedly shoving cast-iron dutch ovens onto the coals, stirring the contents of a deep kettle and adjusting smoke-blackened coffee pots inside the fire pit. It would be a quick beans and biscuits dinner. Meanwhile, the cowboys were rigging lean-tos using dropped branches and canvas tarpaulins. One man was shouting instructions, while the wind did its best to thwart their efforts.

Good. Their rush to eat and get under shelter would make it easier for him to approach unseen. Slowly, Sage began working his way downhill, moving from tree to tree, his eyes never leaving the men below. Just as he got within a hundred feet of the camp, he saw the men pause and look toward the west. Sure enough, Sheriff Smith trotted into camp with Rocky trailing dutifully behind.

Sage searched for Siringo. The cowboy was working at the far edge of the camp, by the road heading east, calmly tying branches onto a lean-to. He was well-positioned to block an escape in that direction. The man who'd been directing the lean-to erection, most likely the foreman, turned to look at the sheriff and then strode to meet him. The two men talked briefly, the foreman resting his hands on his hips and nodding his head. He looked back over his shoulder, straight at a young man who'd been working on the lean-to nearest Sage. The fellow stiffened, slowly dropped the branch he'd been holding and began to back away up the hill toward Sage.

Sheriff Smith must have seen the young fellow's furtive movement too, because he dropped Rocky's reins and spurred his horse forward. The young fellow took off running uphill, abandoning escape by horse since the animals were corralled nearer the sheriff than to him. As Meglit ran, he grabbed for a pistol in the holster that bounced against his leg.

For the first time, Sage wished he was carrying a gun. But he wasn't. Fortunately, Meglit's escape route would take him past the tree where Sage hid. Meglit paused, turned, raised his gun and fired off a shot toward the sheriff. Sage tensed, widened his stance and strained his ears. He'd have to launch his attack at the precise moment Meglit ran past his tree.

Overhead, thunder cracked while jagged lightning ripped through massive grey clouds. The ground shook. In the calm that followed, Sage heard the rasp of the fleeing man's breath and the scrabble of his boots over rocky ground.

When Sage jumped from behind the tree, Meglit was looking back over his shoulder. When he turned forward to see Sage in his path, Meglit's eyes widened and his mouth dropped open.

Even so, his reactions were fast because his gun swung up. Sage quickly seized the man's wrist while kicking his gut with his left heel. The gun flew through the air. Before Meglit could scramble after it, Sage was moving forward, his arms and feet whirling through the air as he hit the man, again and again, suddenly possessed by an unexpected rage. His only thought was of a gentle old shepherd, his dog and his sheep done to death by this murderous thug. At the last moment, seeing Meglit's eyes roll back in his head, Sage pulled his final kick, one that might have killed the man. Meglit fell to the ground and rolled a few feet downhill. Sage slowly lowered his leg, which been frozen in the air at waist height and took a deep breath. Only then did he look down at the camp. A line of cowboys stood there, silent, eyes wide as if they could not believe what they just witnessed.

The sheriff nudged his horse up the hill. Reaching them he dismounted, kneeling to slap a pair of handcuffs on the unconscious Meglit before glancing up at Sage. "Well, that was some fancy footwork. We've never seen the like around these parts," he commented. Smith stood and offered his hand, "I expect Paddy Campbell got a chuckle out of watching Meglit's comeuppance from wherever that old shepherd might be looking down on the proceedings. Thank you, Mr. Miner."

Sage shook hands without smiling. Beyond the sheriff's shoulder he saw Charlie slip into the background and noticed Rocky nibbling on grass. Overhead, the thunder rumbled, lightning flashed and the downpour began. He helped the sheriff load Meglit's still unconscious body onto the horse's back. As they trudged down the hill, Sage realized he felt both guilt and satisfaction.

THIRTY THREE

Even from the Poindexter's lobby, Sage could hear the sounds of celebration. He stood in the archway and saw a dining room transformed. Light-hearted diners trading words and laughter with those at neighboring tables. Sage sat at an empty table and opened his copy of the *Crook County Journal.*

A one-inch headline stretched across the top of the front page like a shout, "Roosevelt To Open Reserves!" Sage scanned the brief story.

> Late last night, Governor Chamberlain sent a lengthy telegram informing this newspaper that relief is in sight for the ranchers of Central Oregon. The Department of Interior will be meeting with local ranchers. The purpose of the meeting will be to develop a method for opening up the forest reserves to livestock grazing. Both sheep and cattle ranchers will be invited to participate. It is hoped that this change in direction will calm the angry waters that have been swirling across the high desert in recent months. It is believed that the President ordered the opening of reserves after some very able lobbying by local citizens during his recent visit to Portland. The time and dates of the meetings are unknown at present but we've been told they will be held in the near future. Check the *Journal's* pages for notices.

Good. Heney had said he'd make sure that the sheep and cattle men were promptly informed of the federal government's reconsideration of its grazing ban. That should stop the range war in its tracks. Sage allowed himself a sardonic smile. Let them think it was their local delegation to Roosevelt that turned the tide. That misdirection served his and Siringo's purposes just fine. But, how stunned they would be to learn that it was really the town dentist running amok and Governor Chamberlain's persistence that caused the change in Washington, D.C. He sighed with satisfaction and flipped the paper over to find a small article below the fold that carried the title, "Fromm Freed, Van Ostrand Arrested."

> Homesteader Otto Fromm, arrested just days ago for the ambush murder of Asa Rayburn, left the Crook County jail a free man early this morning. Prineville dentist and local sheep rancher, Richard Van Ostrand, is said to have confessed to murdering Rayburn. He also confessed to killing the shepherd, Timothy O'Dea nearly two weeks prior. Van Ostrand's business partner in the ranching business, Congressman Newt Thomas, is said to be helping with the inquiries. Fromm had no statement other than to say he is deeply grateful to those who were responsible for finding the real culprit. No further information is available at this time.

Sage closed his eyes and allowed himself to relive those moments earlier in the morning. He and Siringo had been standing beneath the leaves of a great tree, some ways from the courthouse steps when Otto Fromm, his wife and two children burst out of the door. They were hugging and chattering while the *Journal's* reporter tried to obtain a quote. As one, Otto and Lisbeth had spied Sage and Siringo. They honored their promise to remain quiet about who was responsible for Otto's vindication but couldn't resist sending slight thank you nods toward the two men.

"Wahl," drawled the Dickensen detective, once the homesteader family was out of sight, "I expect that will be one happy little household tonight." Genuine satisfaction warmed the cowboy's words.

Sage felt a butterfly sensation take hold in his gut. He had to know, though the knowing might be a stab to his heart. "Speaking of households, Charlie, did you ask the lady for her hand in marriage yet?"

Siringo grinned. "I surely did. She said 'yes.' So, I'll be hanging up my detective spurs and looking to make this country my home."

Despite days of Sage preparing himself for the worst, Siringo's answer was still a blow. Taking a deep breath he continued to push forward, thinking there was no point in stopping until he collected all of the painful information. "She's willing to give up the parlor house business?" he asked.

"Yup, says she's tired of it. The epidemic was hard on her. She said that it made her think about what was really important. I'm mighty pleased to say, I qualify as important."

And Siringo was pleased, obviously elated that Lucinda had agreed to marry him and start a new life. She'd probably be a great ranch woman, Sage thought. Though, she might find that giving up the sociability and excitement of city life a bit difficult at first.

"So when are the nuptials going to take place?" he asked.

"Wahl, first she needs to get the business in shape and sell it. I expect it will be a few months. Will you come back and be my best man?" Siringo asked.

That request made Sage hesitate. It was one thing to pretend happiness when told of the impending marriage. Quite another to stand by and watch it happen. Still, he said, "Why, I'd be honored, though the bride might want me to give her away."

Siringo's brow wrinkled. "Well, I think that Hart fellow might have already agreed to perform that honor. At least, that's what she told me."

Another unexpected stab of pain. He'd known Lucinda longer than Hart. Sure, she and Hart had shared an intense few months caring for the smallpox victims. But still, she'd chose a near stranger over him? He heaved a sigh, and said, "Well, I better be getting back to the hotel. I'm meeting Herman for breakfast. You want to join us?" he asked.

He was relieved when Siringo responded, "Nah, there's a ranch for sale down near Post. I want to go take a look at it. If it looks good, it just might be our new home."

Sage watched Siringo mount his horse and depart. He felt a sense of loss as the tall, lanky cowboy reined his horse around the corner and out of sight.

A spurt of laughter snapped him back into the Poindexter's dining room. He looked again at the newspaper and noticed another small article in the lower corner. This one was titled, "Meglit Arrested" and proved even more succinct.

> Two days ago, an itinerant prospector brought shepherd Patrick Campbell's body into town. He'd been shot and secretly buried out near Scissors Creek in the Ochocos. Yesterday, Sheriff Smith arrested a cowboy named Thomas Meglit for Campbell's murder. Meglit was captured in the Ochocos after attempting to escape. Sources say Meglit killed out of hatred for sheep and those who care for them. The victim, Campbell, was considered a kind and decent man. Meglit, however, has a bad reputation around town.

Sage allowed himself to feel a moment of intense satisfaction. The three stories, taken together, would surely reverse the momentum toward a range war. He gazed around the dining room, noting that never before had he seen its patrons so animated and happy. It was clear they were relieved that they no longer had to contemplate taking up arms against their neighbors. He imagined the same relief was spreading throughout the town.

Herman Eich was crossing the room toward him, his face also alight with pleasure. He took a seat and they ordered breakfast. As they waited, Sage again gazed around the room and finally voiced the thought that had been nagging him.

"How can we ever hope to make this world a better place when so many people willingly ignore their moral compass in favor of ignorance and hate?"

"That's a rather weighty question for first thing in the morning," Eich said drily.

Sage persisted. "The sheep ranchers are standing down now they know one of their own was the bad actor. And, Siringo tells me the sheepshooters are agreeing to meet with the federal agent to talk about grazing in the Reserves. Of course, they are conditioning their attendance on the promise that they will not have to attend the same meeting as the sheepmen."

Eich chuckled. "You are not celebrating. You should. You stopped these folks from getting hurt or hurting someone," he noted.

Spirit crushing resignation weighed down Sage's words as he said, "Look at them. Their hands are work worn, their dress is humble. These people have so much in common. They are decent, courageous people. Salt of the earth. Yet men and animals have died. Neighbor has taken up arms against neighbor. Where was it going to end, if we hadn't intervened?"

Eich's long, gnarled finger gently circled the rim of his cup. "Recently, I read a magazine serial written by a Polish fellow named 'Conrad.'" Eich said. "He called it *Heart of Darkness*."

"Doesn't sound like a ripping comedy," Sage observed.

Eich smiled. "Don't worry, I won't tell you the story except to say it was about one man's inward journey to his own soul. I think that is a journey every spirit has to make. He has to discover his own moral compass, test it for prejudice and share it with others. He has to step out bravely and be guided by that compass."

Sage couldn't suppress a snort of derision. Given the range war that they'd only narrowly averted, one could only conclude that bravery of that sort was missing in a whole lot of folks. "What happened to the fellow in Conrad's story?" he asked.

Eich didn't take offense, just continued his explanation, "In the end, he found light as well as dark. He realized there were points of choice between the two. And, he saw the consequences of choosing darkness. He turned away."

"Happily ever after, huh?"

That brought a rueful twist to Eich's lips. "Happy? I think not. Once you have teetered on the edge, you know the abyss is always there. Waiting. There are always choices to be made until the day you die. And, you won't always make the right choices but you have to keep trying and never become self-satisfied."

Sage gently rocked his cup in its saucer. "Siringo said people are like sheep, so many follow blindly. How is it that they can be led to abandon their moral values, their compassion?"

This time, there was sadness in Eich's dark eyes. "I guess if anyone has wailed that question at the heavens, it is my people. One can always understand the existence of a charismatic, crazed man. But, it is the persistent existence of his followers that wounds human hope. As you said, 'neighbor against neighbor.' Their reasons are many. Again, ultimately, it comes down to choice. The dark or the light. I fear many more mindless hordes will run amok before enough of us have plumbed and learned how to control our own 'hearts of darkness.'"

Sage wasn't ready to let it go. "Sometimes, it's hard to respect people. Even if we had spoken the truth to these folks," he gestured around the room, "they wouldn't have heard. Without Siringo, there would have been a range war. What hope has humanity if so many are willing to follow blindly?"

Eich nodded, saying, "I understand. Often I have asked the question: 'How is it that a demagogue can obtain such power?' You look at these good people and wonder why they do not see and reject manipulating appeals to their baser selves—to their fears, greed, prejudice or their need to see themselves as important.

"My own family left eastern Europe because of the po-groms. For years, we'd lived peaceably amongst our non-Jewish neighbors. We thought some of them friends. And then, a demagogue rose up and spread his poison. Hateful words and rocks flew through our windows. Why? You ask, 'What makes people abandon their compassion, their responsibility to think for themselves?' I believe you and I will ponder that question our whole lives.

"Still, I do not fear the demagogue. If no one will follow, he is powerless. No, I fear the followers themselves. Those willing to surrender their responsibility to think for themselves. Those who lack the courage to live their compassion and instead choose to surrender their will, jump on the band wagon and cause pain to others."

"You're not making me feel better," Sage said. "I am resigned to the fact that it is my lot in life to try to make a better world. That is my purpose, who I am. But it seems a foolish effort when so many are willing to act mindlessly."

"There is no magic answer," replied Eich. "But there are those who grasp their moral compass firmly and consult it often. They are the hope for all of us."

Sage looked at the ragpicker poet. "Did you hear about the wedding?"

"Ah, the wedding. Yes, Lucinda told me about it," Eich said without indicating he'd noticed the abrupt change in topic.

His words delivered a fresh hurt, yet another among the many of this morning. Sage looked down at the table, his hand fiddling with his fork, moving it from side-to-side as he said, "I just can't picture Lucinda being happy stuck out on a ranch, in the middle of nowhere."

"Lucinda?" Eich queried sharply.

The intensity of Eich's response made Sage look up to see puzzlement, followed by realization, cross the ragpicker's craggy face.

"Sage, you poor fellow," Eich said softly. "Siringo's not marrying Lucinda Collins. He's marrying Xenobia Brown."

Before he considered what he thought about that news, Sage felt tears filling his eyes. "But," he started only to get caught up in trying to remember what had led him to such a wrong conclusion. My God, he thought, it was my fear and jealousy that twisted everything I heard.

He stood. "I need to find her," he declared.

Eich reached across the table and gently tugged his forearm. "She left yesterday morning on the stagecoach to Shaniko," he said.

Sage didn't sit down again. Instead, he looked at his pocket watch. "Are you heading back to Portland?"

Eich shook his head. "I thought I'd spend some time with the Gable brothers. See a bit more of the country. Visit with our Indian and Gypsy friends if I run across them. Maybe tell them the whole story and how they helped solve two murders. It will make them feel good, I think."

"Forgive me Herman," Sage said, taking paper bills from his pocket and dropping them on the table, "I have a stagecoach to catch with only a few minutes to spare."

Eich smiled knowingly, stood up and shook Sage's hand. "May you travel in peace, health and joy," he said.

❀ ❀ ❀

Sage ran from the hotel to Hamilton's livery stable, reaching it just as the passengers were boarding the stagecoach. Dexter's grizzled face lit up when he saw Sage. "Well now, Mr. Miner. Will you be traveling with us today?"

"Yes, if I can have a minute to buy a ticket," Sage answered.

Just then a voice spoke, "Well, boyo. Why are ye leaving our fair town like the hounds are pursuing your soul?"

Sage turned toward the familiar voice and there stood a grinning Twill who stepped forward, a young woman's hand in his. "Before you go," he said, "I would like to introduce my lady friend, Samantha Bryce. She's the new teacher up at the Howard schoolhouse." Sage was surprised to see that Twill's new friend was the young woman who'd ridden the stagecoach down Cow Canyon.

Sage grinned and she grinned back. "Oh, Mr. Miner and Iare already well acquainted," she told Twill. He looked puzzled but shrugged it off, no doubt thinking he'd get an explanation later.

"Miss Samantha is an avid student of Willy Shakespeare as well," he told Sage. "And, her school is out in the Ochocos, near where I tend the flocks." His sly wink made clear his intent to woo the new school marm in the months ahead.

Sage wished them well and watched them walk down the street, Twill's step jaunty. He'd miss the Irishman.

Dexter told him to climb up to the driver's seat and soon the stagecoach was rolling down Main Street, past the power plant and across Ochoco Creek. Sage was silent, musing over how swiftly his mood had shifted from downhearted to hopeful. He tried to stifle his exuberance. Just because Lucinda was returning to Portland unmarried, it didn't mean she'd ever welcome Sage back with open arms. But, at least there was a chance.

The stagecoach topped the small hill north of town and Dexter halted so he could take a swig from his flask. Sage twisted to take a final look at Prineville, with its sheltering rimrocks, ribbon of river, green valley floor and distant pine-clad mountains. Large birds wheeled high in a wide and pure blue sky. He felt a pang. Whether it came from the beauty of the scene or from the possibility that he was going to miss the close-knit town and its people, he couldn't say.

Dexter clucked the horses into action and the stagecoach gathered speed, rolling toward the ponderosa pine forest at the base of Grizzly Butte.

THE END

AFTERWORD

THE CITIZENS OF CROOK COUNTY have been blessed with a
number of avid local historians. They also have a great resource
in Prineville's Bowman Historical Museum. The contributions
to this story made by these historians and the museum are too
numerous to detail. It should be remembered, however, that this
is a work of fiction. While I have tried to accurately reveal the
bare bones of the forces at play in Crook County during the early
1900's, I have altered the time line and some aspects of the locale
in order to write what I hope is a compelling story. That said,
all and any historical errors are attributable solely to me and no
one else. Finally, the title *Dead Line* should probably be spelled
"deadline." Esthetics and the need to differentiate from a time
deadline led to the two-word approach.

HISTORICAL NOTES

Smallpox in Prineville

1. Prineville was quarantined for smallpox around the time of this story. A piano box was used to fumigate individuals arriving in town. The other measures included fumigating hotels and the removal of tables and chairs from saloons. A doctor did rush out from Portland to vaccinate a number of people in the Prineville area.

2. The Ed Harbin in the story is based on an actual person of that name. He was, in fact, the hero of the Prineville smallpox epidemic because he did do exactly what is depicted in this story. His wood box stand, however, was situated in front of the Poindexter and not in front of the actual pesthouse.

3. Official town records do not report that it was the brothel madam who first leapt into action when the smallpox epidemic hit Prineville. But later news articles quote residents who remember that the house of ill repute became the first pesthouse in town when the madam set up cots and began caring for the smallpox victims. That madam's name was never recorded nor honored.

4. A stranger to Prineville, Frank Hart, did enter the pesthouse to nurse the smallpox victims. A newspaper article later reported his subsequent death in La Grande, Oregon. The article reported that Hart was a Portland accountant charged with embezzlement and on the run from the law at the time of his death. No one can say whether his work in the pesthouse served as atonement for his wrongdoing or that it was simply a good place in which to hide out. Regardless he provided care to Prineville's smallpox victims.

Charlie Siringo

5. Charles Siringo is the name of a cowboy who, for many years, was an agent of the country's pre-eminent detective agency. At one point he was assigned to Central Oregon at the behest of Governor Chamberlain who wanted firsthand information about the growing range war between the cattlemen and sheepmen. That range war was averted for two reasons. First, because the sheep men did not retaliate despite great provocation. And second, because the federal government reversed itself and decided to allow grazing in the reserves. Meetings were held with both the cattle and sheep ranchers, albeit these were separate meetings. Both sides participated in deciding how to divvy up these grazing allotments and the range peace in Central Oregon became permanent around 1906.

6. Siringo wrote a two books in which he laid out the nefarious activities of his former employer. In one, he relates how he intervened when his co-worker, Pat Barry, tried to frame a man for a robbery that Barry himself had committed. Siringo reported his boss did nothing. Subsequent research revealed that Barry briefly served as Portland's chief of police in 1897.

Illegal Events and Bad Guys

7. The Forest Reserve Act pushed the sheep and cattle out of their summer range in the Cascade Mountains and threatened to do the same in the Ochoco Mountains which were customarily called the "Blue Mountains."

8. There was a Prineville land fraud scheme like the one depicted in this story. A congressman and medical doctor residing in Prineville were convicted of hiring dummy claimants to file on land in the Ochoco Mountains. The doctor served time. The congressman appealed numerous times and the case was dropped on a technicality. The congressman was not re-tried. The two were partners in a sheep ranch and had unexpectedly lost their long-held grazing lease on the military road lands. The evidence showed that they had paid the filing fees for over 100 dummy claimants in a very short period of time. The whistleblower was, indeed, the wife of the chief land agent in The Dalles. At trial, the owner of Prineville's livery stable was one of those dummy claimants who testified for U.S. Prosecutor Francis Heney. No murders, however, were associated with this scheme, although the burning of a rival sheep ranchers' barn was thought to have been ordered by them.

9. The newspapers of that day report that the Prineville sheriff mentioned in this story, C. Sam Smith, was subsequently convicted for scheming to drive the sheep ranchers out of the area by torching their sheep camps and shearing sheds and by cutting their fences.

10. In real life, a man named Asa Rayburn did work for a sheep rancher who is called "Bellingham" in this book. He left that rancher's employ and became a gambling booster in Prineville. Rayburn was a witness for the prosecution against the rancher in a subsequent land fraud trial. There is

no evidence Rayburn was murdered. He simply disappeared from history.

11. The indicted sheep rancher was the called the "Sheep King of Oregon." His attorney was initially charged with facilitating land frauds on rancher's behalf. Later, in 1904, the rancher and his attorney were tried. Numerous witnesses testified that, with the attorney's help, the rancher paid them to claim land as homesteaders with the understanding these false claims would be used by the rancher to add range land to his 20,000-30,000 acre sheep ranch. Both men were acquitted. One of the jurors wrote that the problem was the federal land laws which made such men desperate. This defiant act of jury nullification was based on what history has shown to be an accurate analysis of the causal factors underlying the attempted land fraud.

12. The Tom Meglit in this story is based on a real person who, as an old man, was interviewed by a local reporter. The news article has him relating stories of how he dry gulched and ambushed a number of union men on behalf of mine owners in Colorado.

13. A solitary tree on the prairie near Post is famous in the sheepshooter lore as the place where the Crook County sheepshooters first declared their intention of driving sheep ranching off much of Central Oregon's open range.

14. The fraud connected to the building of the Santiam road happened as described in the story. It is detailed in a book written by a later supervisor of the Ochoco National Forest. The swindle had a devastating impact on the homesteaders who had claimed the land, only to have to abandon it after years of litigation.

Central Oregon People and Miscellany

15. The largest influx of Euro-Americans into Central Oregon came from Missouri. But, there also were immigrants from around the world. The Irish were brought as shepherds to Morrow County which, even today, has a higher per capita percentage of Irish Catholics than most other counties in the state.

16. The idea of Indians selling from tipis erected at the west side of Prineville is based on reports in historical records and photographs. The Indians in the story, however, are based on a band of "renegade" Indians who called themselves the 'Wyam.' They refused to relinquish their land and fishing rights at the now vanished Celilo Falls. Their descendants remain on that land. Many Central Oregon Indians traveled to the Willamette Valley to pick hops, gathering meat and other edibles along the way.

17. The story's reference to traveling bands of Gypsies selling lace and mending pots in Central Oregon came from the brief mention in a Prineville newspaper of that time. Similarly, there were in fact, two Portland-based Jewish brothers who were very well-known in Central Oregon. As stated in the story, for many years, these two men supplied remote ranches with trinkets and small items of necessity in exchange for fleeces.

18. Mexicans contributed early to Oregon's growth. Initially, they worked leading the pack trains that supplied goods to miners. They were considered highly skilled in handling pack animals. When the French-Glen ranch in the Steens Mountain area was formed, Peter French imported a number of Mexicans to work with the cattle because of their reputation as cowboys. With the onset of the SpanishAmerican war, Mexicans were made to feel unwelcome. Consequently, many left Oregon, with the few remaining living in remote

areas or working the French-Glen ranch. The Mexican prospector in this story, however, is a fictional character.

19. A teamster named Steve Yancy did haul the first electric plant into Central Oregon. He made seven trips down Cow Canyon with the equipment, using 2 ten-horse teams each trip. Charges for electricity were based on the number of light bulbs in the house with the standard being 5 cents per month for every 16 candle-watts of use. That five cents powered a light bulb that cast a light about as powerful as a 20watt bulb.

20. Gold was twice found in Scissor's Creek. The first gold strike occurred in the early 1870's. A second try at prospecting the creek, both by placer mining and lode mining, was successful such that gold was being extracted up through 1937.

For a short bibliography and photos, please visit:
www.yamhillpress.net.

About the Author

S. L. Stoner is a native of the Pacific Northwest who has worked as a citizen change agent and as a labor union and civil rights attorney for many years. She lives with her husband and two dogs in Portland, Oregon and Packwood, Washington when not traveling to do research or just see the sights.

Acknowledgments

As noted previously, Prineville's history has been recorded by a number of diligent local historians, past and present. Many thanks go to the Museum's Steve Lent, a meticulous historian, and to the Museum's volunteers for uncovering and preserving the area's history.

Special thank you's are also sent to Denise Collins and Claudine Paris for their helpful suggestions and painstaking proofreading. I apologize in advance for any factual, grammatical or typographical errors and claim them to be solely my own or are attributable to ornery computer programs or solar flares.

I also want to thank the readers of this series and the folks who made prior books in the series possible, including Helen Nickum, Joel Rosenblit, Sally Frese, Denise Collins, Sally Stoner, George Slanina and others that I am sure I have inadvertently forgotten to list. I especially want to thank Alec "Icky" Dunn for his wonderful book covers that capture the essence of each story and the series. Josh MacPhee also deserves recognition for his consistently good layout design. One way or another, this series exists because of these talented people.

This book was written during a difficult year both personally and professionally. I need to thank my dear friends and fam-ily. The love and affection they freely gave to me did much to smooth the bumps in the road. I especially thank Bruce Hansen for his steadfast kindness, grace and strength under fire. I also need to acknowledge authors Anna Johnson and Caroline Miller who have been extremely helpful and supportive.

During the writing of this book I learned that, for over twenty-three years, I have had undiagnosed Lyme disease and at least two other co-infections. Pam Pennington, poet, author and medical massage therapist, kept many of my worst symptoms at bay pending that diagnosis. I owe her a debt of gratitude I can never repay. The Center for Disease Control now estimates that, each year, there are 40,000 new cases of Lyme disease. The Lyme bacteria and its related co-infections are pernicious because they roam throughout the body causing seemingly unrelated physical distresses. At this point, very few doctors know how to diagnose or treat it. I write of this because too many peoples' reports of these types of illnesses are discounted by the medical profession. I learned, the hard way, that is important to listen to your body and advocate like hell for yourself until you get an answer.

Finally, as always, my best friend and partner, George Slanina, deserves much credit for this series and for most good things in my life. I am beyond grateful that I have him and each and every reader, friend, family member, and series helper in my life.

Other Mystery Novels in the Sage Adair Historical Mystery Series
by S. L. Stoner

Timber Beasts

A secret operative in America's 1902 labor movement, leading a double life that balances precariously on the knife-edge of discovery, finds his mission entangled with the fate of a young man accused of murder.

Land Sharks

Two men have disappeared, sending Sage Adair on a desperate search that leads him into the Stygian blackness of Portland's underground to confront murderous shanghaiers, a lost friendship, and his own dark fears.

Dry Rot

A losing labor strike, a dead construction boss, a union leader framed for murder, a ragpicker poet, and collapsing bridges, all compete for Sage Adair's attention as he slogs through the Pacific Northwest's rain and mud to find answers before someone else dies.

Black Drop

Crisis always arrives in twos. Assassins plan to kill President Theodore Roosevelt and blame the labor movement. Young boys are slated for an appalling fate. If Sage Adair missteps, people will die. Panic becomes the most dangerous enemy of all in this adventure.

Request for Pre-Publication Notice

If you would like to receive notice of the publication date of the next Sage Adair historical mystery novel, please complete and return the form below or contact Yamhill Press at www.yamhill-press.net.

Your Name: _____

Street Address: _____

City: _____ State: _____ Zip: _____

E-mail Address: _____

Yamhill Press, P.O. Box 42348, Portland, OR 97242

www.yamhillpress.net